THE VERY GOOD BEST FRIEND

THE VERY GOOD BEST FRIEND

A Novel

TARYN HUBBARD

$$| N_1 \, | \, O_2 \, | \, N_1 |$$

CANADA

Library and Archives Canada Cataloguing in Publication

Title: The very good best friend : a novel / Taryn Hubbard.

Names: Hubbard, Taryn, author.

Identifiers: Canadiana (print) 20240534344 | Canadiana (ebook) 20240534352 |
ISBN 9781989689820 (softcover) | ISBN 9781989689868 (EPUB)

Subjects: LCGFT: Paranormal fiction. | LCGFT: Novels.

Classification: LCC PS8615.U2183 V47 2025 | DDC C813/.6—dc23

Printed and bound in Canada on 100% recycled paper.

Now Or Never Publishing
901, 163 Street
Surrey, British Columbia
Canada V4A 9T8

nonpublishing.com
Fighting Words.

We gratefully acknowledge the support of the Canada Council for the Arts
and the British Columbia Arts Council for our publishing program.

For Esther

March 15

Dear Carolyn:

I've arrived at the mall safe and sound. The bus ride here took forever, but it felt good to leave the city and all my memories with it. I'm ready for this change. Maybe I'll stay in the community longer than I'm obligated to. That's an option we have in the contract. I don't know yet. I'm optimistic that what Matt's doing here is legit. If it's not, well, at least my student loan debt has been wiped clean!

The mall is literally in the middle of nowhere, like I don't think there is even an actual town here anymore. The houses we passed on the drive in seemed to almost fade away in various states of boarded up, burnt, and falling apart. And yet, it's lovely here. The mountains feel so close, as if I could absorb into them and disappear if I let myself. I share a room with Aria, a woman from up north. She was in a similar rut as me: broke ass. She jumped at the opportunity to join Matt and his experiment too. I hope that eases your mind a little.

Matt has rules at the community, the biggest ones being no phone, internet, email, or social media—hence this old timey handwritten letter. I'm a day late sending it because I had to figure out how to mail it. Obviously, mail doesn't get picked up from the mall anymore because nobody knows we're here. Aria told me how to find "the guy" to do it for me. Sounds funny, but that's the way things go here. When we join, Matt wants us to truly commit to the work and that means limiting our access to the outside world so we can focus on radical self-care. I couldn't not communicate with you! I miss you already. I hope you're feeding Sammy well and that you can give him a nice scratch for me. I'll write again soon.

xo,

Rebecca

p.s. Maybe I can have a visitor soon. This place is huge and kind of hilarious that it used to be a mall. It's so '90s. I think my room used to be an old RadioShack. Did I tell you I miss you? xox.

April 19
Hi Carolyn:
I'm feeling more settled. I'm working in the garden, which is arguably the lowest rung on the ladder here, though we are all supposed to be equals. Turns out I'm good at weeding. Who knew? Remember that mint plant we tried to grow on our balcony for our mojitos and how it basically gave up living after three days with us? I learned that it's possible to care for something too much. They take gardening seriously here. I think I'm finally healing after, well, you know. It's still hard for me to talk about what happened. I've been letting myself cry to work through my emotions properly this time. The downside to this is everything feels fresh and raw again, and I'm finding that hard. Matt says he wants to help me. I'm lucky because most people only see him during Performance, but he's been visiting me. He has been vulnerable about his own traumas. I appreciate getting to know him.

About visitors... I checked on that and they aren't letting outsiders in right now. I heard from a friend that vicious rumours are circulating outside about Matt. He's not as bad as you might have read. I think you'd like him. He's kind and generous. He speaks eloquently. I find myself hanging on to his every word and I'm believing in more of what he's trying to do here. He's also deeply wounded from a significant loss and we share that. At night, we have our workshops and everyone in the community attends, no matter where you're placed in the mall. Matt assures us of the work we're doing, that it's difficult and necessary, and requires space away. I don't mind being away from the world, really. But I still miss you so much it hurts!
Your friend,
Rebecca

June 3
Carolyn:
I tried writing to you sooner, but it's harder to find anyone who will risk sending anything out of here right now. Matt has prescribed a vow of silence for the last month. He says it's not mandatory, but everyone is doing it anyway. He wants us to listen to our thoughts and feelings, to discover the core of who we are through what he calls "radical introspection" and that

means shushing external influences. Writing isn't really talking, but that's how things are going. We've stopped writing notes in the garden because nobody wants to be seen holding a pen. Should be interesting to see what we've been growing!

Before we went silent, there were whispers that Matt discovered the mall was bugged. I don't know. Trust me, we aren't that interesting! Though, there have been odd things happening lately. When I woke up two weeks ago, Aria, my roommate since I first arrived here, was gone. Her stuff was cleared out and... it was like she was never here. Did she go back home? The town here is literally just a retro Tim Hortons in the middle of a crumbling road so I doubt she's hanging around main street. It's annoying not knowing for certain, but I'm sure it's nothing. She'll owe him her debt repayment plus interest so there must have been a very compelling reason for her to leave. I couldn't afford that, even if I wanted to leave. I've noticed a few others disappear as well, but it's difficult to tell because the mall is so huge and maybe I'm just noticing new faces?

Matt wants to schedule one-on-one meet-ups with me. He is interested in my computer science degree and all that foolish work I did with para(normal) coding back in grad school. At least someone's finally interested. I was surprised he knew about the technology, but I guess he takes the time to learn about what's going on in the world.

As a group, we do workshops in between Performance basically every night now. Matt says we need to accelerate our radical introspection or we'll lose everything we've worked for. He's acting weird lately, but I think it's the grief. He uses space in the old Target store to bring us together. This will likely be my last letter for a while. So long for now.

Take care,
Rebecca

Aug. 21
Caroline:
Destroy everything I sent you, including this final note. Matt suspects members are leaking out lies about him after someone published the letters they got from some anonymous member here on a blog and he's on edge. He thinks it could jeopardize everything. He says that despite what people think, he's never craved power. He's trying to help people. I haven't

seen the blog, of course, but everyone's whispering about it when they think he can't hear.

People outside the mall are now very interested in us and why Matt is funding this community. They can't believe someone so wealthy would pay off hundreds of people's student loan debts and provide housing unless it was a huge scam. It's ridiculous. Can't someone rich be truly generous? I'm still grateful to be here. The debt was killing me, and despite the strangeness of this place, I don't regret my decision. I'll find another way to contact you. I just don't know when. I've been feeling more tired than normal and nauseous in the morning, but I think it will pass. It's so quiet sometimes I think my ears are playing tricks on me. There's a sound in the distance I hear at night, like a monotone roar. It's probably nothing, but there are times it gets louder, and it feels like the sound is seeping into my brain.

I've moved out of the garden and into a side project on a small team. I'm coding again and it feels great. Matt understands the power of (para)normal technology. He had to fire his original coder. He won't say why. Matt is extremely passionate about the app we're building. I don't think the (para)normal coding I'm doing will work the way he expects and, honestly, it's not ethical, but I'm enjoying the coding. It gives me ideas. It could be a while before you hear from me again, but you will. —Rebecca

Everyone owes money to something. The people I know either let the weight of their mounting debts consume them, lapping up every piece of them, or they forget and go on living and spending and accumulating like that's the most honest thing to keep doing when faced with nothing but more uncertainty.

At least that's what it can feel like on a Friday afternoon huddled in a small cubicle when it's payday.

Cindy tosses an envelope on my desk and continues her way down the open concept office, leaving my cubicle cloaked in an unfortunate mix of patchouli, body odour, and stale coffee. Every two weeks the temps in the law office get a paper paycheque of our biweekly earnings. Permanent staff have direct deposit, but that's more work for the Finance Division and not worth the effort on short-term labour that comes and goes.

"Thanks, Cindy." I say it out of habit. Permanent staff don't typically acknowledge the temps, but I try to be polite because that's what's helped me survive this far in the office environment.

I tear the thin envelope open to look at the disappointing three figures I'll have the onus of depositing into my account later. It's been the same amount for the last three years. The temp agency takes a huge cut, so huge that the arrangement barely makes sense to be doing for more than a couple months as you get back on your feet. I should be more upset about that, but honestly, I don't have the mental capacity right now. Rebecca's letters clearly indicate she's joined some kind of cult and she seems oblivious to this. I can't concentrate on anything else. Most of the time I welcome distractions from my thoughts, but not like this.

The money will stay in my account for approximately three hours on Saturday morning before my automatic bill payments start. Most of it will go to pay for the university education I never really used. In my temp role, I am responsible for removing staples from papers only to re-secure them with clips so it's easier for the lawyer to do his thing.

I shove the paycheque back in the ripped envelope and place it in front of a framed photo of Rebecca and me at the quay. When I look at the quay now, I feel all sorts of difficult things, but back when we were celebrating her completion of grad school, the quay felt like a launching point for new beginnings. She was going to build great things using (para)normal code. She understood the open-source framework even better than her professors, who were hesitant to really dig into this area of coding because there was a chance, if done perfectly, that the language could literally bring back the dead. The story goes that the guy who invented (para)normal claimed it had the power to connect with the afterlife. It has never happened, so it was probably a sham. Just another tech fraud claiming he was going to change the world with his brilliance and then falling short. Rebecca was able to make some neat forensic accounting apps using (para)normal code and her profs were all very impressed, but sadly, once she graduated, her coding skills were brushed off as too niche and she failed to land a job. All she had left was mountains of student loan debt and this paralyzed her.

My desk phone rings. It's the mailroom most likely calling about a package I need to fetch from a carrier. Technically this is part of my job, but I ignore it. It's almost noon, which means I'm practically on lunch.

I blame myself that Matt and his mall even know who Rebecca is.

It was my idea to take that awful personality test on the promenade. He claims he's cultivating an affordable housing experiment in one of the many failed malls he scooped up over the years for cheap. Cheap if you are one of the few in this world who have more money than you could ever spend. He thought he would use the empty retail space to help house people who needed it. It sounds decent, even like a good idea, and one I could get behind in a theoretical sense. But really. There's nothing super suspicious about a very wealthy man trying to start his own special society in secret? Rebecca, so smart, yet so naïve. I say this as her very best friend.

People want to move on, spread their wings, all that positive mindset stuff. Best friends might not stay best friends forever. I'm sad, not in denial. I understand Rebecca needed to do what she needed to do for her own reasons. If I'd known from the start what she was going through personally, I could have helped her. I should have known she was hurting, because any normal person would hurt after what she went through, but I missed the signs and I can't change that now.

But something's not right at the mall and I can't let it go.

Not one of the letters she sent me has a return address, her phone's been cancelled, and she hasn't responded to any emails. I send emails even though she said she has no internet access. I do it in case she's come to her senses and left Matt and his so-called intentional community in the obscurity it belongs. I do it in case she walks out of those automatic mall doors and finds her way back to a world where we communicate and speak with "external" voices because we can, and we should.

She also said I'd hear from her again, and I haven't. It's been months. Okay, maybe one month, but Rebecca keeps her word. She follows through when she says she will.

Before I can spiral any more, I feel a light tap on my shoulder and turn around to see Peter, an analyst who does something with property searches, looking at me nervously. We've chatted a few times in the lunchroom. He has a French bulldog named Pat, which is short for Patricia. He's one of the only permanent staff who talks to me.

"What are you doing on the weekend," he asks, pushing back pieces of his thick brown hair. His voice is quiet and he's looking at the ground. I doubt the temp beside me could hear him. "I was wondering if you," he continues, "wanted to, um…"

"I'm going to the mall." The words come out of my mouth before I fully comprehend what they mean. They come out curt, too, which isn't fair to Peter. We've always been friendly enough, but without a word, he backs as far away from me as he can, his face turning bright red. He quickly disappears down the office corridor and I swivel my chair back to face the corner of my cubicle so I can think.

I'm going to the mall.

Can I just do that? Can I just go find her? Maybe I should. I wouldn't be much of a best friend if I didn't try to find her and guide her back to reality. I've seen enough of those true crime documentaries to know she is not on a good path. Her silence toward me could mean she's in trouble or lost and I can't live with that feeling again. Rebecca might not even know what kind of mess she's in because the appeal of financial freedom after so many years of struggling is numbing her into thinking that what Matt is doing is justified.

I'm certain there's something off about the mall and there's no one out there who will help her but me. If anything, I probably should have left months ago, right after she left. If anything, I'm behind.

And besides, she always hated malls so she's probably having a terrible time living in an abandoned one.

2

If finding Rebecca was as simple as getting into my old car, filling the tank to the brim with expensive fossil-fuels, and driving east toward a spot conveniently dictated to me by my phone, I would. But, beyond the general direction, I don't know where she is.

By Saturday morning, I'm back at the exact spot I let Rebecca slip away. The quay down the street from our apartment building. This is where Matt's people hooked us into taking a personality test, thanks to me. I thought it would be funny. A simple story we could reminisce about for years after it was all done. *Remember that hilarious time?* I can't help but think Rebecca wouldn't be in this situation if I had suggested literally anything else to do that night. A chat with a recruiter of a cult? It seems so wrong now; I'm embarrassed it happened. To my credit, I didn't know then who they were, and mistakes happen when you lack purpose in your day. This I know well enough.

Facing the recruiters again today will be humiliating, but I'll do it for Rebecca. Matt's people made her act all cagey about mall location details, even weeks before she left. She had to deactivate all her social accounts. They told her this was the start of her work, her "vital" work. I think Matt feared a community member might accidentally tag a photo or write something and blow the cover off their whole secret operation.

"It's freeing," Rebecca said the morning she permanently deleted all her social profiles. She raised her hands like a bird. We were in our building's laundry room waiting for the ancient washing machines to stop their ferocious spin cycles so we could toss the sopping wet clothes into the dryers that always needed to be run twice. "I've hated those accounts for years. Everything I scrolled past was a blur anyway. Maybe an intentional lifestyle is a better direction for me. It's worth a shot. I need to do something different."

Our eyes met, and then immediately the lightness of her expression moments before faded. My face flushed as if I didn't deserve blood circulating to my brain. I hoped she wouldn't want to talk about why she needed to do something different. We never talked about what happened. She shook her head and then put some music on and turned up the volume over the roar of the washer instead. I realized we were listening to her new meditation playlist. This was something that came as a recommendation in her welcome box.

I'm not glued to social media, but the fact she needed to *delete* hers and not just abstain as a term of her acceptance to the mall was yet another red flag she couldn't see. They were trying to erase her, piece by piece, before she even got there. If they were making her do all this now, who knows what Matt had planned for when she arrived.

I was sitting on the old plastic lawn chair that had been a staple of this dark laundry room since we moved in and I looked over at her sipping a tea in a travel mug since she had to kick caffeine before she got there as well because "stimulant-free" was another buzzword of her acceptance. "So are you just going to disappear to that mall and never be heard from again? How will anyone be able to contact you? What if there's an emergency or something?" I wanted to say, *What if I need to talk to you.* But I couldn't.

She put her tea down near her feet and looked at me. She spoke slowly and gently like she had done so many times throughout our friendship. It was one of those things I appreciated about her. She wanted me to understand. "I don't know yet, but I'm sure they'll let me know how it'll all work when I get there. Please don't worry. It's just a short-term lifestyle change as I work some things out on my own. I'm not going to vanish."

The word *vanish* stung. I can't deal with someone else I care about vanishing again. My sister Jennifer disappeared when we were kids and Rebecca knew that. Jennifer was my whole life and then she was gone. I miss my sister as much as I miss my best friend, even after all these years.

That's why I'm out here today when I don't want to be. Even the thought of seeing the recruiters again had me up all night.

But I'm here. I'm doing this.

The quay is almost empty today even with clear blue skies and sun above. I take a deep breath as I reach the worn walkway of thick wooden planks to steady myself. If looking in the mirror had even crossed my mind before leaving my apartment, I'd be staring back at blood-shot eyes and stringy unwashed dark blonde hair pulled into a messy bun. Not my finest look, but it'll do for now. I'm alive and I'm human. I normally try to keep myself somewhat presentable. It helps me to blend in better, but I haven't been sleeping. I haven't had a restful sleep since I was a kid, but it's gotten worse since Rebecca left. I stayed up late last night because it was Friday and that's what workers do when it's the start of the weekend, even permanent temps like me. I fell asleep on my small loveseat, but only for a few precious hours, and then I was up again in the early morning. Thinking. Over-thinking. Going over the never-ending catalog of details in my head and then falling into another vivid dream about Jennifer. I never remember my dreams for long. For this, I've been grateful.

As I make my way from the walkway to the back parking lot where I know the recruiters will be, my phone vibrates with a new message. I pull it out and read a text from an unknown number: *I'M CALLING YOU BACK BECAUSE YOU LET ME GO. HOW COULD YOU? I'M CALLING YOU BACK. I'M CALLING YOU BACK. LOOK ME IN THE EYES AND TELL ME YOU'D DO ANYTHING TO HEAR MY VOICE AGAIN.*

I'm getting so many of these spam messages these days. Most of them claim I'm a rich heir entitled to millions. If only. This one's a bit weirder than most, but everyone is trying to get more creative these days. I delete it and block it anyway. I must keep walking. There's a small group of parents and their shrieking toddlers wandering around the playground and a woman in her 70s dressed head-to-toe in a flowy white cotton dress walking a limping Scottie. Seagulls and crows jump from pile to pile of garbage to peck and claw at the scraps left behind by picnickers long gone.

I'm relieved about this lack of foot traffic. It means Matt's recruiters will have more time to talk to me, to tell me exactly where the mall is. I need an address, that's all.

When I came here with Rebecca on what turned out to be the day we were tested for what they called "community suitability," I thought it was all a big joke. We were practically tackled from the walkway to come over to their booth, *just for a chat*, they said. The booth turned out to be two brightly painted vintage Boler trailers, one turquoise and the other lemon. Easy-listening music drifted through the windows to complete a wistful, slow-living vibe. It was just too perfect. We should have run right then. The mall recruiters dressed like they were selling home-made kombucha at a Saturday morning farmer's market in the country, all naturally dyed t-shirts and faded denim. Looking back, it was another thing that seemed too perfect, too calculated. It was all designed to disarm us, to seduce us for a lifestyle we didn't know we were nostalgic for. They promised to pay us once we finished the chat, in cash. Twenty minutes. Twenty bucks. The recruiters seemed friendly enough and we needed extra money. Win-win.

The recruiters handed us each a small brochure and told us we had to read it before they could invite us in. They needed to make sure we understood what the mall was, at least a little. I skimmed the glossy pages and read about community-style living and gardening. The headline read: "Unlock your best life with *intention*." I laughed when I read it, but the money was easy and we didn't have anything better to do.

"Let's try it." I looked at Rebecca and smiled to gently nudge her to try something new. I was hoping she'd be charmed by the ridiculousness of it. That's what we've done together for years. A mall that was basically a collective of exhausted people who were tired of the scarcity and debt they've been balancing for the last fifteen years or longer and wanted to give up, and, what, garden in the idyllic country? It seemed absurd, but I thought answering a short questionnaire was harmless, even fun.

If only I knew then. Rebecca had been so sad those days. This was a rare outing for us.

Instead of laughing, she glanced at her brochure and shrugged. One shrug was enough consent for Matt's team, and we each followed a recruiter with a clipboard into a trailer.

Today, the same trailers are here in the parking lot, arranged in the picture-perfect positions they were before. Everything looks the same, but the recruiters aren't outside actively soliciting people to take the personality test like they had been the night we saw them. The doors and windows are closed, but there's two lawn chairs out front and a half-drunk mason jar of coffee on the ground beneath one. Someone will be inside. I'll have to knock on the door. It's an extra step. I had imagined the recruiters out here, like they usually were, but I can go to them.

I knock on the lemon trailer, step back onto the curb, and wait. I've rehearsed what I'm going to say. I'll keep it simple and direct. The address. All I need is the address. The trailers are still. I listen for movement inside, but I don't hear anything. As I wait, I notice a knot of rust rotting out the chrome bumper on the turquoise trailer. It's a smudge on an otherwise fully curated look I hadn't noticed before. A bee buzzes close to my ear, and I try to brush it away, but the sound stays. It's level and even like the bee is perched inside my ear. I swipe at it, but it doesn't stop. It's my nerves. This happens to me sometimes. The key is remaining calm, something I find very challenging to do.

I look back at the park as I wait. Everything's peaceful out here until a loud cry pierces through the quiet. A woman shouts and runs across the playground. She's waving her hands and looking all around like she's rabid. A crowd of caregivers surround her, they're calling out now, only quieter. They're all saying the same thing, like a chant.

"Kyle? Kyle, where are you? KYLE?"

Hearing this, my lungs seize, and I feel like I've swallowed a small balloon. My cheeks flame hot. I want to go over there and help find the boy. I want to rescue him, but I can't move my feet. I can't leave this curb. All these years later, decades even, and I still can't get up and go. What if my help could change some sort of disastrous outcome? What if this mom needs me? I need to move.

"Kyle, mommy's looking for you. Where are you?" I watch Kyle's mom throw herself against the railing and look down at the rushing river below. We always jump to the most extreme conclusion first.

She'll be alone forever. I push the memory down. Not today. Not out here.

The woman's voice gets louder, more uncontrollable, more feral, with each scream. It's hard to listen to. I'm not used to hearing so much emotion anymore. I'm feeling suddenly cold and I wish I had brought a sweater. A few people who live in the townhouses nearby have walked out from their doors to see what's happening. No one comes out from the trailers.

Where is he? I manage to loosen my stance on the curb and step down onto the sidewalk. I can help. I take one step toward the playground and stop.

"Kyle!" Her tone is different now, relieved but trembling, like she's finally ready to let her brain process what just happened, what could have happened if the outcome wasn't as swift, if in that instance life was cruel enough to turn into her worst nightmare.

The mom scoops up a boy, maybe four years old, into her shaking arms and hugs him, burying her face into his dark hair. The woman walking her dog waves and tries to explain. The boy had been visiting the Scottie outside the playground. He'd opened the latch to the gate himself and wandered over to make friends with the dog. It was a misunderstanding, a foolish call to adventure that only a preschooler would accept. The caregivers are all laughing now. Everyone's safe and where they should be. It's suddenly a normal Saturday again, as if someone hit the play button and the day's activities were allowed to resume as expected. Lucky them. It's not always so lucky for some of us. Another chill runs down my spine and I try to shake it off.

I turn back to my own business, my reason for being here, with my heart still racing. Rebecca, I need to find Rebecca. This is a situation I can control. I feel the balloon in my lungs slowly deflate again. Good. It's been a while since I've felt that balloon and it's never a good sign. I need to watch it. I need to keep moving. I need to start driving east. I walk to the turquoise trailer this time and knock harder. I don't have time to waste. The road is calling me to find Rebecca. Before I reach my secure spot on the curb, the door swings open with a squeak.

"We're not seeing people today. Come back another time." The voice, weak and timid, comes from within the trailer. I can barely hear it. It's almost a whisper.

"I'm looking for my friend who joined the mall a few months ago. I have some important news I need to tell her," I lie. "I've got to get a hold of her. Can you give me the address of where she is?"

No response. I take a step closer, but not close enough that I can see inside yet. "Please, it's about her brother." Another lie. Rebecca's an only child, unlike me who's a sisterless twin with a try-hard brother. "My friend's brother is in the hospital. Hurt from a motorcycle accident. A hit and run. He's lost a lot of blood. She'll want to know right away."

I could go on, sometimes the lies come easily, but something shifts from inside. I approach the door to look. There's a woman, maybe in her late twenties, hunched over a honey-coloured Formica table. I don't recognize her as the person who interviewed me or Rebecca for the mall. She's alone and working on a crossword puzzle book, like the kind you'd get from the dollar store for someone stuck in the hospital or bedridden at home without good TV.

"You know I can't tell you where they are," she says, scribbling a letter down and frowning. She crosses out her ink with a huff. "That's part of the beauty of unplugging. It's about being completely separate. Detached. Free." She says *free* like even her mouth could not contain the concept of it. It seems to float past me.

"But, it's her brother..." I stop myself, the lies being too much even for me. This woman doesn't care and I've always been a bad liar.

She looks up at me for the first time and stares. Her wide eyes are intense and I feel myself start to sweat with a flash of panic. I look down at my toes sticking out of my sandals and the cracked purple polish I need to redo, and pull my hand through my hair, embarrassed at what she must be seeing. I haven't felt like myself lately. It's the stress. When I get home, a shower is in order or maybe a nice bubble bath. I'll try to get some rest, for my health. I've told myself to focus on the little things recently and it's time I start listening. Rebecca was always the one who reminded me to take time for myself.

"I remember you. You've been here before." She tosses her pen down onto the table, and it rolls across the shiny surface before falling to the floor.

"Just once."

"If that's what you want to believe."

"I believe it because it's true."

I shake my head. She's changing the subject. Matt has trained an army of manipulators. I sensed it the first time we met them. This interaction confirms it.

"I've seen you here multiple times. This is the first time you've spoken to me though. The other times you…"

"There's no way," I interrupt. This woman has mistaken me for someone else and I have no time for it. Petty mind games are the cheapest way to distract me from the disaster that is their so-called community.

She scoffs and pushes her tortoiseshell glasses back up the bridge of her long nose. "Whatever," she says with a sigh, leaning down to grab her pen from the black and white laminate floor and bringing it back up. She pulls her book closer and writes another few letters. "It's not a good idea to go looking for something you haven't been invited to," she says without looking up from her puzzle. "It's not brave. You won't be doing yourself any favours trying to find someplace you don't belong, don't understand. You wouldn't be welcomed if you got there. And, besides, you'll never be able to find it. The location is not public and there's a reason for that. He doesn't like anyone from the outside world trying to visit. We're working there. He has a way of making it very unpleasant for those who try to interrupt that work and he has a way of knowing a lot more than he should."

She laughs at this, then quiets. She looks at me again and tilts her head to the side like she's trying to figure me out. Her thick dirty blonde hair just about touches the table when she does this and suddenly I feel sorry for her. This poor woman. What did she study in university that put her in so much debt that choosing to spend her days trapped in a stuffy, miniscule trailer recruiting vulnerable people for the absurdly wealthy in a quayside parking lot seemed like the best escape plan?

She taps the butt of her pen a couple times on the table. To the left of her, there's a stack of envelopes. The top one, at least, is addressed to someone. I wonder if these envelopes are filled with equally peculiar messages handwritten on cream-coloured notecards like the one I found in Rebecca's room. I'm tempted to lunge for the stack and tear each envelope to shreds so they never reach their destinations. The army of manipulators use notecards as a tactic to persuade a would-be member to trust them, that, and the promise of living without debt for once in their adult life. It's too much to resist.

Then this woman grabs my attention again, as if catching my thoughts and trying to divert my suspicions.

"Do you know a nine-letter word for *hopeless* beginning with the letter d?" she asks.

I consider the question. I've never been good at puzzles. I don't like games. Games require a level of patience and surrender I don't have. I'd rather walk somewhere or read or clean or do just about anything else. But today a word comes to me quickly.

"Desperate."

3

"I'd do the same thing, you know," Rebecca said the day before she left for Matt's community. We had just walked to the grocery store down the street from the apartment. She was helping me carry the bags because I was still recovering from the injury on my arm. It was another expensive haul, where even basic vegetables were unbelievably pricey. Rain poured as I held a faded purple umbrella over my head. "If I had all that money, I'd one hundred percent buy back people's loans like Matt Maxis does. I'm in awe of his work," she added.

In *awe*? The word felt innocently dangerous, like accidentally pricking your finger on a forgotten pin buried deep in a drawer and pulling it out to see a gush of blood you weren't expecting. The biggest news stories that week were about the ongoing billionaire space race, the money being spent for a few minutes in orbit was unfathomable to me, so I could see that in comparison Matt's mission to buy student loan debt seemed downright altruistic. But Matt doesn't pay off the loan and leave it at that. He paid it off on the condition that the beneficiary must leave their life behind and join his private community at the mall. The excessively rich can't help themselves from driving an exchange that's stacked in their favour. It's what they're accustomed to, and for people like the Maxis family I've learned, it's hardwired from birth.

From my research, I discovered a potential community member must live at the mall for one month for every $1,000 Matt paid off. For Rebecca, that meant she'd be there for eighty-five months or just over seven years. Leaving early was always an option, but it meant she'd owe the community major interest on the original loan. She couldn't afford that. If she decided to leave the mall and pay, she would be right where she started financially if not worse, but she'd have her old life back and that's got to be worth something to her. It would have been for the old Rebecca, the one who had her own thoughts and dreams. The Rebecca she was before she lost something she desperately wanted.

Rebecca, I wanted to scream, *this is forced labour.*

But I held my tongue this time and instead posed a question that had gnawed at me since I found out about the details of the contract. "If you had this kind of money, why wouldn't you just pay off the loan and let the person live how they wanted to live? Like, you pay their debt and you both move on. Maybe you offer them a place to live, but it's completely on their own terms. You do it because you can. Because you have so much money it's ridiculous to hoard it anymore. I can't see you trying to put together some secret society where everyone does what you say and you are the ultimate ruler. You're too human."

She shook her head and laughed. "Matt is human, too. Part of what excites me about this is the community he's building. It seems like a good way to live, and you know I can't stay here anymore. It's getting harder each day." Suddenly she sounded as if she was on the verge of tears. Her mood was shifting. Her eyes darkened and took on that far away look I was getting used to seeing. It was never good. She swallowed. "You have to understand that by now, right?"

I wasn't ready for this talk. "Do you know what you'll be doing there?" I asked, trying to change the subject.

"It's embargoed until I arrive. I have no idea, but it doesn't matter. Part of the deal is I have to go to the mall, so that's what I'm doing. Once this is done, I'll be free." She let out a deep sigh, but it didn't sound like her usual signal of defeat, but as if she was cleansing her body with breath, like she was doing yoga breathing. Rebecca hated yoga so this new style of breathing was concerning. Old Rebecca would have laughed at someone randomly yoga breathing on a walk. "I'm sorry to leave you with all the rent. I feel terrible about it. Will you be okay?"

Despite trying to brush it off by telling her I'd be fine, the truth was, it'd be a stretch. A significant one. I knew it from the minute she told me she was leaving. I would struggle with keeping everything afloat.

I found out later that she knew more about what she'd be doing there than she was telling me. They'd been sending her things, details on what her life would be like, what she could expect, and how she'd grow as a person at the mall. Before she left, she left her computer open to a virtual tour given by a member who'd lived in the mall since it began five years prior. Rebecca wasn't home, so I watched it.

The tour guide identified herself only as *Sophie*. The harsh overhead lighting gave her pale white skin a freshly bruised look. She closed her eyes briefly before launching into her story. She was originally from Halifax. She'd studied in a four-year journalism program because she wanted to tell the stories of her people, to dig deep into the issues impacting her home. Then the economy fell from the sky and, despite what she tried, Sophie could not find paid work, only demoralizing unpaid internship after unpaid internship she couldn't afford to take. She was rejected again and again. She struggled for years, she said, in jobs that didn't suit her and would keep her broke and didn't fulfill her with what she wanted to do, which was serve her community.

That was until she learned about the mall one night when she was alone on a walk to clear her head.

"When I joined the mall, my whole life changed. I could see clearly who I'd become, and I didn't like her." As she was talking, she looked off camera as if someone was whispering something to her. She raised her eyebrows, then looked directly into the camera with a new focus. She spoke slower now and with a specific emphasis on each word like she was trying hard to get back to the pre-approved script. "I was bitter. Defeated. Sad. Anxious. And, most of all, broke. I could barely cover rent. My credit was down the toilet. No bank would give me more money even if I tried. I was treading in quicksand. I couldn't juggle it all anymore. Matt calls it "spectral burnout" because a part of our core being is missing. I deserved a change. I wanted better for myself. Somehow."

The video then cut to her sitting in a lush vegetable garden, with rows of greenhouses just behind her. She had a straw hat on, which made her look carefree and happy. Far in the background, right at the edge of the frame, there were tall dark walls, but that was all I could make out.

"It took a lot of time to allow myself to believe I was worthy of something, anything." She said this as she put her foot on a shovel and pushed down into the ground. I admit the sound of the metal crushing into the fresh dirt was oddly satisfying to hear.

The video cut to Sophie in her room. It had the cold and sterile quality of a hospital room. She had a roommate, but they were not part of the video. Each of them got their own twin-sized bed that looked like it was made of cardboard and topped with a thick slab of foam. There was also an unnerving lack of personal belongings, no photos or art on the walls. No books or electronic devices.

"I'm happy now. Free from everything that pressed down on me from my before life." Sophie spoke directly into the camera again, her pupils small and reflecting the ring light shining into them.

Before life? The words cut me. I couldn't be a part of Rebecca's before life. We shared a life. There has never been a before or after. There's just us.

"Matt knows. He really does know. I owe him so much. More than he understands. I have so much appreciation for him and his vision here at the mall." She wiped a tear from her eye, then blinked back into the camera. "I love the path I'm on."

Good overall production quality, but I didn't believe a word of it. Matt must have written it himself. Her script sounded like it was torn from the mass-produced pages of a gratitude journal bought in bulk at Costco. *Spectral burnout?* Please.

"I never think about my debt anymore. It's made a world of difference for my self-esteem. Seeing the interest bump up each month on my debt left me heartbroken day after day. I was tired of being sad. That's all over now. Again, I thank Matt and his community for that. It's his vision. His work. I've made some of the best friends I could ever expect here. I think I'm going to stay longer than my contract states because I love the mall. It's my home. I belong here and this is the work I should be doing for the rest of my life. I can't wait to meet you!"

She ended the video by leading her viewer through a guided meditation, complete with breathing exercises. So that's where Rebecca picked up that pretentious breathing. Only in the last scene could I see her rubbing her belly because she was pregnant. Giving birth behind an abandoned food court doesn't do it for me. However, she didn't just smile the whole time, she beamed, which is when I felt the physical need to stop watching and lay down a while.

Our *before life* took place in a 1970s barebones apartment rented from a woman who rents a place in a better part of Metro Vancouver than uptown New Westminster. This way my land-lord has the equity she so desires and the lifestyle she feels she deserves, which from what I can glean from her social media is paddleboard yoga in Deep Cove and charcoal flavoured soft serve in South Granville. She likes to post photos of her latest boyfriend, a tall man with glasses who looks a little like Joshua Jackson when she applies the right filter. At least she's never increased our rent. For that small mercy, enjoy all the gourmet ice cream you want, Shelley! Now that I'm covering all the rent for this place, I'm in a situation where almost seventy percent of my income is spent on rent alone. No financial advisor worth their salt would advise this, but I don't have any other option. I wouldn't know where to begin if I pressed reset on my whole life. This is why a small part of me can understand the appeal of Matt's community to people like Sophie who are, in her own words, sad and anxious. But Rebecca? She's talented. She can code (para)normal better than anyone in the world. Literally. She just needed more patience. Things were eventually going to go her way.

My unit is on the second floor beside the coin laundry room and smells musty when it rains too much, which means it always smells musty because it's always raining on the West Coast. The carpets are thin and blue and scratchy, but it's home. I thought I'd be somewhere better now, somewhere with a bathtub that wasn't the colour of homemade split pea soup or had a kitchen with cupboards that stayed on their hinges when the heat register beneath them started blowing. I thought I might even have a husband or a serious partner at this point in my life, someone who looked out for me, and me him, but here I am. Unit 202. Double-locked cheap door. Queen-sized mattress on the floor.

Rebecca's room is now where I keep her deflating yoga ball and a small bookshelf filled with books collecting dust. These books represent a mausoleum of half-baked hopefulness: college texts for courses in the Humanities, paperbacks on how to live on a budget or as a vegan, and Best Hikes on Vancouver Island 2013. I should donate them, but then the room would be almost empty and that's just wasteful when I'm paying this much money to live here. There's also a photo of Jennifer and I that my mom took in the driveway just before we left for the camping trip. She's in a pink jacket and I'm in a matching purple one. It's our last photo together. We smile at the camera, even though Jennifer's eyes are red from another argument with dad. It was a long weekend and my mom insisted we have a photo, even though no one was in the mood because dad was mad about something. When I look at that picture now, I wish I would have taken my sister by the hand that day and never let go. If I had done that, maybe she would still be here with us. Instead, I let her walk away because that's what we all did when we went camping. We naïvely went into the forest alone as it was nothing. As if we had the power to shine through the darkness of a thick blanket of trees and wildlife even though we didn't. I keep this picture to remind me of what it was like to stand beside her.

Near the window of Rebecca's old room is a wooden rocking chair, one of the few things she didn't give away before leaving. She bought it a couple weeks before we took the personality test. I guess it's mine now. She also left something that I don't think she meant to leave, something I keep with her letters even though it disturbs me. A week or so after she moved out, I noticed a thick cream-coloured notecard stuck between the chipped baseboard and the wall in the corner of her room. She forgot it, and since she was gone and I had no way of reaching her, I flipped it open and read a handwriting I didn't recognize. It said, "*Conjure her and she will come. She'll become alive just like she should have if reality was fair and true and had a bit of grace. She will be with you, just like she needs to be from the other side. I'll show you how. I'm tired of the world playing sides. Life, death. Right, wrong. Good, bad. We need relationships with the people we have true connections with without boundaries. The pain will stop when you see her. I know how hard it is, dear, to lose someone. People like us deserve to be with the ones we love no matter what keeps us apart. Death no longer do us part."*

The note wasn't signed. I found the words confusing and I couldn't make sense of them. Was this even a note for Rebecca? It must have been because it certainly wasn't for me.

I thought about destroying the note right after I read it the first time, but I stopped myself and put it away instead. I wanted to know why someone sent it too much, and, besides, I agreed with the sentiment of the words on a level so deep and powerful I was ashamed of myself.

4

When I get home from the quay, Sammy comes to see me at the door with a purr and I scratch his head. This place is a mess and seeing the stacks of books and piles of laundry now tires me. I shouldn't live like this at this point in my life. I'm sure it exhausted Rebecca, too. Even before she left, she was getting rid of things, making way for the change in her life she needed. As far as I know, she only brought one suitcase that contained some clothes and a small pink box. When I saw the box sitting with her suitcase by the door the morning she left, I went back to my room. I hadn't realized she had a box like that and seeing it there all lonely broke my heart.

Now that I'm home from the quay, I need to tidy up. I pull the worn quilt across my bed and attempt to fluff the old pillows. Good enough. I grab my phone and see I have a missed voicemail from an unknown number. I'm so eager for Rebecca to be calling to arrange a ride home that I almost don't want to check it because I'm afraid I'll be disappointed. She's not allowed a phone at the mall, I know this, but maybe there's a chance she found one and she used it to call me.

Before I can think more about what the message might say, I punch in my pin and listen to the voice on the other end. My heart sinks. It's not Rebecca, it's the droning voice of my older brother Chris, my one family member I'm still vaguely in touch with, no thanks to much effort on my part.

"Hi, Carolyn! I'm just calling to remind you about our dinner tonight. The girls are looking forward to seeing their auntie." He had me on speakerphone I can tell from the noisy but familiar din of an office in the background. He must be working on a Saturday. How very on brand of him.

"We'll have, um…" he continues. "We'll have cake. You know, birthday cake for you…"

No, no. I look at the date on my phone. It can't be that time of year already. I hear him start singing and quickly toss the phone to the foot of the bed. "Happy birthday dear Carolyn…"

My brain fills in the part I heard for nine years and that I loved hearing for those years.

…and Jennifer.

This brain of mine can be so cruel. I almost succeeded in not remembering that today is my birthday and the fact that Chris went out of his way to remind me of this when I've told him repeatedly not to, makes the sudden realization worse. If only he listened to me. I make a significant effort to forget it every year and usually it's easy enough to do, especially when there's no one in my life who knows it. Even Rebecca didn't ask me much about it and we never celebrated together because she understood this part of my life was off limits in our friendship. I've found most adults don't care about other people's birthdays past a certain time in their lives. Fine with me. After sharing my birthday with someone for nine years, celebrating it on my own had become so painful that I decided one day in my early teens to just pretend I had come to exist on this earth without a start date. I also arrived solo.

But now that I know what day it is, I can't stop my brain from doing the calculation.

This is the hard part. The calculation is why I stopped remembering my birthday in the first place. I'm 31 today. Now my brain starts on the next part of the calculation, the worst part of the whole birthday process. It's been 22 years since I last saw my sister. She's still that little girl in the pink jacket, while I'm this adult. It doesn't seem fair that I've had to go this long without her, to go this long without talking to her or know what really happened to her out there. Over two decades later, missing her hasn't gotten any easier, but that's a thought for another day. I need to find the mall. I need to do it now because Rebecca is not safe there.

I look over at my desk where all my research on Matt is lying open. I also have some printouts from the internet and a small

Letter to the Editor cut out from our local newspaper wondering why city bylaw officers haven't shut down a "cult" trying to recruit at one of our local parks. Then there's the copy of the blog posts Rebecca mentioned in her third letter. I was able to find them right away. A woman named Rane created a blog about losing her sister to the mall. She posted daily until she went cold about a year ago. I emailed her anyway to see if she had reunited with her sister, but it was another dead end. She never replied.

Then there's my intel about Matt. *Matt knows*. I sit down at the desk and start reviewing everything once again. I must be missing something.

When Rebecca told me she was leaving town to join a community run by Matt Maxis, I set out to find as much information about him as I could. I did this for assurance that she would be okay there. I was trying to do a background check, like anyone would once they got a whiff of this guy. I can't be the only one not buying this totally unregulated student loan buy-back program, served up with a side of free housing during a crippling affordability crisis.

The first thing I found was his work profile. His picture wasn't available to anyone who wasn't a connection and I didn't dare add him to my profile, which I barely used anyway because people found very little value networking with temps. Matt had a few noteworthy items publicly available for the world to see. He worked for the family company Maxis Ltd. in Ottawa right after he finished his commerce degree at the University of Toronto. According to its business profile, Maxis Ltd. was established in 1919 as a major supplier to Canada's burgeoning auto industry. From there, it diversified and became one of the largest importers of plastic gloves and products for use in homes, medical facilities, and industry. "To this day," the profile read, "the company stays true to its roots of supplying the hardworking Canadian people with the daily conveniences they deserve." Maxis Ltd. products, it went on, could be found in grocery and hardware stores across the country.

I probably have a pair of gloves imported by his family in my apartment right now. I felt oddly used when I first realized this because it means I have contributed to his otherworldly prosperity and his ability to experiment with people's lives in a literal dead mall by virtue of purchasing a pair of disposable dishwashing gloves.

Beyond the boiler plate narrative around his incredible family, there are a few things that aren't sitting right with me about his story, no matter how hard I try to ignore it.

The first being why he broke away from his family to pursue his own thing in the first place. It would have been so easy for him to stay, collect an obscenely large paycheque for doing close to nothing, and wait in line for his eventual turn at the helm of a self-driving machine of the likes of Maxis Ltd. Instead, he started M2 Enterprises and it's thin what he did from there. With my temp law admin skills, I was able to find some not very exciting court documents about his uncle trying to sue his dad for massive amounts of money because of a joint business venture gone bad. Beyond the strife of a rich family bickering in the court of law, I couldn't find any websites or press releases mentioning Matt's own company.

The second part that isn't adding up is why he focussed on investing in dead or abandoned malls. I haven't found anything to suggest he is interested in redeveloping the land. I found an industry magazine published seven years ago citing Matt Maxis as one of the giants in mall revitalization efforts because he wants to keep them intact. The article said, "If you've ever walked into a mall in British Columbia, it's probably owned by Matt Maxis, the young entrepreneur who is also trained in yoga and meditation. He moved to the south coast of British Columbia from Toronto to enjoy the laid-back vibe and beautiful mountain vistas from the front of his family's many estates..."

I drop the papers on my desk and rub my temple, trying to soothe the start of a tension headache. I've read through all these materials dozens of times and still I've found nothing. At the sound of my papers, Sammy jumps from my dresser onto the desk and all my research spills to the floor.

"Sammy, come on. Please be careful." He slinks out of my room. I kneel to gather the papers. I've read them over and over many times looking for something, but all I see is a rich kid running through life like it's a carnival. It's exhausting to absorb myself in. Under my desk, I see a slim book with red cardstock covers poking out from beneath a pile of manila file folders that contain pieces of marketing work I did when I was trying to make a name for myself. I haven't had the heart to throw my portfolio away yet even though it is getting outdated. I know instantly what the red covers mean. I pull it out and see Rebecca's thesis from her computer science degree. She called it: "The Future of Community Wellness with (para)normal."

I place the book on my desk and set it down, brushing my hand gently on the textured cover before opening it. She poured herself into this thesis. She spent countless hours writing about how (para)normal technology could support people with grief by creating meaningful connections with the dead. I flip through a few of the old pages. I'm probably one of the only people in the entire world to have read this thing. It's all just theory, ideas that only she truly understands. I read through a couple pages.

> "…there are people who need to connect with their loved ones who have passed over or else they can never move on. Without moving on, their lives are in stasis. They are in pain. But they do not need to be. This technology has the potential to improve community health and wellness by providing short and meaningful simulations with the deceased for long enough to unleash important serotonin that can lead the way to healing…"

I flip to the front of the book and read her dedication page. *For Carolyn, my very best friend. If I do this, I'll do it for you first. Just watch me.* I never understood most of the technical stuff she told me about what she was trying to build, just that she thought she could connect a griever with their late loved one with her unique understanding of (para)normal coding. She wanted me to see Jennifer again. I never told her much about Jennifer or what happened, but she understood without me saying that I would never recover from losing her.

Still, all of this was a decade ago and nothing became of it. I shut the thesis and set it down beside my other research. Time to get ready for my bath and then a much-needed rest before going to Chris's house for a birthday cake. I promised myself some self-care time earlier on the pier, and I need to start following through. I walk toward the kitchen to put the kettle on to make tea and stop just as I step into my small living room.

Something feels off. My skin prickles with fear. The sensation that someone is here, that someone is watching comes over me. It's impossible. This isn't a ground-level unit and there's a large courtyard between this building and the next. All this thinking about Rebecca must have reminded me on a subconscious level that I'm alone.

Even though I know this on a logical level, I can't fight the feeling that I'm being watched and need to will myself to turn toward the balcony to see it with my own eyes. The balcony will be empty. I listen to the thumping of my heart and repeat to myself, *When I open my eyes, the balcony will be empty and I will continue to the kitchen to make my tea.*

I open my eyes and my legs tremble. The balcony is not empty. A shadowy figure is standing behind the old drapes. Someone's watching me. Someone's in my home. I'm stunned in place, too scared to move. The best I can do is close my eyes. Unlike the blue skies earlier today, now it's a rain typical of early fall. Even though I remembered to lock the door like Rebecca always reminded me to do, I hear it slowly slide open and the pounding of the rain gets louder, closer. So this is how it ends. A home invasion before leaving for my brother's house to have a birthday dinner I don't want. I take a step back, unable to keep my composure any longer, and stumble into the corner of the couch.

Sammy is startled again by this and jumps from the couch with a bang, pulling down my lamp with a crash.

My eyes immediately dart to the lamp. When I look back at the balcony, it's empty. The door is closed. The rain is pattering dully outside. Everything is normal.

Did I imagine what just happened? I walk over and carefully tug the door handle. It moves. It wasn't locked. I slide it shut and push the latch down. I swear I locked it before going to the pier, but maybe I didn't. My mind has been consumed with so many things that it's possible I forgot such a small but important thing. I pick up the lamp from the floor and return it to the table.

Time to get out of here.

I hurry out of my unit and walk to the entrance of the building to check my mail. Rebecca might have sent me something by now. Then I can stop worrying and move on. It's clear to me after what just happened that I need to start focusing on myself more.

I open my mailbox and pull out a single piece of junk mail. I turn it over and see a big, shiny airbrushed photo of someone I haven't seen in years. Steve. Oh, not this guy. Not today.

Before I rip up the flyer and toss the pieces into the recycling bin below the mailboxes, I read it. It appears Steve is now focusing on the "sizzling, FOOL-proof passive income market" of helping millennials purchase investment condos to rent to university students. The ridiculousness of it floods my body with a strange and welcomed sensation, almost like relief but wilder, and I laugh so hard one of the seniors who lives in the unit outside the mailboxes opens his doors to ask if I'm okay.

5

Steve was not my finest moment. Even seeing his face on this flyer and reading his name now fills me with a million emotions, none of them healthy. I haven't forgiven him. I also haven't forgiven myself for what I did to get rid of him. It takes two to royally screw things up. I know in my heart that every part of it was necessary, but I only wished Rebecca had seen it the same way, but she didn't.

Rebecca dated Steve on and off for close to two years. He'd break up with her for a few weeks, see the woman he'd been courting on the side since the start, and then come crawling back because he remembered that he really loved her this time. It was for *real* this time. He was good at sounding sincere, like he was a nice guy deep down.

I knew he wasn't. Anyone who paid attention would know that too.

The break-up, make-up scenario happened so often that I even witnessed it once when he "accidentally" ran into us at the quay, where he never went but fine, and confessed his undying love for her alongside the dog training session going on in the park to the right of us. She welcomed him back, and every time she did, I had to deal with his presence yet again. His unpleasant smell that was apparently a deliberate result of expensive cologne. His hair thickened with goopy gel. His polyester tracksuits that, honestly, seemed a size too small. Despite all that, it was his personality that bothered me the most, and the way he continued to treat Rebecca after the honeymoon make-up period was over, like she wasn't the most special person he'd ever met. This really bothered me. He didn't deserve her, but she never asked my opinion on the matter so I kept it all to myself. I had to bottle up some really toxic feelings, and that's not sustainable. At least not in me.

Steve was studying to become a real estate agent through correspondence. He was going to make a lot of money, he claimed, and probably he has. Good for him, I guess. Sell those properties! I see his face now and again, which is more rounded than it used to be and permanently red, but there's the same crooked smile, on bus benches near busy intersections in the city. *Move With Steve!* Whenever I see his bench, I can't help but study his face, even though it's likely been edited to look unfairly youthful and bright because there's no way age has been so kind to him. He wasn't a particularly vibrant guy, but Rebecca loved him for reasons beyond my understanding, so I tolerated him for the time I had to.

When they were together, he was over almost every night to the point where I wondered if he rented his own place anymore or if Rebecca invited him to live with us and failed to mention it to me.

"Helloooo," he'd say to me when I walked through the door. He'd use a cartoonish voice, like greeting me this way would put me under his charm. Most people liked him, but I couldn't. I'd seen too much of him to ever like him.

It was at this time I was trying to make it as a freelancer and rented a small desk at a co-working space in Gastown. I could have done the same amount of work from home, as my client list was laughably low, but I thought I would network in the co-working space, meet people, collaborate, join a team. I was wrong. I was awful at networking. Allergic to making small talk. Hopeless at connecting with anyone who wasn't my one and only best friend. I kept my headphones in and my head down for most of the time I was in the office. When my six-month contract was up, I didn't renew it and I left without saying goodbye to anyone.

Seeing him in my space when I got home each day was the last thing I could handle.

"Hi, Steve," I'd say upon this greeting. He'd usually be sitting at our kitchen table, taking up the entire space, with his thick textbook open to look like he was studying for his exam, but he was just texting the whole time. I hated it when he was over when Rebecca was still in class. She gave him a key. The kitchen would be messy with his dishes and the packages from the food he made himself earlier in the day. I knew from experience that he wouldn't be taking it down to the recycling bins. It stressed me just seeing him there.

One day Rebecca was home when I got back from my dreary co-space desk and not Steve. The kitchen was tidy.

"Helloooooo," I said and laughed. She looked at me, confused, and that's when I saw that her eyes were red. "Are you okay?"

She put her hand on her forehead. This always meant something was worrying her. "Steve and I broke up," she said quietly. I almost missed what she said.

Even though I could tell she was hurt, I added the word "again" mentally but didn't say it. Steve had dumped her many times before and they always reconciled before long, before I ever got used to the joy of walking into my apartment and not seeing him sitting right there.

I told her I was sorry to hear that, which wasn't true because he was awful and she was so much better off without him but what else was I supposed to say? She loved the guy, and who someone decides to devote themselves to is a personal decision. She then told me about the text message she saw him sending to some girl, and that was that. She ended it this time.

She sniffled and I handed her a tissue. I thought it was really over.

Days after the breakup, I was borrowing her phone because the screen on mine had smashed and I couldn't make any calls or afford to fix it until I got paid again, which would have been weeks away. I was talking to Chris about his latest promotion. He liked to keep me up to speed on all his career moves and I always felt obliged to listen out of some strange sibling duty.

Mid-conversation, Rebecca received a text message. I heard it come in with a ding. I didn't mean to look, but the preview showed it was from Steve and I couldn't help my curiosity. What did this loser want? Rebecca was out of the house grabbing a coffee down the street. I clicked on the message.

I'm so sorry babe. I miss you like crazy. I'm an idiot. You know I'm an idiot. I love you. I think I got scared of the thought of us moving in together. But I'm ready now. I even found us a place with room to grow. I can't wait to spend my life with you. Can we talk?

I stared at his message. She hadn't mentioned she was thinking about moving out and we didn't keep secrets like this. Was this one of Steve's delusional attempts at getting her back? It's possible one of them casually mentioned the prospect of moving in together during one of their honeymoon periods when they were *so* in love. There was a pattern with them. Break-up, make-up, break-up, make-up. Enough. I could have easily changed the status of the message to unread and left it at that, but it was from Steve and Steve needed to be put in his place. A feeling welled up in me just then. I was the only one who would step in and help save Rebecca from a nightmare waiting to happen. If she saw it, she'd call him and they'd be back together before she finished that coffee she was buying. I hated how Steve treated Rebecca, but I knew Rebecca would go back to a relationship that did not serve her. It's like she thought she didn't deserve the absolute best.

I stopped listening to Chris go on about the view of the North Shore mountains from his new office window, the number of high-res computer monitors he had, and the selection of organic coffee and fresh fruit available in the staff kitchen for free. Then I started to type: *Steve. Never contact me again. It's over.* I read the text over, realized I could do better, then added: *I hate everything about you. Stay away. Bye Forever.*

I sent it and felt good afterward, like a soothing balm had been applied all over me. He didn't reply and Rebecca never mentioned anything to me about it, which made me know it was the right decision. Best friends do each other favours.

I had hoped she saw it that way.

If that was truly the last time Rebecca heard from him, this might be a different story and I wouldn't need to look for her in this urgent matter. But it wasn't.

6

That night, I tear down the highway for dinner with Chris's family at their hillside house in a sidewalkless suburb an hour away. Driving has always helped clear my head. I can't replay the balcony scene anymore and what I might have seen. I'm tired, under stress. It's understandable that my imagination is going off on me. But it seemed so real. Impossible, but real.

I pull on to their quiet street of executive-style homes. Each home is safely pushed in from the road with a long, private driveway.

My sister-in-law recently redecorated the sprawling five-year-old home in the style of a faux old farmhouse, with white paint everything. I adore my sister-in-law, Farrah. I follow all her attempts at transforming herself into a beloved lifestyle and motherhood influencer on social media. Their daughters are curious and intelligent, and I love that they are my nieces. They're the real reason why I keep in touch with Chris. Despite my love for them, being here tonight is overwhelming. I agreed to the dinner weeks ago, not realizing that this was Chris's sneaky way of getting me to participate in something remotely related to celebrating my birthday. For someone who makes a living developing software for the future of medical technology, he's oddly sentimental for the past.

I park in the driveway behind their two white extra-large SUVs. I walk up the steps and read Farrah's latest boutique jute welcome mat that says in black script, *We Hope You Brought the Awesome!* I wipe my sandals across the text and knock. My brother answers the door in his work clothes, dark olive chinos and a pale pink oxford, and pulls me in for a hug before I can say hello.

"Happy birthday, my dear sister." He's at least one full foot taller than me and, since him and Farrah joined the local CrossFit gym last year and swapped half their meals for high protein shakes mixed with designer alkaline water, this hug feels more like the Heimlich remover.

"Before I step in there," I say, pushing away, "you need to tell me there are no surprise guests tonight. Can you do that? I would be disappointed not to see my nieces, but I can't see mom and dad right now, got it? It's been too long and now is not the time."

He furrows his thick eyebrows together and he looks just like dad did. Or what I remember him looking like. It's been years since I've seen my parents. "I would never ambush you like that. I wish you would think better of me. Please come in."

As soon as I enter, Lucas, their chocolate lab, is pawing and sniffing me. This happens every time I visit, not that I mind. It's Sammy's scent that he's most interested in.

"Good boy, Lucas." I scratch his head and kick off my sandals toward a tray of perfectly lined Hunter boots, one for each member of the family. They wore them as they stood in a dry field for their Christmas card portrait last year as more of a unifying prop than functional attire.

"Keep your shoes on, we're sitting out on the patio tonight. We bought an outdoor heater last month, and it has definitely elevated our outdoor living experience and honestly changed our lives." He's dead serious. Farrah has been posting about this new patio furniture for weeks. It must be lovely. Soon I'll be curled up in the new chair swing, listening to the gentle hum of the highway at the bottom of the hill. I always appreciate the comfort of their home, even if I don't fully feel like I belong to this family.

By the time we pass through the kitchen, my nieces are both circling behind me, readying themselves for the inevitable pounce. Even with my relationship with Chris being strained at best, coming here is like walking into a warm cuddle.

"Where's Rebecca?" my seven-year-old niece Sandy asks. Her golden blonde hair is divided in two braids that reach her shoulders. The question catches me off guard, though it shouldn't have. My nieces loved it when Rebecca and I babysat them, which happened only seldomly because my brother prefers to "date night," as he calls it, at home on their overstuffed white sectional in front of a TV as big as a Mercedes-Benz Sprinter and within arm's reach of a fully stocked wall of wine. "You're always with Rebecca," Sandy adds in a matter-of-fact tone that I admire for its confidence. Well, yes, we are always together, until we're not.

"Um…" I can barely get the words out. I'm sure I told Chris she moved out. Maybe I didn't? No, I don't think I've gotten around to it yet. "She's…" My throat catches, but I think I manage not to look upset. Last time I was here, Rebecca was with me, and we promised Sandy and Ellie we'd take them to the pump track park down the road with their sparkly pink scooters, just us.

Ellie, a nine-year-old, joins in on the stare down. When they were smaller, Farrah would dress them in these matching organic linen outfits with bonnets, and they looked so similar that they were often mistaken for twins. Farrah told me she did this because it made Chris so happy he'd cry when he thought no one was looking. It reminded him of his own twin sisters, she'd said. I've never known what to do with this information about my brother, so I buried it down alongside everything else.

"I saw you yesterday from the front yard when we got home from school. I waved and waved, but you didn't respond. How come?" Ellie says.

I shake my head. "It wasn't me. I was at work." I need to visit these two more. This must be some huge hint.

"It was you. You just stood there staring at me and not moving. It was kinda scary." She looks hurt.

I kneel down so we're on the same level and I look at her sweet eyes. "I haven't been out here in months. I would never not visit you if I was in the neighbourhood."

"Oh, you're here already! My apologies for not greeting you at the door."

It's Farrah. Thank God. She holds a small box and hands it to me. She smiles and wishes me a happy birthday. I'll talk to my nieces about what's going on with Rebecca and I later, not that I have much to say. "For the birthday girl," Farrah says, batting her new classic set eyelash extensions, a purchase, she revealed in a recent social media story, that is good for both her self-esteem and her brand. They do look stunning, like Betty Boop if she was doing the boho mommy thing.

I unwrap the delicate paper and pull out a lipstick in a tube that's so shiny and silver it looks like a bullet. I take off the lid and twist the tube to see a cheeky fuchsia colour in matte. It's not anything I would normally wear, but I thank her anyway and quickly shove it in my purse.

"I was thinking perhaps we could work on your dating profile after dinner? I could help you spruce it up." Farrah says. Last time I saw her, she started one for me. I haven't opened it once. I shrug and that's all she needs to let the topic go for now. Dating profiles aren't for me.

We eat veggie burgers and fennel salad on a deck lined with twinkle lights. It's lovely out here and for a moment I think I really am enjoying the sound of crashing waves from the ocean instead of their new motorized fountain. I'm enjoying the company of others. I haven't seen many people since Rebecca left. I'm only realizing that now. Even my neighbours rarely leave their units and I doubt Peter from work is going to be talking too much after I blew him off yesterday.

The conversation moves from what the kids are doing in school, to what I've been doing. This isn't my favourite topic and Chris has a way of guiding any conversation back to work. I'm surprised he's here tonight since he's notorious for committing to a 60-hour work week.

He takes a big sip of his drink. "Refresh my memory. What is it that you're doing these days?"

It's the same as before and he knows this. He runs his fingers through what looks like a freshly trimmed beard. The crow's feet around his eyes look a little fainter than I remember. It looks like even Chris can't deny the allure of filler and Botox. Farrah has dabbled for years. Some people have too much money.

"Same." I don't want to talk shop. The lawyer is boring and my long-term temping is demeaning, but I have no desire to change right now. If things weren't so complicated, maybe I could refocus my life. Follow through with self-care. Find a boyfriend. Change careers.

"What about home?"

Or move.

"Same." I also don't want to talk about my new spare bedroom or the burden of extra rent that puts me in such a fragile financial position that any unexpected expense will cripple me.

"What about Rebecca? Anything new with her? Or you and her? Any trips planned?"

Here it is again, the question on all their minds. They're wondering why Rebecca isn't here but are too polite to plainly ask it.

"Yes, actually," I say, flattening a wedge of overcooked egg with my fork. I've never liked egg in my salad, too squishy. "Yes, there is something new. She moved out."

"Moved out?" He looks at me suspiciously, like maybe I've just been hiding Rebecca in the car this whole time and this is a joke.

"Really?" Farrah chimes, clearly waiting for me to spill some major dirt.

I nod and take a bite of my salad. It's too creamy and does anyone actually like the texture of hemp hearts? The taste is all wrong, and I don't feel hungry anymore. I try to hide the salad under a chunk of brioche bun but end up letting my fork slip out of my fingers and onto my plate.

He raises his eyebrows. "That's got to be an adjustment."

You have no idea, brother, but I keep quiet and hope this conversation will politely blow over and into the more palatable realm of updating me on their upcoming vacations. Last year it was the Caribbean. They've hinted at Italy before. But maybe I can't stomach even that level of conversation. The glass patio table we're huddled around feels too small. There's no room for my elbows. I push my chair back for air.

Farrah puts her fork down and leans over to me. "Did she finally move in with that Steve guy?"

The sentiment is like a slap in the face. "Steve? Not a chance."

Farrah and Chris exchange a look that's too quick for me to decipher. Steve was their realtor for this gaudy palace. They still have a bullseye *Move with Steve!* magnet on their perfectly finger-printless stainless steel French door fridge.

"Where is she?" It's Ellie who says this. Ellie with a smear of ketchup across her adorable cheek. I never realized before how small nine-year-olds are. The age is seared in my mind as significant and mature, like a nine-year-old should be able to take control of any situation. But seeing my sweet niece, I realize I wouldn't let Ellie walk to the mailbox across the street by herself, let alone walk into a forest. If she did walk to the mailbox and managed to get lost, I wouldn't stop until I found her. The thought pulls me in and away from this table until I notice everyone is looking at me for an answer.

"I don't know," I say, keeping my eyes on Ellie only.

"Must have been some fight then." Farrah takes a sip of white wine from a goblet that says *Mommy Juice* and looks to hold half a bottle when filled halfway, which it was when dinner started.

"Not a fight." At least I don't think it was. It was more like a crossing of boundaries, but I don't want to talk about it here.

"Oh, come on. After all those years, something between you two must have snapped." Farrah bats her eyelashes at me.

"Just tell us what happened," Chris demands in a tone that I can only imagine is the exact straight-shooting one he uses to command the boardroom and impress the senior executives.

If Rebecca was here with me, she would lightly kick my foot and if I replied a certain way, that would be our cue to make an excuse and go. *No worries. Happens to the best of us.* It was code for: rescue me from this place and these people.

But tonight I don't have anyone to conspire with, so I face the question. "Fine," I say. "She's joined an intentional community somewhere in the country. I don't know where she is beyond that." It's the first time I've said it out loud. I look down at my plate, feeling oddly vulnerable by the statement I just made. What kind of friends don't know where the other one is?

Chris's big laugh fills the space between us. Farrah scolds him but can't stop a smirk from creeping across her ageless face. The girls look confused.

"I'm surprised you didn't go with her," Chris says. "You two do everything else together. Why not join a cult at the same time?"

I watch how he tosses his head back as he laughs. Jennifer used to laugh like that too and I never noticed that Chris did the same thing until now. Seeing the familiar mannerism sends a shiver down my spine. I still miss her so much and would do anything to see her again. Being friends with Rebecca meant I could have a connection with someone without any of these familial triggers.

"You don't know where she is? That, that seems not good," Sandy says. She's always touched my heart. She's the only one here who shares my concern for my best friend and the seriousness of the situation. "This makes me feel sad and worried."

I study Sandy's face, managing to somehow keep the gawking looks of my brother and sister-in-law out of my peripheral vision. "I'm going to look for her. She was sending letters and I haven't received one in weeks, practically a month. She would contact me if she could. I'm going to help her come home."

"I like to help people, too," Ellie adds. I nod and she smiles at me. I really should spend more time with these two. They are refreshing to be around.

"I saw something about a new intentional community in the news the other day…" Chris butts in, interrupting my moment with Ellie.

"Oh?" I attempt to take a small sip of water, but my hands are shaking too much so I put the glass down.

"Sounded like nothing more than an intense multi-level-marketing scheme to me," he says. "No one's that generous. I mean, I would be, if I could."

He read an article about our dear Matt. Even my brother, as a striving workaholic with annual bonuses as large as my annual income, knows people with money are not that generous. They always want more.

"Those pyramid scheme things are just awful," Farrah says, starting to slur a little. "Sheila got caught up in the shakes. She kept DM'ing me to buy them. I heard she has a whole garage full of them at home. Spent Conner's university fund because she was told it was a sure shot to double her investment and, of course, it wasn't. My heart breaks for her. I'm grateful that Chris handles all our investments. I hope Rebecca isn't involved in some scheme. She was always so smart with her computer programming or whatever she was doing. I always thought she should make an app, something useful that everyone would use." She takes another gulp of her wine then looks at me for an answer I can't give.

I have no idea who Sheila and Conner are, and Chris and Farrah have no idea what they're talking about. They don't know Rebecca like I do. Chris reads these articles on his tiny Smartwatch at 2AM because he has insomnia. His mind gets going about work and all the things he's responsible for but are ultimately meaningless and he knows it, and he stress-reads the news to get his mind worked up about the bigger pre-apocalypse world we're all sinking in.

"This situation is different. She needs my help," I blurt out.

Chris stiffens and pulls his body straight. Another authority position stolen from our dad. "She's an adult, Carolyn. She'll be okay. These communes are not earth shattering, half the time it's just people too tired of paying rent and want to play anti-capitalism for a bit. She's probably just mending clothes or feeding chickens on a farm or something. She can decide how she wants to spend her time. It's not a lifestyle for me, but we all make different choices." He takes another generous gulp of his cocktail.

"I don't know exactly where she is, but I know the direction. It's enough to get started and it's Rebecca. I need to do this for her. She'd do it for me."

"It would be like looking for a needle in a haystack, except for a perfectly content needle that just wanted to move on with her life. You two had been hanging around each other for years and, hey, maybe you were both keeping each other down. You're 31 now. It'll be good for you, too. It's time for a fresh start. Farrah said she'll help you with the apps. It's been a while since your last boyfriend. It's time for you to move on, too. There's still time for you."

The boyfriend he would be referring to is Adam. Nice enough guy, but there's not much of a story there. We got together because we both rode the train at the same time. I feel like one of us just stopped contacting the other or we both faded on each other at the same time. It wasn't exactly the romance of the century. Even still, I haven't met anyone since. I'm open to love. It just hasn't happened yet.

I'm not surprised Chris looks down on my life from his perfect hilltop perch on what little I've accomplished in my time on this earth. I will probably never own real estate. It's not looking good that I'll ever have children. I may never find a life partner. I might, but it's not looking likely. The one thing I tried to do, start a business, ended unsuccessfully years ago. I'm still paying off my schooling that didn't lead me anywhere. My parents are estranged. My twin sister who I love is forever lost in the woods. But there's no way I'm losing my best friend, too. This part he doesn't understand. I'm putting my foot down on that one. Now is not the time to get in my way.

"You think I don't know how to look for someone who needs to be found, who needs help?" It comes out more like a growl than a sentence and my dark tone surprises even me.

You could have kept looking.

"I didn't say that," Chris says, his voice a touch gentler now. He knows how I feel about the inadequacies of Jennifer's search. All the missed steps. The talk of a plan that was never actioned. We abandoned her. We left her in a forest alone. Farrah keeps her head down and starts gathering everyone's dirty cutlery in a pile in front of her wine glass. "I just don't want you to get hurt. She's probably safe. Isn't that a good thing? You want your best friend to be okay, right?"

"I don't know for sure. I've been doing some research about the community," I start, but Chris interrupts me, sounding more and more like dad the longer this conversation goes on. I should have skipped this dinner. I shouldn't have come here.

"All you have to go on is she hasn't sent you a letter?" he booms. "That's nothing. People get busy, Carolyn. She's not just sitting in her hippie place thinking about writing letters to you like it's the 1970s or something. She left. She has a new life. Deal with it."

Stop, just stop right there. We're turning around. Get going.

"It can take me a month just to reply to an email sometimes," Farrah adds gently. Her smile is kind, but she is still echoing my brother.

As much as I hate to admit it, his words poke at something I haven't wanted to admit. She ghosted me.

It's been four weeks since I heard from her. Suddenly, this doesn't feel like a long time. I push my plate away in frustration. My nieces copy me, pushing their plates in front of them. Their love for me brings a small smile to my face.

"This time of year is hard for you, it always is. Last year you sat there telling us you were going vegan. Imagine! We grew up slaughtering our own pigs on grandma and grandpa's farm, and you liked it." Chris knocks back his glass, draining the dregs of what was a double vodka water.

I lasted six months as a vegan, but he doesn't need to know this. It's something I want to do again when things get settled. It's better for the climate. Chris is also misremembering the farm thing. I cuddled the piglets, and because I'd just lost my twin, our grandparents let me do it for as long as I needed. I basically lived at grandma and grandpa's after we lost Jennifer because I couldn't stand to be around mom and dad. My grandparents were the only people in my life who never told me to *just* get over it, which is exactly what my brother is doing now.

He sets his glass back on the table, the remaining ice cubes clink together. "Have you talked to mom and dad? They asked me for your number again."

"You didn't," I say sharply. If I get a call from them, I'm never talking to Chris again. "Tell me you didn't give my number to them. You need to respect my feelings on this. Please."

"Of course not. Forget I mentioned anything. I know the rules."

Chris and Farrah clean up our dinner plates and go back inside. I hear the hiss of water hitting their industrial grade kitchen sink. Chris is right. One missed letter doesn't mean much beyond the plain fact that Rebecca hasn't bothered to contact me in four weeks. For people not watching their mailboxes, four weeks is not long at all. If I look for her, I won't know where to go. I'll be wasting my time. Tears gather in my eyes and I blink hard to shove them back inside me.

I walk inside to tell Chris I'm not feeling well, lie about it being a busy day tomorrow and that it's time for me to go home. I thank them for dinner and give the girls a hug and kiss. My brother walks me to the door.

"You'll miss mom and dad one day, you'll see. They are family. Blood bonds are deep," Chris says. He goes in for another hug, but I step out onto that tacky welcome mat before he can. "You don't want to keep everything all bottled up until they die. Talk to them while they're still here. You'll want to tell them how you feel."

I shake my head in frustration. Every visit ends like this. A plea to reconnect with the last people on his earth I want to see. My parents.

"Dad can't change the past," he continues. "Turning around with you was the hardest thing he ever did. He's told me many times. Imagine if you and him went missing looking for her. It happens. These are hard, hard decisions. I can't sleep some nights just thinking about what I would do if, god forbid, the situation happened to me. Give him a call and talk to him about it. It might help you move on."

I slip my purse over my shoulder. My car keys are ready in my hands. I can't get out of here fast enough.

Chris sighs again. Farrah follows us to the door, her now almost empty wine glass in hand.

"They're getting older. Things can happen fast," he says. "Don't wait until it's too late."

"It can get expensive, too," Farrah pipes in.

I look at her. "What do you mean, expensive?"

"Trying to commune with the dead, like you would have to do if you don't talk now. My girlfriend does it all the time to talk to her dead mom. Lines up to get a spot with this, like, psychic in West Vancouver. Pays hundreds of dollars each time. There was a lot of unresolved issues from her childhood. Her mom was a theatre actor and went through many…seasons. I don't understand it myself." She steadies herself on the door handle. "It's also weird. She claims her mom talks to her through this psychic, says these things like she's talking to a ghost. It can get very emotional for her. She usually needs a full week away at her cabin on Pender Island just to recover. She wishes there were a better way. I guess they have a lot to work through."

Sharing my thoughts on the ridiculousness of what Farrah just said would only backfire to keep me here longer.

"I'll be okay with the status quo," I say over my shoulder as I walk down their steep driveway to my dusty car. "Besides, I've always been more scared of people than the idea of ghosts."

7

In the middle of the night, I wake to the sound of my phone ringing. I don't know what time it is. My room is dark. I fumble for my phone on my nightstand and see, through still blurry vision, an unknown number. If Chris was lying about giving out my number to our parents, I'll be furious. I consider not answering, but since there's a sliver of possibility that it could be Rebecca calling for help, I do.

"I'm calling about the email you sent me about my sister?" Her voice is loud and raspy, like whoever is calling isn't sure whether she should whisper or scream.

With the mention of my emails, I'm suddenly awake. "Hello? You're calling about my email?" I kick my covers to the side. This is someone who understands firsthand what I'm going through. Her sister joined Matt's mall and she also went silent.

There's a pause. "This is Carolyn, yes? It's Rane."

My body surges with energy. Rane blogged her sister's letters for the world to see just how unsettling the mall is. I can't believe she's getting in touch with me. I freeze, like I'm going to forget how to talk. This could be the break-through I need to find Rebecca. Rane is going to tell me the location or she's going to tell me her sister is okay and that Matt is fine and the mall is a good place I don't need to understand, just trust. I take a deep breath. I don't know if I'm going to laugh with relief that I'm finally talking to someone who knows what's happening or cry out of fear of screwing it up. This is the biggest break I've had.

She clears her throat. "Did I wake you? I didn't even think about looking to see what time it is there."

I tell her it's no problem and, thankfully, she continues talking. I flip on my bedside lamp and grab an unused dream journal

I received in an office Secret Santa years ago and a pen I hope still has ink.

"I've had a few emails like yours. I try to answer as many as I can if the person seems legit. Sometimes I get people reaching out to ridicule me on my sister's mistakes, that she deserves whatever happens to her because she couldn't own up to her responsibilities at home. Some will say she needed to look after herself, that she was responsible for her loans solely. *No one's paying my debt*, they say. It's awful. Where's the empathy? One guy keeps asking me to let him interview me for his crappy true crime podcast. At least they were more interested than the police. They couldn't care less, no matter how many times I called. Anyway, I'm sorry to hear about your friend. It sucks."

Her voice is grave, with a tone like she's calling me to send her respects. Or, worse, her condolences. There's something off-putting about Rane that I can't put my finger on. I open my notebook and fold back the page. She knows something otherwise she wouldn't be calling.

"Have you found her," I ask, and then with a slight hesitation add, "your sister."

She's quiet again. I'm worried she might hang up, so I blurt out, "or have you heard from her at least?"

There's another long pause. I think I hear something in the background. A train maybe. I imagine her sitting in a dark room overcome with worry and anger about the situation. Her call to me is her way of staying connected to her sister, to her cause. Obviously she hasn't heard from her. She would have deleted her damn blog and put the horror of not knowing where her sister is out of her mind for good.

"No, I haven't. Not yet." Her voice is tight. I think I understand this woman. I get it, the hopefulness, the mounting disappointment. It's not knowing what happened to a loved one that destroys a person from the inside out with a rot that starts in the heart. It's impossible to move on. I've lived that with Jennifer every single day since she went missing. It never gets easier.

Time to refocus the conversation. Talking about her sister is too real, too raw. I get that, so I get straight to the point. "Do you know where the mall is?" She must be calling for something, especially if she hasn't heard from her sister yet. I wonder what time she thinks it is where I am. Where is she calling from? How far will Matt's recruiters go to find the perfect person for the community?

"I know it's somewhere rural," she answers in a distant voice. "Somewhere there's horses in the pastures, big mountains. We don't have mountains where we are, it's flat, so Andrea said it was beautiful there. She said it reminded her of the time we spent with our parents camping. When our mother passed away when we were in our early twenties, Andrea took it very hard. In retrospect, I should have been there for her more. We could have avoided this. She needed support while she grieved. But I was grieving, too, and I needed to look after our family as the oldest sister. It was too hard. Now I'm grieving for my mother and my sister." She sniffles. She'll be hanging up soon. I can't keep a stranger talking when all it does is irritate her wounds that haven't healed.

"Was there anything else you remember her saying, besides the mountains?" It's British Columbia, we're enclosed in sharp peaks and valleys pretty much everywhere. This detail isn't enough. "Any stores or street names?"

"Nothing like that. She said once that the buzzing was getting to her. She heard a lot of buzzing. Some nights it felt like it was in her head. She was always sensitive to sound. I tip-toed around her as a kid because she was always waking up and she didn't do well with a lack of sleep."

"Buzzing?" Rebecca mentioned buzzing in one of her letters now that I think of it. "Was it like a chainsaw sound?"

She laughs a little. "No, no, gentler. It was like a louder bee buzz. I think that's what she meant. It was just loud enough to drive her crazy. She couldn't get away from the sound. It was keeping her up. It wasn't long after that I stopped hearing from her."

The pain of losing a sister is one I know too well. Nothing I say will comfort her. "Have you tried to find the mall yourself?"

"Wouldn't you look for your sister?"

The hairs on my neck stand up. I want to tell her I would, of course I would. It's not always so easy. Sometimes there are things or people standing in your way.

Before I can answer, she sighs. "When I went looking, I couldn't find anything. I was just driving around. There's so little to go off that would lead me to the mall. Not a day goes by that I don't think about going again though."

"What stops you?"

She takes a deep breath. "Weird things started happening as soon as I left. I thought someone was following me. I could feel someone lingering around me, but I couldn't see them. I became all paranoid and I'm totally not that person, so it scared the shit out of me. But I started seeing things, like flashes in the mirror. I couldn't be alone anymore. It was so disturbing that I had to go home. It was a terrible feeling, but I have a family to think about. My kids worry about me. I'm still anxious that I'm being monitored in some way. But it's baseless."

This is the first time I've heard about anyone associated with the community being stalked. Matt made them delete their social media, but maybe this was only the start. He could easily have a team of stalkers ready to scare people. "When was this?"

"Two months after I stopped hearing from her, so about six months ago. I couldn't stay away. I had to know how she was. We always talked before she left, almost everyday. That's how I know something's not right. She promised me she would keep in touch, and when she didn't…" Her voice goes quiet. "They weren't allowed phones anymore."

So the people living at the mall originally had phones and he clawed them back.

"I totally get it. You're sisters. That means something." Chris's words echo in my mind. *She's an adult.* Maybe he's right. My best friend doesn't owe me anything. It's not the same as being a sister. I should be happy that Rebecca found a new life. And, I would be under normal circumstances, but not like this. It's so secretive.

"Okay, I want to share something with you. That's why I called." She takes another deep breath. "I'm going to send you something, but it's for your eyes only. Do not share it with anyone. I mean it. If you do, I don't know what will happen. I don't trust those mall people. They're sketchy. Can you do that?"

"Absolutely."

"Promise?"

"With everything I've got."

"Watch your text."

I thank Rane for calling me. After she hangs up, my phone vibrates a moment later. She's sent me a link and I click on it without hesitation. My video player pops up. The video is shaky because it was likely recorded on a phone, but it's in high definition so I can see what's happening clearly. The first few seconds I'm watching the back of heads. The video pans a crowd of people, could be over a hundred, maybe more. We're in an audience, but it's quiet. It's strange to hear a crowd this large deadly silent. I can't make out much of what this audience is. The person recording aims the camera to the ground in what might have been a fumble but manages to come back up and frame a man walking to the front of the room and jumping up onto a small riser. He introduces himself as Matt. This is the mall. I'm watching Matt take his spot in front of his debt-burdened disciples.

He keeps his head down, the audience somehow becomes quieter than before. If I was relying purely on audio, I wouldn't think there was an audience at all and it gives an eerie feeling.

"Thank you, everyone, I needed a minute to clear my head before coming out here. I've been waiting for this for a long time. It's intense to see the mall come to fruition like this. I've dreamed of this for many years, of a place where people can come and just be themselves. We are doing something special here, something incredibly important. I hope you feel it here now!" He raises his hands to the ceiling as if to make his presence bigger.

The audience claps and cheers, the video jumbles around. How did someone get a phone in to record this? Or is this old and from when they were allowed phones? Maybe I shouldn't trust this, but I can't look away. How did Rane get it?

"Everyone, everyone, shhhhh," he says, and the crowd immediately stops. "The past is not for people like us. We feel things. Our worlds are full of pain, mistakes, and the people who plague us, who haunt us every single minute of our days and nights. They haunt us because we need them and they want us. This place, what we are doing, is about the future. It's about coming to unity with the past, bringing it all together so we can survive another minute of reality. Why should we suffer when we don't have to? We will forget about our grief and the shackles that have held us back from our potential as a productive member of society. We will be whole once more."

The speech catches me off guard. It is a bit dramatic for a commune where they co-manage a vegetable garden. How are they all so empty inside?

He pauses, takes a moment to survey the room. The video doesn't give a close-up of Matt, but his eyes pop in front of the dull curtains he has behind the riser.

"Are you feeling free?" He pushes up the sleeves of his slim-fit cotton shirt, revealing one full arm of tattoos. I pinch my screen to zoom in and see the outline of vines.

There are a few *whoops* again, but all that stops when Matt looks straight out into the crowd. He narrowly misses making eye contact with the camera. His pale blue eyes are icy and calculating, and they send a shiver down my spine. I feel nervous for whoever was holding this camera.

"I know how the onus of debt can bring us down, crush us, deprive us of our true callings. People like us, people who feel, shouldn't be brought down further. It's not right. I am in a position to help, and so…"

Now people are pumping their fists in the air. A few have started stomping their feet.

"It's my pleasure to provide this important space," he continues, nodding his head slowly as if he's taking the time to absorb the admiration and enthusiasm of the crowd. "Truly, it is. I can do this work for you, so I do. It's my privilege and my duty to serve you. You have all been selected for the mall for a reason. Everyone here is special. You all need to heal. Your healing can help move forward something this world hasn't seen…"

You all need to heal. The sentiment could apply to me, yet his method is appalling. The video suddenly cuts to another clip from this stage. It's the same speech, same everything, but I've missed something. The stomping is ten times louder. Something was cut. I missed a clip of something happening. The video timeline shifted. Why was this video edited?

"I need you, all of you, to make me a promise right now," he yells above the stomping. It's getting harder to hear him. "You'll each continue the silence I prescribed you last week. Only silence will help you find and connect with your authentic self. At this point, this is the most important work you can do. It's the first step. I know everyone is excited about our community and eager to get to the next step. I might be the most excited. But we need to keep listening to our innermost thoughts or we will fall into our old toxic patterns. That's part of what our purpose here is, our work. Please let the silence rein. It's good for you. And if you have memories of loved ones long past, don't fight them."

The room goes quiet. Why are they listening to him? What did I miss?

"Thank you, don't you think it's easier to think when it's quiet? To listen? I always find it so much better. The outside world is too loud, too busy, too greedy. I've been in competition with everything, my family, my friends, my colleagues, my neighbours for my entire life, and when the time came for them to care for me when I needed them, they stepped over me instead. They saw my vulnerability as an opportunity to exploit me. They couldn't understand why I refused to feed the money machine. It hurt. No more. That's part of why I started the mall. First as a retreat, then I found someone special who could create what I needed. One of you."

The audience is completely silent and still now. The video zooms in closer to Matt and I notice a small hearing aid in his right ear just before he places his hand on it and closes his eyes like he's collecting himself, but I get the unsettled feeling he's listening to a feed.

"Now pay attention," he says slowly. "We are all going to line up in front of the tables to your left and get yourself a tablet.

This tablet is how we'll communicate with each other in the mall during our frequent and necessary doses of silence. We will share our thoughts, feelings, and musings. Our grief and wounds. Be raw. Be you. Everything we share will be run through a special algorithm working to make our lives together better and more comfortable. The network is local to these walls. This is for all our security and your privacy. I know it's hard, but this measure protects our work here. If your communities on the outside listened better to your suffering, you wouldn't need to be here to heal. Anything you want to say, can be shared with everyone, out in the openness of the mall. There are no secrets here. Secrets lead to misunderstanding, often catastrophic. Secrets can be deadly. Not everyone can go back and make things right, but I think we will accomplish that at the mall with our work."

He takes a few steps back from the foot of the stage, looking like he's about to exit.

"You want to talk about secrets?" screams a voice from the back, a woman's voice. "What happened to Sarah? She was my roommate and she disappeared. All her stuff was gone one morning. We deserve an explanation!"

Rebecca mentioned her roommate disappearing in one of her letters. A trickle of fear knots in my stomach. Rebecca herself is someone's roommate. I feel the balloon in my lungs inflate again, and I try to breathe.

The video has stayed fixed on Matt this entire time and I watch with a sinking feeling when Matt goes completely still at this question. His voice is drained of all the eagerness and confidence he had moments before. He's cold and seeing his reaction freaks me out. He's like a completely different person. "What benefit do you gain from asking me this? From breaking your silence? From interrupting everyone's thoughts and healing for your selfishness? We can all hear the accusation in your voice. When you speak, we miss hearing what we need to, what we want to, what we'd die to hear again. The, the, the…" He jumps off his makeshift stage into the crowd.

The video shakes and then ends right there. I save the video to my phone and rewatch it, worried my access might disappear any moment somehow. I scan the backs of all the heads for Rebecca again, but I don't see her. By the third viewing, I'm certain I see Matt's face twitch when he says *there are no secrets here.* He's lying. He's hiding something.

I redial the number Rane called from, and it rings and rings. I need to know who took this video and how Rane got it. She might know something about the missing section. What did he tell him? I call her again. Still more ringing. She's gone. I toss my phone aside, and surprisingly, I don't feel awful anymore. The morning sun is starting to drift through my blinds. Sammy pokes his head up for a scratch. This is one of the first mornings in a long time I've felt rested and refreshed, despite only having slept for three hours. I have a meaningful purpose to my day now. If I could talk to Rane again, I'd thank her. Talking to her has helped me unlock my innermost thoughts and they are telling me if I don't go looking for Rebecca now, I'll never forgive myself. And, in keeping with Matt's sentiment in the video, why should I grieve the loss of my best friend when I don't have to?

8

It turns out that even non-permanent, disposable employees like me are entitled to the illusion of a life apart from work. This is to say my temp coordinator at the agency approved my request to take five unpaid days in a row without issue. With this, I'm feeling like the white-hot flames of a million smoldering buildings could not keep me from finding my friend. Rebecca is east. She is surrounded by mountains. She is being held by an egomaniac with means beyond my wildest dreams in a crumbling mall. I will find her.

My new sense of purpose is making me feel all sorts of gratitude and connection. I thank my coordinator and start to tell her about my journey to find my best friend, but she cuts me short because she has a meeting with another temp in five minutes. That's okay! Next, I ask our neighbour Terry to look after Sammy. Terry agrees. She loves cats! I bring over all his supplies and give Sammy a big kiss on his head. I tell him I'll be back soon and I think he winks at me for good luck. Afterward, I check my credit card and feel relieved that if I spend wisely, I will have enough room for a very cheap motel if I eat most meals from a grocery store. Yesterday I made a payment and it will be posted in a couple days. I'm doing the best I ever do financially. This isn't a holiday. It's a rescue mission. I'm set.

While I wasn't successful in getting an address from the recruiter on the quay, I do have something that can help me. The postmark on her letters says Valley Falls. I'm not sure if this means she's in Valley Falls or nearby. Matt's people sent her a bus ticket to Nelson. That was all she would tell me about the location. There's a two-and-a-half-hour drive time between these two places. It can't be that hard to find a boarded-up mall in the middle of a small town, especially one where people from across the country are visiting and never seen again. This can't go unnoticed. Then again, I know I don't pay much attention to my neighbourhood or even this building that I live in. Terry is the only neighbour I've ever really engaged with. I push the thought away. It's better to keep this new positive mindset going as long as I can. Deserted malls are everywhere now, and a town the size of Valley Falls with less than 15,000 population could only have one mall as it is.

It's ten hours of driving from here to a post office in Valley Falls. I'll drive Trans-Canada East for a big chunk, then Crowsnest Highway. When I get there, I'll be in a new time zone and a new city. It will be a recipe for a new me. I'm trying very hard to stay optimistic about this journey. If I let my usual fear shake me, I won't be able to do this.

I ease my 1996 white Saturn onto Trans-Canada East and drive straight. My surroundings blur past me and it feels like a blink and I'm through the Lower Mainland and driving straight past Hope. If I keep up the speed, I'll be in Valley Falls in time to check into a hotel and get some rest for the next morning when I need to make some leads.

After five hours of straight driving, I pull off the highway into a gas station to stretch my legs and eat the granola bars and apples I had the foresight to pack. I buy a coffee and chug the caffeinated sludge I paid three dollars for back in my car. By now, some of my initial energy I felt infused with when I saw Rane's video has faded and the lack of sleep is hitting hard. The road feels big and long, and I'm doing everything I can not to feel drowsy and overwhelmed.

I eat quickly, slam some gas on my credit card, and get back on the road.

The next thing I hear is the piercing sound of the semi truck's longhorn jerking me awake. I perk up just in time to steer my car back into its lane without smashing into anyone. I must have drifted across the centre line. I don't remember doing that. Did I really fall asleep on the road? I try to replay what happened, but I can't bring it back. My bumper just missed him. My heart pounds and my hands are shaking. I can hardly hold the steering wheel. I check the clock. 2:28PM. I've only been driving for one hour since my lunch break at the gas station. I had coffee. A big one. I was feeling awake. I hadn't felt as tired when I got back into the car, but now my body feels heavy, like I'm lying underneath a lead apron awaiting someone to x-ray me. The last thing I remember is hearing something loud, but I don't remember what.

I grab hold of the steering wheel long enough to signal to get off at the rest stop area just up ahead. I'm careful not to make any more driving mistakes. I smile and wave at the semi driver in the lane beside me who witnessed the whole thing, and he gives me the finger. Solidarity. Okay, I deserve that. I pull into the rest stop and park.

What I need is to give my head a shake and wake the hell up. I need to make it to Rebecca's mall alive for her sake and mine. I blink my eyes. They're dry and gritty, like sand blew in them. I must be more tired than I thought. My chronic lack of sleep is finally catching up with me at the absolute worst time.

Standing outside my car, I close my eyes for a moment. When I look up I notice a family sitting at a picnic table. A mom. A dad. Two toddler boys and a baby girl. The baby sits on mom's lap trying to keep her head up. They're eating sandwiches. No one is talking. Maybe they're on their way home, or maybe their family vacation has just begun. I'm not sure which would be better for them considering how miserable they all look. Except the baby. She's smiling, but no one's looking at her. Everyone keeps their eyes down and on their food.

I've always been hypervigilant in anticipating when someone is in a bad mood and it's best not to say anything. It's a feeling that people who regularly experience explosive moods understand intuitively. Best to just stay as quiet as you can to not trip any hot tempers. My dad had a way of always letting us know that he could unleash his temper at any time. *Just watch me.* What would set him off this time? No one wanted to find out. His mood was a controlling tactic and it always worked to keep us in line.

My hands shake again. I put the right one over the left to stop them from moving and turn my attention back to the awkward family lunch to distract myself with the misery they are displaying for everyone here.

Now I'm curious, which one of them is upset? Is it overly tired mom? Or an overly tired dad? Who does the family not want to upset right now? Who is trying to take control? I sit on the bench near their table and watch them as I give myself time to settle down. After a few deep breaths, I slowly feel my heart rate relax.

The baby starts to cry. The boys fight over the juice box. Why is there only one?

The dad finishes the last bite of his sandwich and, one by one, licks each of his fingers to clean the mayonnaise off.

"Let's go. Now!" The dad stands up and walks toward a silver minivan hauling a tiny red egg trailer. The boys stop fighting and start eating the rest of their sandwiches. The wife closes her eyes, her food untouched. She's been nursing the baby.

I try to practice a breathing exercise one of the other temps at the law office taught me a couple years ago when I was nervous about messing up some important paperwork for the lawyer. She told me that the best way to clear my head was to try to count back from ten while keeping all other thoughts out of your head.

"It's easier said than done," Gail said. She was an older woman, with a streak of turquoise through her white hair, who took the temp job after her retirement savings started to run thin after one of the many market crashes. "Each time something pops into your head, you start from the beginning. It's about focus and patience. This little exercise has helped me many times in my life. I hope it helps you, too."

It's worth a try. Anything is better than the balloon feeling in my lungs. That's harder to recover from, especially on the road when I don't have time to calm myself down.

10... 9... 8... My thoughts float to what happened in my car. Why had I nodded off? It's unlike me. My heart beats faster. This counting isn't working. I start again because I don't know how else to get a hold of myself.

10... 9... 8... 7... 6...

"Are you okay?"

The question breaks my concentration. I glance up. It's the mom from the family eating that tense lunch looking straight at me. I point to myself, not sure if it's me she was asking that, and she nods, managing a weak smile. "You okay there?" she repeats.

"Oh, I'm fine. Totally fine." She must see my chest heaving. I wrap my arms around my torso to hide my chest. I feel like I've just sprinted five kilometres, but just my heart. I'm not out of breath, but my heart feels like it might run ahead and leave the rest of my body behind.

"Are you sure? I'm asking because your arm looks like it's dripping... blood maybe? Did you cut yourself? We have a first aid kit in the van with band-aids. Want me to run and get it?"

Her baby cries again, and she automatically does this little bounce to try to soothe her. The baby responds by crying harder. The woman stands up, raises her eyebrows at me as if to ask the question again. She has dark circles under her eyes. How this woman can keep it all together and try to help me, I can't understand. Her kindness could put me in tears if it continues like this.

I need to get away.

I look at my arm and see a familiar nick above my elbow oozing blood. My blood. I didn't feel a thing. Not a sting, not anything. I move one of my shaking hands to hide it. My shirt is drenched in blood.

"It's nothing," I say, forcing a smile. "Thanks though. I must have caught my arm on something in the trunk of my car. A hook or something. I didn't even feel it. It's worse than it looks. Just packed too many things."

The woman nods, then looks down at her boys, who have been quietly observing our entire interaction but have now lost interest and have gone back to tossing small bits of sandwich crust at each other. She's already on to the next thing. While her head is down, I run to the bathroom. Inside, I hold out my bloody arm to examine it in the dirty mirror. I grab some paper towel, wet it under the sink and dab the blood away. The towel immediately turns pink. This cut is months old now and I thought it was completely healed. It happened when Rebecca was still home. We were in the kitchen together. It's impossible for this cut to be fresh. It can't be the same one from over five months ago, but I don't recall cutting myself since. I grab more towels and put pressure on the gash.

I catch my reflection in the mirror. My forehead is slick with sweat. I flick some water on my face and try to tousle my limp hair, an unsuccessful attempt to look less dead. I place my palms on my cheeks and tug down to reveal a gaunt looking me. It's something I've done for years when I feel bad about my existence. I stare at my pale face, then let go.

The road is waiting for me. I need to get back on my schedule.

Just as I turn to leave, an ice-cold hand grips my shoulder. Someone is here. I hadn't heard anyone. A rush of embarrassment washes over me. Has the mom from the picnic table followed me in here to make sure I'm okay?

Before I can look to see who it is, the pressure increases and coldness radiates into my muscle, freezing me to the spot. I'm too stunned to do anything. Whoever is behind me is holding me back from leaving. I struggle to pull away, but I manage to break free.

"Hello?" My voice echoes through the dark bathroom. I hold my breath and expect someone to jump out of a stall to grab me again, but nothing happens. It's quiet. No one is here. I must be more tired than I realized. Time to get back on the road. I'll sleep as soon as I get to the motel. I need a reset. Seeing fresh blood from this old cut has stirred something within me. It brings me back to a moment with Rebecca I can't get back. This is all related to stress. I lost track on the road and now this feeling in the bathroom. Focusing on driving will help me stay grounded.

I take a step to the door and stop when I hear the sound of running water. Water suddenly spatters from one of the taps behind me, jagged and laboured, like a person choking. Fear prickles the back of my neck and I push myself through the door and to my car without looking back.

I'm not sticking around to find out what is happening in that old bathroom. I twist my key in the ignition. Nothing. The engine doesn't kick in. I attempt again. Nothing.

"Not now, not now, not now." A tow truck is not in my budget. I have gas. My oil change is current. What more could a 25-year-old car need? I mean, it's only two and a half decades old! I slam the steering wheel. "Seriously?"

The movement triggers something in my arm and the cut starts stinging. Maybe I should have gone and got stitches back when it was fresh, but then the doctor would have asked how it happened and I didn't want to talk about it because I want to forget it ever happened. Drops of blood fall on my jeans.

I try the engine again. Still, nothing. Perfect. I pull the latch for the hood and get out of the car. I struggle to lift the hood up and look inside, but I manage it. The bits and pieces that make up my car are all there as far as I can tell. Nothing is smoking. It's not leaking, at least that I can see. I couldn't tell if something was broken if I tried. I step back and kick my front tire.

"Damn it!" I say, loud enough that a few people near their cars look at me. "Sorry, it's just my car…"

They shrug then go back to what they're doing, which is good because I don't need an audience. I dip back under the hood, keeping my head low so no one else will see me wasting time here. I don't know what else to do.

"You need some help over there?" It's a strong voice, a clear voice. A voice that can help me, I hope. I turn around and there's a woman sitting in the bed of her truck with the latch flipped down. She's sitting on a rolled out purple sleeping bag and eating a bag of apple chips.

"Car won't start," I manage to reply, even though all I want to do is cry. "I don't know what to do. I'm useless at this kind of stuff." And at life in general. And keeping in touch with my friend. And at using rest stop bathrooms without freaking myself out because I'm scared of being alone. These inadequacies I'll keep to myself.

She hops out of her truck bed. Her work coveralls are covered in oil. A good sign.

"It's your battery. I heard it right away when you were testing it. It's like squeezing the toothpaste tube when the stuff's long gone. I can give you a jump. But you gotta promise me to get it replaced as soon as possible. It's dangerous to be driving a vehicle with a spent battery," she says. I notice her tattoos look like black and white sketches of a garden with vines of peas, carrot tops, and strawberries all wrapping around her forearms. She notices me looking and rubs her arm. "You like these? My brother and I got them when our mom died. She was like a master gardener. Not really, but really could have been. My brother designed them himself."

She holds out her arm, an apple chip still clutched in her fingers. "I always loved his creativity." She studies her arms for a moment as if it's been a while since she has looked at them herself. "If only he knew how talented he was."

"They're beautiful," I say. That's what people with tattoos want to hear. "Hey, thanks for your help. I'll get the battery right away, if my car ever does start." Please start. *Please start.*

She nods and walks back to her truck and pops the hood. Then she leans into the back cab and pulls out a small set of jumper cables. She attaches them to her battery, then she walks over and attaches the other half to mine. I am grateful that she has clearly assumed, and rightfully so, that I wouldn't know how to hook up a jumper cable if my life depended on it.

"Now we're going to have to work together on this. Alright?"

She gets back into her truck and revs her engine. I do the same and, like magic, my 25-year-old car is running again. It may be on life support but it's breathing and that's all I need to keep driving east. I leave the car running and get out of the car to thank her.

Before I can say thank you to her, she's staring down at my arm now. "What the hell happened to you?"

I tell her the same thing I told the mom, then I blurt out, "I'm driving to get my best friend. I'm on a road trip, in a way."

"I've always liked a good road trip. Are you two heading out somewhere after you pick her up?"

"Not exactly…" I'm not sure how much I should say and then suddenly everything comes spilling out. "Actually, I'm going to help her get out of this intentional community she joined. It's around Valley Falls in a boarded-up mall. That's where I'm heading. I don't even know where it is."

She's quiet and I'm not sure if she heard what I was saying, then she gets this serious look on her face. "You need to be careful."

And just like that, talking to this helpful stranger has descended into the typical conversation I have with my brother and virtually everyone else I meet. "I always am," I say. "Thanks for the jump."

She shakes her head. "I mean it. Be careful. My brother joined a community around there two years ago and I haven't heard from him since. It was probably the same one because, like, how many of those damn shames can there be."

She looks over her shoulder, then looks back at me. "It had a total cult vibe," she whispers. "Struck a rift between him and I whenever I mentioned it. I didn't think he should go. I thought he should try giving his art a go."

"Really? Can you tell me anything more?" I try to keep my voice calm, but I'm screaming inside for more detail. This person could be my first lead on the road.

"It is what it is." She pulls a small joint from her bag, lights it, and takes a long inhale. "He thought he needed to revive himself," she says as she exhales. "He'd been in and out of jobs for years. He owed thousands in student loan debt, yet couldn't land a job. He loved to code, could live off nothing but energy drinks and praise if he was trying to figure something out. Still, no work. He felt his life was over, until he didn't. Matt gave him 'purpose,' he called it. Matt believed in his talents. Blah, blah."

"Matt?"

"It never made sense to me," she continues, looking off into the trees, as if she didn't hear me. "My brother, who was smart and talented, found some rich jerk who'd take him in because he felt he needed the boost. This Matt guy offered to pay his way and pay his debts. All he had to do was answer some questions in a personality test. If something's too easy, it's probably a scam, right? My world is heavy duty mechanics and I see it as black and white as anything in an engine manual. It either works or it doesn't. It's starting or it's not. That place clearly only worked for one person and it wasn't my brother. It's no surprise. The world has been run by men like that for hundreds of years." She looks at me from under the filthy brim of her hat.

"Where was this place?"

"No idea." She studies my face as if looking for something in it that she's not finding, then she squints at my car. "Okay, let's take the jumper cables off. I think you're good to go now. Remember, you need a new battery. The one in there is a disgrace and should have been swapped out years ago. Years."

She opens her truck door and walks between our cars, disconnecting the jumper cables from both of our batteries.

"I don't know what I would have done if you weren't here," I say. "Can you tell me more about what happened to your brother? I'm going to find the mall right now. That's why I'm on the road. I can tell your brother to go home or at least call you, too."

She gives me a stern look and blinks slowly.

"Okay," I say. "I'm going to the community *after* I get the battery. Thanks for your help by the way. I hope your brother gets out of that place."

"Never mind the battery," she says, as she walks back to her truck and climbs into the driver's seat. "The guy who runs the community, Matt, he's got the money to back up his little experiment, but he's lacking in overall raw talent and charisma to lead people. People didn't understand where he was coming from. You can't buy trust. That's where my brother came in. He was the brains. He was likeable."

Rebecca has only mentioned Matt at Performance, never a co-conspirator. The part of the video when Matt starts listening to a feed in his ear comes back to me. This could have been this woman's brother.

"Did something happen to him? Did your brother leave?"

"He didn't just leave," she says, looking down at the tattoo of the lettuce on her forearm as it hangs out of the window. "He ran for his life because he was scared shitless."

"Why?" I search her eyes for any sense that she's lying but her expression is as black and white as an engine manual, too.

She waves her hands in exasperation. "Because he started seeing visions. He saw our mom and she'd been dead for almost five years by then. That mall does something to your mind. I think it's the spirit of all the failed stores, the people who lost their jobs, the rise of the cult of Bezos. Pain. Stress. Mass-produced junk. All that shit lingers. I don't know. I've never been one to go to malls. I buy clothes and wear 'em until they fall apart. I don't know what's happening at the mall, but there's a spirit there, and it's not happy." She flicks some ash from her joint onto the cement below her window.

"Come on? The mall has a spirit?" This should be the time I turn around, get into my car, and start driving. She helped me, but the weed she's smoking has gone to her head in record time.

"The visions were fine," she says, blowing smoke out the window. "Even nice. Who doesn't like seeing their dead mother from time to time? They always got along really great when she was alive. A bit of a mama's boy, but in the best way."

She laughs, looking off into the highway for a moment, then shakes her head and a strand of grey curly hair falls out of her faded baseball hat that reads YUMMY in hot pink stitching.

"The real problem," she continues, giving me a hyper-focused look, "started when he began feeling our mother's cold touch on his skin. At first it was sometimes and then it was always. He couldn't stand it, the jabbing and prodding. He couldn't escape it. He stopped sleeping, he never ate. After a while he left the mall, and that was a big one because he told me in a letter that no one ever leaves the mall. Once you're in the community, you stay there. There's apparently a tiny footnote in the contract about it, like those Terms and Conditions no one reads. I haven't seen him since I took him to the bus stop. He could be hiding out in the woods somewhere because he owes all this money to that fake visionary guy and maybe he's worried he's going to have his thumbs broken or something, or maybe something else finally got him. Maybe he turned to ice. Maybe he's hanging out with our dead mother watching reruns of Dr. Oz together on some rose-patterned sofa in the sky. I don't know. I hope he's alive. He's my brother after all. The only family I have left." She tosses the end of her joint out the window and puts on a pair of cherry red aviator sunglasses. "Anyway, good luck with your friend. I hope you find her. Bless up and out."

Bless up and out? It's like Offred from *The Handmaid's Tale* collided with a Beastie Boys lyric mid-sentence. My face must betray these thoughts because she chuckles to herself.

"It's something my brother started saying before he left for the mall. I say it now as a way of keeping him close. I don't know where he picked it up. Good luck, eh?" She shrugs, then rolls up her window and drives off, the gravel crunching under her tires.

Before I shift my car from Park into Drive, I touch my shoulder. Had I really felt that icy grip earlier? No. The bathroom was empty. It was my nerves. I've been under so much stress since Rebecca left that it's acting out on me physically. What happened to me was nothing more than a physical manifestation of my stress. I pull my car back onto the highway, hoping that I'll make it the rest of the way without it dying again.

9

Surprise: I skipped getting the new battery because my car is running fine now. Totally fine. I hadn't budgeted for any car repairs and buying the battery would mean I had less time on the road. This is math I understand.

I drive straight to Valley Falls and check into a single-level highway motel with slime green doors. The nightly rate is a touch more than I can afford, and since my credit card minimum payment hasn't been posted yet, I ask the desk host if she'll check me in one night at a time. Immediately the pleasant voice she greeted me with moments before disappears.

"Normally we charge the full stay and a deposit." She looks at me like she thinks I'm going to ask her to throw in free reign on the lobby vending machine next.

"My card will have all the room on it the day after tomorrow. It's just for the first two nights, really." Please don't make me beg or waste time finding another hotel. I smile in a last attempt to look friendly even though all I want to do is collapse on the bed after that drive.

To my relief, she looks over her shoulder and slides the key over. I thank her and leave the lobby to find my room. Once I'm in there, I drop off my stuff and walk toward the little downtown I drove past to look for something to eat.

Down the street from the motel, I find a small diner with lots of room and get myself a booth in the corner. I order the nightly special, a mushroom burger with fries, and a tall glass of water and sink back into my seat.

On top of a stack of crumpled magazines and brochures near the cash register, is their local newspaper. I flip through a few pages and hold my breath when I read the headline: *Matt Maxis: A Modern Millennial Prophet in Ray-Bans and Blundstones Triumphs Over the Retail Apocalypse*. The server places my plate in front of me and I read the article slowly, devouring each word before even touching my food. Most of it summarizes what I already know, but there's something gratifying about seeing it all laid out. His family business connections, his interest in yoga and mediation, his work buying student loan debt, and there's mention of a long-term partner and a daughter. The daughter is the youngest of his ten kids. Ten kids, okay I didn't know that part. It seems like just another advertorial for a family-man-entrepreneurial-genius, but I keep reading. Half-way through the article, the tone shifts and I squeeze the article so tight I could rip the newsprint to shreds.

Matt Maxis has business in his blood. Hailing from a long line of entrepreneurs with connections to some of the biggest industries in Canada, it was only a matter of time before he'd follow in the footsteps of his father and grandfather. That was until he traveled to Vancouver for a yoga retreat with his late partner, international supermodel Barbara Chan, and saw first-hand something he hadn't experienced before: nature, meditation, and silence.

"It changed everything for me," he said. "It felt radical after the life I'd been living."

Maxis's critics aren't so sure he's really the philanthropist character he claims to be. One source who would only go on the record if they remained anonymous for fear of legal retaliation from the powerful Maxis family, revealed that Matt Maxis focused on helping people in exchange for free labour at an extremely high price. The source said they have evidence suggesting that once you commit to Maxis's community, it's extremely difficult to leave. It has the "grip of a golden handcuff," they claimed.

When asked about these allegations, Maxis is quick to brush them off.

"It's easy to criticize what you don't understand. Tell me who said these things, and I'd love to sit down with them for a respectful conversation."

The exact location of the community is limited to those involved, but it's rumoured to be near or within Valley Falls.

I pull the article from the fold of the newspaper and take a breath. Confirmation at last. The mall is near. My server comes back to fill my water.

"Everything taste okay?" She smiles and pushes a few strands of loose orange hair back behind her ears. Her name tag says *Debbie, 2002.*

"It's great, thank you." I put my hand over my cut. I'm wearing a long-sleeved shirt because I don't want any questions if the cut starts oozing blood again. So far it has remained dry.

Debbie, 2002.

Debbie might know something. This is a small town and she's worked here for well over twenty years. Members could have come and gone through here. Maybe some locals joined the mall. Old colleagues. Children.

Before she steps away from the table, I say, "Hey, um."

She turns around and smiles, which encourages me to ask my question, so I continue, "have you heard about that intentional living community run by a rich guy taking up in some old mall around here?" I pull up the article and show it to her. She flinches when she takes in the picture of Matt's smiling face

Her friendly expression fades. She leans toward me. "You're not the first person in here asking about that, that cult," she says in a low voice. "I don't like the idea of it, especially not around here. Living like that. Who even knows what they're doing. It's not right. They should have never closed that mall. We have nowhere to shop and for what? Some freak show."

"My best friend joined a couple months ago and I've stopped hearing from her. I was getting these letters every so often and they stopped coming. I'm worried something is going on there and I need to find her."

"One of the girls got a job here after she left that place. She lasted a couple of days before she stopped showing up. A weird one. Looked like a wounded bird with light, feathery hair. The few things she said were related to her boyfriend back home. Well it turns out he had died years ago in a brutal car accident. She talked about him like he was still with us," she says, shaking her head. "That's all I know. It doesn't seem like a place that's worth anyone's time. I wish the city would earn our tax dollars and shut it down, but you know how it is." She leaves and I watch her fill the water glasses of the couple beside me.

I carefully fold the article and put it into my purse. Thank you, Debbie. I quickly eat my food, leave Debbie the best tip I can, and walk back to my motel room. My mind's still going over the details of the article. The reporter found someone to interview. A source like this is a breakthrough. Could it have been Rane's sister? Or that jumper cable person's brother or the wounded bird from the diner Debbie told me about?

I search the newspaper's website and find the contact information of the reporter who published it. Ian Flynn. Before I psych myself out of it, I send him an email asking for his help to find my friend. I tell him about the four letters I received over the last five months, all stamped at post offices in Valley Falls. I give him my contact information, take a breath, and then press send, and I try to go to bed. Just as I begin to relax, my arms throbs. I go into the bathroom to change the band-aid. In the artificial light of the bathroom the wound looks fresh again, even though it stopped bleeding earlier and I thought it was healing like it was the first time. I run cold water over a starchy white face cloth and gently dab it over the spot. When I'm finished, I apply the fresh band-aid I found in the trunk and go back to bed.

I toss and turn. The memory of the cold fingertips on my clothed shoulder from the drive plays over and over in my head. That woman's brother felt the same thing, then he started to see his dead mother everywhere. Is the icy touch a warning or is it my imagination or is it my gut telling me to turn back? I'm nervous. My mind plays around with me when I'm nervous.

I hear my phone vibrate with an incoming message. I reach over to the bedside table to grab it.

TAG, YOU'RE IT!

Enough with this spam. I delete the message and turn my phone to silent. Then, I roll over and try to sleep.

Only I can't.

My mind rolls back to the night at the quay when we each took a personality test.

Her name should be Smiley. That's what I thought when Rebecca and I were approached by one of Matt's recruiters to take their community personality test.

Her actual name was better than smiles. It sparkled. I fell for everything they were curating like a row of perfectly placed dominos.

"My name is Diamond and I'm going to ask you some questions. Don't worry, I'll make it fun. This isn't a *test* test. It's a way for me to get to know you better, to understand if you would be a good fit for the mall and a good contributor to our project, to our community. I hope we can make this a conversation and have some fun during our time together this evening." Diamond smiled some more, and I noticed her dimple was enhanced with a glittery piercing. Diamond shone, just like the woman from the video tour did when she led her meditation at the end.

"Can I do this interview at the same time as my friend? It will save you time." Most of our answers would be the same anyway, I was certain of that.

She laughed and tilted her head, as if to get a better look at me. "Everyone gets their own interview. It's better that way. It allows us to talk one-on-one and to be more authentic with each other. Our community is special and we need to make sure everyone will fit. Sounds okay?"

I nodded because I wanted the twenty bucks.

She flipped through some pages, then flattened them out. She studied me a moment before launching into her first question.

"Do you wish you could go back in time to relive a happy memory?"

"Sure." I can't be alone on this. I think it's safe to assume most people want happy memories instead of disastrous ones. Happier memories from my childhood were harder to extract, there was always something lingering, some tension or anger, just out of reach.

However, I'm sure there was a pure happy memory somewhere in my brain. My memory of meeting Rebecca in university was one.

She ticked the yes column and continued onto the next question without asking for details.

"Do you look to food or alcohol for comfort after hard news?"

I nodded.

"Is that a yes then?"

"Yes." My mom needed her trusty friend wine when she was dealing with something and I learned that chocolate helped me make life more palatable. I've hidden it in drawers, desks, cupboards. When Rebecca saw me gnawing on cheap grocery checkout chocolate she knew something was up. What was Rebecca's telltale sign? Getting back together with Steve? I didn't know. I wondered how her conversation was going in the next trailer.

Diamond looked me in the eye, inviting me to add more, and when I didn't, she sighed and continued down her list of questions. I was clearly failing this test, but it didn't really matter.

"Do you need to talk through your thoughts out loud with a friend or family member in order to process them?"

I paused. Did I need to talk through things? I liked to get a second opinion on things. I liked confirmation about what I was thinking. Rebecca was someone I turned to time and again. She was more than a sounding board. I valued what she thought of me.

Diamond sighed again. "Don't overthink it. Just go with your gut." I caught her glancing at the short line up of people waiting for their tests. She wanted to get me out of there.

"Yes," I said confidently. Rebecca was right there with me whenever I needed to make a decision.

She ran her pen through the yes box, and made another note. I thought I saw a frown. I must have been answering incorrectly. *Yes* may not have been the best choice. I felt my palms sweat. I couldn't make her notes out. It looked like shorthand, a code only the recruiters would understand. I was dying to know what she thought of me. I shouldn't have cared, but I did.

"Last question, you're doing great." She didn't look up. "Do you regularly talk to your family?"

I said yes simply because I didn't want any painful follow-up on my complicated family situation. I didn't know where my parents lived anymore. This doesn't happen when you are close with them.

Diamond cleared her throat. "Okay, well…" She looked at the paper where she had sloppily written my name. "…Carolyn. Right. Carolyn. Thank you for your time today. I'm happy we had this special moment of conversation. I hope you've found it as meaningful as I did. Do you have any questions or anything you'd like to add?"

"When will I know about next steps?" I would be declining any offers immediately, but I still wanted to know about the process. To get my $20 participation fee, I wanted to pretend to be invested.

"We have your contact information. We make the recommendations quickly. We'll be in touch. Is there anything else? You can tell me anything." She tried to make that intense eye contact again.

Something in the way she said it—*you can tell me anything*—unarmed me in a way I hadn't expected. I don't talk to many people about anything real. Before I could think better of it, I started telling her about Jennifer and how the loss has impacted me my whole life. I hate that this stranger knows something so personal about me.

She nodded in a kind way. "I'm so sorry you've experienced this. You have been strong and brave for telling me about your grief. We, as a collective, feel that grief is not fair. It's one of our main mandates. How do you feel about grief?"

"I hate that it fills every part of me, even all these years later." Tears welled in my eyes. I hadn't meant to be so vulnerable with this woman I only met ten minutes ago.

"Grief is a process we feel deeply about at the mall. We understand that people have, and rightfully so, long-term and significant issues resulting from grief. In our work, we seek to lighten the load in our small way. Would you be open to telling us a little more about your loss?"

Before I responded, she started shuffling through her papers. She fastened a blue piece of paper to the clipboard and passed it to me. I took it and reviewed the questions: *How old were you when you experienced this loss? What happened? What do you wish happened? How has grief impacted you...*

I filled out each question, putting in details I haven't thought about in years. I did it quickly. If I thought too hard about any of this, my whole night would be ruined, maybe even my next week, too. I would spiral and I wasn't good to be around when I spiralled. I looked at my bandaged arm. My cut was fresh then. I pushed people further than they want to go. I made everything about me.

When I was done with the questionnaire, I handed her back the clipboard and stood up.

"Oh, you just need to check that box and sign right there." She pointed to the bottom of the page.

I took it back, ticked the box, and scribbled something that resembled my signature. My vision was blurred from the tears. She smiled, handed me the twenty-dollar bill she owed me for participating, and I waited for Rebecca on the street. When I pocketed the money, it felt so insignificant and hardly worth the price of telling her so much of my story. Even Rebecca didn't know everything I told them. It was always better for me to dwell on memories of Jennifer on my own than face them. I never overshared, until that night with Diamond.

"While you wait," Diamond called out from inside her trailer. "We have free Wi-Fi you are welcome to use. It's fast."

I had a measly data plan and I used almost all of it during my long commute to the law office to distract myself with mindless TikToks. I thanked her and connected to the network. I didn't have anything pressing to look at, but the glow of my screen, the act of endlessly scrolling, was soothing at that moment. Mindlessly absorbing social media posts helped me get my thoughts off my dead sister, who was likely lying somewhere in the woods decomposed at that very moment and there was nothing I would ever be able to do about it.

I push these memories aside long enough to fall asleep in the unfamiliar motel bed.

10

I slept for a total of four hours, maybe. Lumpy bed. Stress thoughts. I grab my phone and check my email, a ritual I've done every morning for years. There's an email from Ian Flynn sitting unread in my inbox. I click on it before I have my eyes fully open. He'd be happy to connect with me and asks if I'm available to meet him at a coffee shop at 11AM this morning and to bring the letters with me. He mentions wanting to see my letters twice. I take this as a good sign. He knows the value of them, just as I do. I email back, *yes, I'll be there.* This is progress. My first full day of searching for her in Valley Falls is starting off wonderfully.

I have a quick shower, careful not to get too much soap on my cut. The wound looks deeper than before, with the flesh around the two-inch gouge red and raw. I should get stitches to finally take care of this, but there isn't time while I'm on the road. After I blow dry my hair, I dab under my eyes with concealer, then apply some blush and mascara. As I reach for my normal beeswax lip balm, I see a flash of silver at the bottom of the bag. It's the lipstick Farrah gave me. I fish it out and swipe the colour over my lips. It's bright, but I don't hate the way I look with it applied. It complements my features in a bold way I wouldn't have considered myself. I may be on a rescue mission, but that doesn't mean I can't have some fun with colour.

By the time I get to the coffee shop, I'm five minutes late. I don't know who I'm looking for because Ian's profile was the only staffer on the newspaper website without a photo. I look around and see a man, mid-thirties, with blonde curly hair sitting with a copy of a daily newspaper, a thick notebook, a pen, and a handheld digital recorder. This must be him. Ian is either this man or the older man in the corner who brought his granddaughter along. I take a chance and walk toward his table. As I do, he looks up from his notebook and immediately I forget how

to put one foot in front of the other and I stumble. Not enough
to cause a major scene, but enough to know that my cheeks are
probably as bright as my lipstick. I shouldn't have worn this
colour.

"You must be Carolyn. Please sit down." He looks up at me
through thick-framed glasses with spotless lenses, and gestures to
the chair across from him. "Can I get you a coffee? They do a
good Americano here, surprisingly for a town like this. Let me
buy you one."

"Sure, that would be lovely." He nods and gets up from the
table. I sit down on the wobbly wooden chair across from him,
my heart beating fast. I'm worried I'm going to feel that balloon
in my lungs start to fill again and I won't get the contact of his
anonymous source. I watch Ian order my coffee from the barista
and try to calm down. He seems friendly enough. He drops some
change in the tip jar and waits at the bar for my drink.

His small black notebook sits across from me, open. I see his
loopy writing. *Carolyn Jones. Friend of community member. Has four
letters written from within the mall. Travelled from Metro Vancouver.
Motivated.*

Motivated for what? Before I can think about what he means
by that, he's approaching the table with a steaming cup of coffee.

"I wasn't sure if you liked anything in it, so I asked them for
cream and sugar on the side." He sets the drink in front of me.
Then he flips the notebook over and pulls it closer to him.
"Thanks for meeting me here. Your email about the letters.
Incredible. You're a good friend coming all the way out."

"Thank you." I lift the hot drink and take a careful sip. He's
right, it's good and the ritual of drinking it puts me more at ease.
I waited too long to take this trip. Ian knows something is going
on, too. For the first time in weeks, my shoulders relax.

Ian gets right into it, asking me for the letters before I even
set my mug down on the table. I hesitate because I haven't
shown them to anyone.

He rests his palms on the table and smiles. "It's okay, I'm a
journalist. You can trust me. I'll be careful with them. I understand how these would be important to you. She's your friend."

I glance up at his blue eyes. He has stubble like he's been up around the clock. It looks so nice on him. He catches my eye and smiles. I feel a flutter in my belly. Oh god. I look down at my hands and try to focus. He might see something in Rebecca's letters that I don't. It will be okay to let him see. I pull them out and lay each letter on the table. I haven't shown them to anyone and having them on the table like this feels naked. He might read them and tell me exactly what Chris said, she's moved on with her life. I don't think I can handle that.

"Here they are, in the order I received them," I say, pointing to the one on the left with my free hand.

A different kind of smile spreads across Ian's face, one of satisfaction, and I see underneath his stubble that he has a dimple on his left cheek.

"May I?" he asks, hovering his hands over the letters. I notice he's not wearing a wedding ring. Not that it matters. It's just an observation. All the male lawyers at the office are married, even the younger ones who act like the old ones. "Can I read them to analyze the tone?"

I hesitate, and he notices right away, adding "I understand they're personal. You can trust me to keep the specific content confidential."

"Help yourself." I gesture toward the letters like I'm signalling toward my first born.

He swoops in to pick up the first letter, examining it from top to bottom before gently opening it. It's strange watching someone I don't know open my personal letter. Part of me wants to yank it back from him and run out back to my car. I could continue my search for Rebecca and the mall on my own. I don't know if I can trust this guy. The mechanic at the rest stop told me to be careful. Debbie the server from the diner looked over her shoulder and Rane thought she was being followed. How is meeting Ian so openly like this being careful? I look at the grandpa and granddaughter sharing an oatmeal cookie, laughing at each other as they each take bites of their respective chunks.

"Hmm…" he says after reading one of the letters.

"What? What do you notice?"

"Oh, huh?" he says, keeping his eyes on the letter in his hands. "I didn't realize I was saying anything. I make these noises when I'm thinking about something. Drives my colleagues crazy, but I can't help it. I'm someone who gets absorbed fast. The rest of the world fades away and…" His voice fades and he's back reading the letter, his concentration fully on Rebecca's words.

Absorbed. I feel like that sometimes. He's wearing a pewter blue button-up shirt. It brings out his eyes. His shocking blue eyes. I drink more of my Americano. Delicious.

He returns the first letter to its envelope and continues through each of the others. The caffeine has kicked in and I feel a little more settled. Maybe we can help each other. There might be potential here. He runs a hand through his finely coiffed hair and I look away trying not to stare.

He leans in closer as if he's about to tell me a secret. "I hear he buys them boots when they arrive, something that will last. He wants so-called sustainable clothes. Long wear, not fast fashion. But they all wear the same kind. Brown leather boots because they are his favourite. Total power trip."

I haven't heard anything about what the conditions were like in there and it's likely that Rebecca didn't know this thing about the shoes before leaving. I do recall the footwear of Diamond or the other recruiter. The boots didn't seem odd to me because literally everyone in Vancouver wears Blundstones. Even the lawyer I work for wears them to court.

"Who was your anonymous source? Are they local and can…"

Before I can ask more questions about the source, he puts down his mug and sighs. It's a frustrated sigh. He closes his notebook this time and carefully puts it back in his satchel.

"I'm sorry, but I can't tell you," he says sadly. Our eyes meet and it feels so intense I can feel my eyes start to water. It's been a long time since I really looked at someone and it's a lot to handle along with everything else going on. I glance down at my empty mug.

"It's part of my journalism ethics," he continues. "Using anonymous sources isn't ideal, but for a story like this, my editor let me run with it. It's possible the source could provide me with more information later on, that's why I can't jeopardize it by talking about who my source is. It's not that I don't trust you. It's how this works. It's about getting this story told. It's important and I think you, out of anyone, knows that."

I never thought about it from a journalistic perspective before. Still, it's disappointing to hear. I don't have a lot of time. Everyone I have met along the way has been an outsider. I was hoping Ian would connect me with his source because they had actually lived there.

I pull my letters toward me.

"Now, where should we go from here?" he asks, watching me handle the letters.

"We?"

Coming out here and finding someone to work on this had never crossed my mind. I guess if he knows how to contact the source, then it is as good as me knowing who they are because we're working as a team.

"Well, you contacted me for a reason..."

Having a partner could cut down the time. We could share research. I only have a couple days of money left to fund this, so I need to make headway. I need the location of the mall soon or I'll run out of time.

"Let's work together," he says and extends his hand confidently toward mine. I stare at his hand for a moment before reaching out and shaking it. "Perfect, we'll make a great team," he adds.

He leans over to grab his bag again. "Can I interview you for my next story? It's a series now. The angle of the very concerned best friend would definitely be interesting and would put a human face to this whole thing."

"I won't go on record talking about Rebecca." She would never forgive me. She's a private person. Even showing Ian the letters was crossing a line, something I've promised I would never do again. Also, I'm still a marketing and PR professional and I know when to decline an interview from a reporter who's too motivated. Even a cute one.

He shrugs and leans back in his chair.

"The letters are a solid lead," he says, looking out the window onto the street. "My source didn't have anything produced from within Matt's community. Artefacts. That's what you have. The community is not this special commune where capitalism ceases to exist and everyone works for the common good. Did you know Matt could be a billionaire if he wanted? He's that connected and wealthy. He hasn't become one yet because he's been busy getting this mall set up. Once it is, I think he'll try to scale his efforts like a good MBA would."

"So, this person, your source, left voluntarily? People can do that? They can leave without a major issue?" Or unreasonable interest on an already large chunk of debt.

"I didn't say that," he says with a laugh. "The source from my article left. I'm not sure how it went down."

He looks at me again and this time before I can look away to save myself, I blush.

We plan to meet again tomorrow morning. His day off. I can barely contain my excitement. "We have a lot of work to do," I say. "I'm only in town for a couple days. That's all I could afford to take off, but I think it's enough time." I need it to be enough time. I haven't let myself think about the possibility of turning around without making contact with her, without knowing for certain she is okay.

"My editor will only give me so much time to pursue this story, which I find totally unbelievable," he says. "I have to fill the paper with the usual amount of community stories, local politics, and events coverage or we're at risk of losing advertisers. I'm doing this on my own time now. I don't think my editor really realizes how huge this story could be. If she did, she'd let me drop everything to get it. Or maybe she does, and the reality is keeping advertisers happy is what matters. I'm not going to be at that paper forever. Not after I break this story. Telling the world about this abuse is too important. People need to know what's going on. I have a bad feeling."

"I've studied Matt," I say. "I want to expose the truth about him too."

He looks at me curiously, then nods his head. I don't tell him what that woman said about her brother, that he saw visions and felt the cool touch of his dead mother on his body. I haven't felt those icy hands on my shoulder again. Maybe it never happened. I'm tired. It could have been my mind playing with me. I may have felt the breeze coming through the window and not realized it. I'd been driving a long time; it could have been my circulation acting up.

I glance over at Ian as he stares at his notepad. Yes, working with someone will help.

"I think we're going to work well together," Ian says, as if reading my mind. "We'll make good partners. Meet me tomorrow at 10:30AM at the post office on 10th Avenue."

I nod and this time he smiles into his long-empty mug.

The next morning I'm startled awake by a shower of terrifying knocks on the door. I stay in bed with the covers pulled up and I wait for whoever it is to go away because they can't be looking for me. Ian wouldn't be at my door. I'm meeting him at the post office and no one else knows I'm here.

"Ms. Jones?" a voice from outside shouts over the onslaught of knocks. "Please open the door, it's the front desk. There's a matter I need to address with you immediately."

I slink out of bed, pull a hoodie that was on the floor over my pajamas, and open the door. The morning sun forces me to squint.

"Good morning Ms. Jones. I hope I didn't wake you?" It's the woman who checked me in. The friendliness from earlier has been replaced with a frown and crossed arms.

Before I can tell her that, yes, she did wake me, she's talking again. "Do you have another credit card, Ms. Jones? I tried to put through your card for today's stay, as you asked me to, but I'm getting a message that says the cardholder needs to contact the company? My boss is very concerned that you can't pay. He wasn't happy that I agreed to charge you this way as it is against our policy."

I'm instantly awake and regretting the fact that I never did get a backup credit card for situations like this when my card malfunctions. Chris used to check in on these things with me when I was in my twenties because they were good to have as *an adult* he used to say. He eventually gave up, but not before making clear they would never lend me money if I got in trouble.

"Thank you for letting me know." I try to shut the door, but she puts one of her patent leather orthopedic shoes in the way. "I'll have to look into it. My card is good. There's room for tonight's stay. I can pay." I did all the calculations and I could afford the week. If I spent wisely, I could do this.

"As of right now, your check out time is this morning at 11AM. That's one hour from now. Thank you for staying with us. I hope you have a pleasant day." She manages to bring back that sing-song tone from when I checked in just at the end.

This must be a mistake. As soon as she leaves, I open my laptop and sign into my bank. I scan through the purchases. I must be a victim of fraud. Even I can't be this broke when I work full time. Then I see it, my recurring payment to my dentist for an emergency root canal I had last year. I don't have extended benefits so I had to put it on a payment plan. How could I have been dumb enough to forget it was coming out? Managing money like a proper adult eludes me. My bank account's almost empty. Forget about not being able to afford another night in this hideous motel, I won't be able to etransfer my landlord my rent money or pay for gas to get home. Before I can sink into this feeling, the alarm on my phone goes off. It's time to meet Ian. I quickly get dressed, pack my suitcase, and get in my car. Now more than ever, I need to keep going with what little time here I have left. I'll have to return home this evening. I shove the key in the car and will it to start. When the engine starts, I take it as a sign that the best thing to do is put my foot on the gas and drive away without a second thought.

When I reach the plaza, I park in the back. As I walk to the entrance of the post office, I hear a short honk. I look up to see a large black pickup truck that appears even bigger because of the small stall its parked in. Ian's behind the driver's seat waving at me. I walk to the passenger's side, open the door, and climb in. The truck is immaculate on the inside and smells brand new. I glance over at him. He looks fresh in a brown button up shirt rolled up to expose his forearms. His strong-looking forearms that I somehow failed to notice yesterday.

"This is for you." He hands me a take-out cup of coffee and I thank him. The warmth from the paper cup is what I need right now to ward off the feeling of failure after my credit card declined. I take a small sip and lean back in my seat. I can't worry about my accommodation. For once, I'll try to be in the moment.

My phone vibrates. Without thinking, I open it up and find another peculiar text message. *BOOKS IN THE TRASH CAN. YOU CAN'T CATCH ME.*

I stare at the words, trying to make sense of them. Did one of my nieces get a cell phone and these are messages from her?

Before I can think further, Ian looks over. "Anything important?"

I shake my head and toss my phone back into my purse. Maybe it's time I reply to these, but later. Ian's satisfied with my answer and goes back to whatever he's doing on his phone.

It's a quiet morning in the plaza. Older adults come and go, there's a FedEx pick-up, and the occasional person runs in while keeping their car idling in the parking lot.

"I hate it when people keep their cars idling when they could easily turn it off," I say.

"Yeah," Ian says, barely looking up from his phone. "It's like, what about the climate crisis? The world's on fire but they don't want their car to lose the air conditioning or something."

"Unbelievable."

We watch in silence as a few mothers with strollers walk up from the street, more older adults, and then another big delivery.

Ian tosses his phone in the cup holder beside my coffee and looks at me with a sudden interest that puts me off guard. "You know," he says. "I don't know much about you, Carolyn Jones? What do you do for work?" His voice is casual yet pointed. Great, a person skilled at interviewing strangers wants to learn about me.

To some people being asked what you do could be seen as the most basic of questions, but to me it scratches at my disappointment with how my career failed to launch. "Well, right now, I work in a law office in Vancouver."

He drums the steering wheel, returning his eyes to the parking. "Wow, that's incredible. So you're a lawyer?"

This is how this conversation always goes.

"Oh no, not a lawyer, just someone in the office. I work with papers."

He nods and drums his fingers on the steering wheel. I hope that's the end of the questions about me.

"That must be fun," he says, looking into his side mirror. I guess my temp work is interesting after all. I look at my side mirror. There's nothing out of the ordinary going on in this parking lot. My sense of calm is fading fast. This is starting to feel like a waste of time.

"Before going back to school for journalism," he continues. "I worked in construction for, I don't know, fifteen years or so? Maybe longer if you count the summers I had to help my dad on site."

"What drew you away from construction?" I was more interested in hearing about his life than in talking about mine. I'm tired of rehashing why my business failed and why I'll probably die with only a mountain of debt to keep me company.

"The weather mostly." He glances in the rearview mirror and adjusts the collar on his shirt. "Working in the heat or the rain or the snow. I hated it. Also the ebbs and flows of the economy took its toll most clearly in construction. Being laid off was expected and it was starting to annoy me. Some people in my family didn't need to work like me and dad did. It wasn't fair. The family was making decisions, big decisions, without even consulting us. Besides I always wanted to be a writer so I finally took an online journalism class. The Valley Falls Times took me on, but it's not where I want to be forever."

I haven't met anyone who was where they wanted to be forever. Everyone I knew was transiting through life, hoping something better eventually came along, something that clicked for them in a way that made them feel like work could be meaningful. Rebecca hadn't wanted to make her career in a tech kiosk in a mall that had over 70 percent vacancy. She wanted to build important applications. She wanted to use the (para)normal technology to help people process their grief on their own terms. She also wanted a family. As for me, maybe temping was as serious as I got. I haven't let myself dream beyond that in a long, long time.

"Where do you want to go after The Valley Falls Times?" The more I keep Ian talking about himself, the less I'll have to talk about myself.

He combs back his hair with his fingers and looks out into the parking lot. "I'd love to write features, to expose the truth about what's really going on in this country. I need more experience to do that. I guess it's a "brand" I need. I don't know. It's a bad time to get into journalism with the industry being absolutely gutted though. I don't know if it will ever recover. Even at my paper, if the ads aren't bought, the junior reporter, aka me, could very easily get let go. In the six months I've worked at the paper, there have been times I've hung on by a thread. The thin line between working and not has been central to my existence for most of my life. Didn't need to be this way, but that's how it is. Some people, people like our Matt Maxis, get to wield their power as if there are no consequences."

"Sounds stressful." And all too familiar. I haven't connected like this to someone in forever, not since Rebecca.

He laughs and when he nods his head I can smell a note of his piney aftershave. I take a sip of coffee. It's been years since any man cared about my caffeine levels. I have completely ignored dating since my last boyfriend. And for what outcome? I deserve to be with someone. I steal another look at him. When he notices and our eyes meet for a flash of a second, I turn to look out my window hoping I've hidden my blush this time.

"At the eleventh hour," he continues, "an ad buy comes in from a local realtor or a pizza place and I'm so grateful." He laughs. "I don't even like fast food or real estate."

"You've got to love those coupons." I wasn't sure what else to say, but it's an existence I relate to. At the temp agency, I could be cut at any moment without notice. I've found the best way to deal with that is to forget it's even a reality. It's amazing how much of my work week I can accomplish on autopilot. I am good at my job, but sometimes I can't even remember how I made it from Sunday night to Friday afternoon.

"Also, as a junior reporter, I am paid a low wage for the level that is expected of my work. That's another reason I'm focusing my attention on freelancing to make up the difference. I've had some pretty good luck so far, but it's not easy. I feel like I'm always working." He gestures toward his small notebook on the dashboard, as if it's waiting there for him to fill it up.

He opens the door and gets out of the truck to stretch his legs. I lean back in my seat and try not to think about where I'm going to sleep tonight.

Just then, Ian opens the door and whispers, "Look, these might be our people."

He points to three men walking toward the entrance, then he grabs his notebook, phone, and voice recorder. The men are all wearing brown leather boots. Beyond the similar boots, they don't look like a unified group. Before I can say anything, Ian's already outside the truck waiting to go in after them.

I open my door and quietly close it, not wanting to look too eager in case anyone is watching. I scan the parking lot, half expecting to see something that is so obviously from Matt's community to confirm these men are connected, like a brightly coloured van similar to the youth group vans I'd see around town when Jennifer and I were kids. But nothing here strikes me as unusual.

I follow Ian inside the store, and we split up to look less obvious. The three men also split up and we're officially outnumbered. One man stands in line at the post office, one man waits for prescriptions and the other looks through the magazine stands. Ian takes a picture of the man in line at the post office. The man has a large stack of white envelopes in his hands. I wish I could see if they had return addresses on them. We need the mall's address. This is our chance.

I'm closest to the man getting a prescription. He's sitting in the waiting area now, flipping through the newspaper. Unlike everyone else sitting there, he's not looking at his phone. This is probably because members aren't allowed to have phones. A shiver runs down my spine. It's them. I just have this sense of it. These guys are from the mall and I'm running out of time. They will know about Rebecca.

"Hey you!" My voice cuts through the noise of the store and everyone, from the woman stocking cereal boxes to the teenager standing at the pharmacy counter, turns to stare at me. "Where is she?" I shout.

The man waiting for the prescription looks over his shoulder but doesn't seem too interested in me.

Before I can say anything else, Ian shoves me down the toilet paper aisle. "Are you out of your mind? You're going to ruin this whole thing. We're going to follow them, okay? Don't talk to them."

"We need an address."

"I know we do, but we aren't going to get one by screaming our demands across a pharmacy." He gives me a slight smile, as if he's more amused then upset with me. "We can still recover but be quiet please."

I nod and I follow him out of the aisle. The line up at the pharmacy has cleared out, and our guys are gone.

"No, not this." Ian starts speed walking out of the store. Outside on the sidewalk, the parking lot is back to near empty.

"I'm sorry," I say. "I don't know what I was trying to do back there. I let my panic get the best of me."

Ian looks ahead to the street. "We might have been close to something, but who knows. Those might have been some other guys. We can't let this setback get us down."

I sit down on the curb and I can't stop myself from crying. The last thing I want is for Ian to see me emotional right now, but I can't help it.

He sits down beside me. "It's okay, Carolyn. There's no need to be upset. We'll find them. You have a few days left, right? We're partners now." He manages a chuckle to lighten the mood, but it sounds forced and why wouldn't it be, I messed up our opportunity to follow these guys back to the mall.

I wipe my tears on my sleeve. "I'm done. My credit card has reached its limit and I can't afford another night here. I need to go back to work. All my stuff is in my trunk." I hate talking about how broke I am like this. "I already checked out."

Ian reaches into his pocket and pulls out a crumpled napkin and hands it to me for my tears. "I think you need to see this through. It's important. If Rebecca is anywhere near Matt, it means she's in danger. You can't turn back now."

His words feel like a punch to the gut. "I absolutely want to see this through," I say. "I want to find Rebecca and make sure she's okay, but there's nothing I can do. I don't even know if my ancient car will make it home, let alone out of this parking lot." Ian's old napkin is no match for all these tears. I dab my eyes with the shreds anyway.

Ian reaches for my hands and holds them. "I have a couch. I have food. I have Wi-Fi. What more do a couple of amateur detectives need?" His hands are warm and comforting and surprisingly what I need right now. "Don't go home. We're going to find the mall and we're going to find Rebecca. We're doing this together. We're partners, remember?"

I've never had someone be so generous with me, but I've only known Ian for less than a day. It's not like me to trust like this. I also don't want to go home without finding the mall and sleeping in my car isn't an option I want to explore.

He squeezes my hand. "Come on, let's go to my place. We're done here. What do you say, partner? Are you going to come with me?"

I don't say anything, just nod, but that's enough for him because before I realize what's happening, he's walking me back to my car. He says he'll see me soon and I watch him walk back to his truck and jump in. I sit behind my wheel, turn the key, and follow him out of the parking lot casually, as if staying with someone I just met is completely sensible and safe. It's so easy to go along with this, to let Ian lead the way toward Matt and his community, toward Rebecca. It's easy because I don't know what else to do. Turning around isn't an option, but everything about this trip so far has been hard.

A couple minutes up the road, we hit a red light. Ian's truck idles in front of me and I look in my rear-view mirror to wipe away the mascara that's probably streaked down my cheeks and my heart almost stops.

It's my face reflected in the narrow mirror, but my skin has turned grey and looks swollen like it would be tender if I touched it. Drops of congealed blood fill the corners of my lips. My hair is longer than normal and wild, caked in a thick layer of dry mud. I don't know what's going on, but these are my eyes. This is my reflection. My heart beats faster and suddenly my body is overwhelmed by sound, like this noise has fused to my cells and it's coming from within my head. But the sound isn't human, it's mechanical like a vibration. I look in the mirror and blink, but my eyes don't move. I do it again, still my eyes are staring back at me. I'm freaked out and a flood of nerves seize me. I bring myself to pull up my hand to touch my face, my grey face. It's not reflected in the mirror. My hand is not showing in the mirror. This isn't my face, but it is, of course it is. Before I can scream, someone in the car behind me lays on the horn and it distracts me just enough to look away. When I look back in the mirror, I look how I expect myself to look. Tired, but me. No swollen face. No blood on my lips. The sound is gone. I pat my hair, feel my lips again, move my eyes. My face is still my face. The guy behind me won't let off the horn. When I look back to the road, Ian's already a block ahead.

I yell out of frustration then take hold of the steering wheel with my shaking hands and drive through the intersection. I glance again at the rearview mirror. I still look normal. Everything is as it should be. Everything is normal.

Rest is what I need.

I couldn't have driven home tonight if I tried.

12

Ian's main piece of furniture is a teetering black-brown book-shelf filled to the limits with books. His coffee table is piled high with the latest magazines in topics ranging from politics to woodworking. Glancing through his collection helps keep my thoughts off what happened in the car. Or what I imagined happened because there's no way I saw myself like that. Maybe I'm suffering from an apocalyptic episode of body dysmorphia. This must be a new condition. I don't know. I've been stressed. I flip through Ian's dog-eared copy of *Atomic Habits* and listen to the splash of his kettle being filled with water in his small galley kitchen. He's humming to himself and for a minute, I feel like I'm at home in my apartment with Rebecca waiting to share some tea together. Instead of feeling comforted by the memory, it sears my mind as just another reminder about how much things have changed. I shove the book back into the case and sit down on the couch.

I pull out my phone and see there's an email notification. It's a message from my landlord. The subject reads: *Did you get my notice?* I open the message and learn I'm being evicted with the minimum legal notice time. My landlord and her boyfriend are each selling their investment condos and will be making the step to buy a hobby farm on the Sunshine Coast to achieve their "life-long dream" of pursuing "organic husbandry," while also hosting "rad" Airbnb guests from "all over the world." Okay, Shelley and Todd! She goes on to write: *We found a super smart realtor, Steve, who will be coming by on Saturday with his fabulous designer to take some initial photos of the place. These will inevitably be the "before" shots, as we need to do some extensive renos to get it liveable before we put it on the market...*

My landlord goes on about the fine details she and the love of her life Todd will add to my hovel of an apartment to make it desirable when she lists. I email her back a one letter response: *K*, and put my phone back in my purse. Searching for adequate housing is not something I have the mental space to be doing right now. I rest my head in my hands. What is the vacancy rate these days back home? 0.05%?

Ian comes out from the kitchen with a tray and sets it down on his small living room table.

"Help yourself," he says, gesturing toward his beautiful black tea pot. My fingers will smudge the handle, it's so shiny, but I pour myself a small amount anyway. I'm not in the mood for tea or small talk. The ramifications of Shelley's email are sinking in. I need to find a place to live and I need to find one that I can afford alone. Rents have increased exponentially since I moved into my place.

When he's finished pouring his mug, he sets it down on the table then reaches into his pocket to pull something out. It's the voice recorder he had at the café. He sets it on the table then points to it and smiles. His dimple is showing again and despite feeling exhausted and stressed, I feel my heart flutter. He's so cute. "I was hoping I could interview you now," he says gently. "You're the first person I've met who knows someone living in the mall." He pulls up his notebook from a side table and places it on his lap. He uncaps his pen. "You will be able to add some new perspective to the story that everyone wants to hear. It will help Rebecca."

I blow on my steaming mug of tea. He's forgetting that he knows someone there as well. That person I need to talk to. "Except the source you know. The one I'm not allowed to know anything about."

I'll need to talk to them soon because Shelley and Todd are coming down on me hard.

He laughs. "Yes, besides my source. I'll only ask a few questions. I promise."

"I still want to talk to your source." If I talk to Ian's source, I'll be able to live with myself that this trip was worth the humiliation, failure, and expense. I tried to find my friend. I failed, but at least I tried. *Wouldn't you look for your sister?*

He shakes his head. "I'm the only one who can talk to them. I'm sorry, it's like what I said before about trust. You have to trust me, for your own protection."

I take a sip of my tea and the scalding hot water trickles down my throat. I set my mug down on his coffee table. "I'm not in this to be interviewed. All I'm trying to do by coming out here is find my friend." This whole trip is feeling more and more like a failure and now I've got to get back to my place to let Steve in. I'm sure he remembers our address for all those months he basically lived with us. All my old furniture will be sitting there exactly the same, signaling to him that I've been stagnant for years. The balloon starts to expand in my lungs.

Ian reaches for his recorder and puts it back in his pocket. "Okay, I understand. Maybe we can do an interview later. Your perspective on what Matt is doing is an important voice in this story. I think there are other people like you, friends, or family members, who are worried. You have a chance to speak for them. You can help tell the story. But only when you're ready. I won't push."

He reaches for his TV remote and turns it on. "We can watch the news for a minute. That always relaxes me."

Watching the news is the last thing I do to relax, but I lean back into the couch anyway. I'll need the rest before starting my drive home tomorrow morning. I don't trust myself driving now. The way I saw my face when we were leaving the strip mall didn't make sense. I feel terrible and exhausted, but that was such a bizarre exaggeration. I breathe in and out, and feel the balloon start to deflate.

A flashy commercial for home equity loans fades out and an anchor with perfect hair and red lipstick starts reading her teleprompter with a slight squint. "We're live on scene in a small forest community in the valley waiting to hear from officials about a body that was discovered earlier this morning by dog walkers. A content warning for viewers, some may find the details of this story disturbing. Shauna?"

Ian turns up the volume.

"Thank you, Sandeep. I'm here with witnesses who say a body of a male who looked to be in his forties was discovered right here on this path." The journalist stands in the middle of a tree-lined path, her turquoise rain jacket flapping in the wind. "I'm here with Philip whose friend was one of the dog walkers who made the gruesome discovery."

The segment cuts to an older man in a faded denim jacket. He immediately reminds me of my dad. They would be similar ages. Thinking of him is the last thing I need. I push it out.

"I'm here to support my friend. She was the witness, not me. The guy, the body I should say, well, it didn't look natural." The man is pale and wide-eyed. The camera closes in tighter. "After she called the police, she called me and I'll never forget the fear in her voice. She told me the body was leaning against a tree like a doll. Someone positioned it that way, I say. When she got closer, she could see...bruises around his neck like he had been choked. He had full sleeve tattoos, very distinct like vines of a garden and carrots wrapping around his arms. Probably a weird gang thing if you ask me. I'm saying it first because cops are always wishy-washy on this: this path is not safe. Do not come here. Some freaks are out here."

The vine tattoos. My mind goes back to the woman who helped me in the rest stop. She said her and her brother got the garden box tattoos when their mother died. She said it was an original design.

They cut back to the reporter, who's brushing her wind-blown hair out of her face.

"Can you tell us anything else? Did the police say anything to your friend about what they think might have happened?"

"I have no idea. My friend said it was a man that somehow looked like a doll. Not sure how that would work." He shrugs and then suddenly he closes his eyes tight and scrunches up his face like he's in pain. He puts his hands over his ears and he's shaking. "What on earth is that sound?" he manages to say in a strained voice.

The camera fumbles and shifts from the man to the reporter. She is standing there with her hands over her ears. "I can report

I am experiencing a very high-pitched sound, and, oh my god, there is a stench that has just enveloped this area and…" She gasps for air and the camera falls to the ground with a thud. Over a shot of gravel and dirt, all we hear is the reporter muttering, "I, I, I…"

"What the hell did we just see?" Ian looks over at me. We hadn't heard a high-pitched sound over the broadcast feed.

They cut back to the studio. The anchor's mouth is wide open in disbelief. After a moment of staring into the camera, she manages to say in a shaky voice, "We…we will find out what is… happening over there after this short break."

A commercial for luxury retirement living blasts from the screen.

"Please turn it off," I say. He does and the room is quiet. "I think I know who that man is, the one they found dead."

Ian looks at me. "How? They barely said anything about him."

I get up from the couch and pace the room. It's a small room, but I need to move, even a couple steps will do. "On the way here, I had car troubles…"

Ian pulls out his recorder. "Please let me record this. I won't use it. I just…it helps me stay calm when I know everything is properly documented."

I nod and he presses the button. "There was this woman who helped me and she asked me where I was going, so I told her and then she told me about her brother and how she doesn't know where he went. He started seeing their dead mother." I tell him everything she told me, including the details about the tattoo.

"You found a witness like that and didn't tell me!" he says in shock.

"I didn't think too much of it, plus she said my car was going to die any minute so I wanted to get out of there. Plus she was high."

He stares at me with confusion. "Tell me you at least got her contact information."

I shake my head and sit back on the couch. "I'm awful at this. Please turn off your recorder now."

He turns it off and puts it back in his pocket. Suddenly the room feels too small. Ian notices my discomfort and assures me everything will be okay. I've stopped believing people when they say that. I want to believe Ian. Believing everything will be okay seems like a fantasy at this point. There's something going on and I'm certain the mall is at the centre of it, but the closer I get, the further out of reach it feels.

Ian turns the TV back on and I hear the monotone drone of a police spokesperson flatly say they are trying to figure out what happened, they take the events very seriously, and they don't think the public is at risk. "If anyone knows anything, please contact our Crime Stoppers number…"

If the man found dead on the path is the brother of the mechanic I met, it means he never escaped. Something got to him. This could mean that Rane's sister, Rebecca's roommate, and the others never got far either. Maybe I haven't heard from Rebecca because she actually tried to leave, and…I stop myself right there.

Water, I need water to help settle down. I get up to get myself a glass of water from the kitchen. Ian doesn't look up.

I open the cupboard over the sink and find a neat stack of plates and bowls. Four each. I open another cupboard and see a single steel colander. It's amazing to me how I can never anticipate the way another person organizes their kitchen, even a kitchen as sparse as Ian's. In the next cupboard, I find a few glasses and pull one out. I turn on the tap, let it run for a moment until it's cold, and fill it up. As I take a sip, I notice a pile of mail beside the coffee maker. Ian's still glued to the news so I step toward the pile. I won't touch anything. I just want to see, and besides I need something to keep my mind off whatever happened on the news a minute ago.

As I take another step, something else catches my eye, something out of place. Beside his toaster, there's a long, sheathed knife with a thick handle. The engraving reads: Winkler Knives. I take a step back as if even looking at this object could harm me. Ian's a hunter. Or is he? This is the only gear I see. The knife scares me and reminds me I know nothing about him. The man whose house I'm at could be anyone. Panic rushes over me. I pour the rest of the water out in the sink and leave the glass on the counter. It's time for me to go home, to get away from this place. I need to grab my suitcase from beside the couch, walk to the door, and drive straight home.

I stand in the doorway of the kitchen and watch Ian watch the news.

A commercial for hip replacements animates the screen. My heart is beating faster and I force a level and calm voice. "Thank you for inviting me to stay with you, but it's time for me to go home. There's been some emergency with my landlord..."

I grab my suitcase from behind the couch and pull it toward me.

"But wait, no." He stands up and takes a step near me. I take a step back. I'm not sure anymore about any of this. Nothing about this trip feels safe. "You can't go just yet," he pleads. "We need to help your friend. Look at this!" He gestures toward the TV. "She needs us. Look what's happening. You know this man was connected to the community. You just said it. He just has to be. No one understands the danger Matt is causing except us."

I know turning around without Rebecca will haunt me for the rest of my life, but I can't stay here. I don't even know who Ian is. I pull my hand away and put on one of my boots while holding my suitcase for balance.

"Please stay. Please. I know where the mall is," Ian says. The words are coming out of his mouth fast and I can't believe what I'm hearing. "At least I think I do. I'm almost one hundred percent sure."

I pull my second boot on and stand up straight. He *knows* where the mall is all of a sudden? The news confuses me. All I've wanted is the address and he only tells me now. "Why haven't you gone yet and why are you only telling me this now?"

"I needed to know if I could trust you. What Matt is doing needs to be exposed but I'm lacking evidence. If this doesn't go down perfectly, the story dies and Matt gets away with everything. Then he gets another unfathomably large inheritance and his ability to screw over the lives of more people becomes even more probable. It's not fair. You know, he's still going to inherit millions, well probably billions now with inflation, from the Maxis family. Just think of all the lives he can manipulate and ruin with even more money. He owns at least a dozen malls already all over the country. He will scale up, creating his own secret society to keep power over people he says are indebted to him. But there's more going on there. I just haven't figured out what yet. And, now with you, I think we can do this together."

A rich man's secret society won't be good, I've felt that from the start. I hadn't factored in Matt getting more money from his family. His wealth has been the most abstract part of this whole thing for me. The extent I know is he is wealthier than I could ever comprehend. He has the opportunity to take away the financial burdens of virtually everyone in the country, but instead of helping them he chooses to cloister them away from everyone they know. But why is he doing it? I need to see it for myself. *We* need to see it for ourselves. It's the only way we can put a stop to this, whatever it is. And now that man on the path. His position against the tree. The choke marks. The sound. My heart sinks thinking I might have heard the same sound in the car. I touch my face. I haven't been to the mall so it's not possible that I'm being impacted by something related to Matt. My issues are stress related. They have to be. I study Ian's face.

"I want you to stay. I need your help. I want you to find your friend." He sits back down on the couch and pats the spot beside him. "Come on, let's plan our next steps. We're going to find Rebecca."

I really want to find Rebecca and Ian knows where the mall is, but this entire time I've trusted his word and maybe I shouldn't have. I think about the knife I saw on his counter. "Why do you have that knife in your kitchen?"

He laughs. "Don't all kitchens have knives? I mean, I don't cook too often but at least I know that much."

I take another step toward the door. "I saw your knife beside the toaster. The, uh, big one." I'm kicking myself for being too trusting, for not questioning anything about this man. I've taken everything he's said at face value and maybe I shouldn't have.

"Oh, that knife." He smirks. "It's nothing, seriously. I'm waiting to sell it. I got it from someone I was interviewing recently. They were going to chuck it and I thought it might be worth something. Have I mentioned how crappy my salary is? It's nothing. I promise you."

I understand Ian's money issues more than I understand Matt's excessive wealth. A few bucks from the sale of the knife would make a difference. That's why I wanted to do Matt's personality test in the first place. Something's not adding up. If he struggles with finances so much, how is he affording such an expensive truck?

"My car is almost three decades old because that's all I can afford. How are you driving that truck?"

He laughs again. "That truck? That was a left-over from when I was in construction with my dad. Call it a severance package. I can barely afford the gas."

"Is there anything else you need to tell me?"

He shifts in his seat and a look crosses his face that I can't place. Maybe there is something he needs to tell me, but instead he shakes his head with the same enthusiasm I've experienced since meeting him. "Nope. I'm just a journalist looking to crack a story about an abuser." He lifts his arms up in an innocent shrug.

His words put me at ease enough to take off my boots and join him on the couch as the news anchor tries to make sense of the murder and everything unfolding on the trail. After a few minutes, Ian leans in close to me and softly says, "We'll leave for the mall in the morning. Let's relax tonight. We make a great team."

His breath on my neck doesn't scare me, it comforts me in a way I haven't felt for a long time. For the first time since the start of my trip, I feel optimistic again. Slightly. I take his hand without overthinking it and he gives me a strong squeeze. He pulls me in for a cuddle and he smells very good. When he looks at me, we kiss. It's a kiss I feel all the way to my toes. It's not what I was expecting to happen when I left to come here, but this is my one chance to find her and I'm not going to waste it by listening to my gut. My gut got us on the quay that night so they could discover Rebecca. My gut urged me to do something to Rebecca that would hurt her all the way to her core. It's time to trust the process.

13

"So, is Ben your ex?" Ian looks over at me before returning his focus back to the road. It's late the next morning and we're buckled into his truck and driving on the highway toward where he figures the mall will be. There should be some unspoken rule that if someone hears a person they barely know sleep-talking that they keep it to themselves.

"I don't know, honestly. Are you sure you heard right?" I move my neck back and forth in an attempt to stretch it. I'm sore from sleeping on his tiny couch, but for the first time in a while, I slept for multiple hours. He offered me his bed, but I didn't want to make things more awkward.

"Pretty sure. You said the name like half a dozen times. Ben. Or maybe Glen or Jen? It was something like that. I was pretty exhausted so maybe I was dreaming. Do you want to talk about it?"

Jen. That's what dad called her. She hated the shortened version of her name, but dad had two modes and teasing was one of them. I liked the teasing side better because the controlling side was so destructive. Now I see them as two sides of the same personality defect.

I shake my head. "Not a chance but thank you for asking." We're together to find Rebecca. He doesn't need to know about Jennifer. I wasn't aware I'd been dreaming about her again. Dreams are never a good sign. This has been a stressful situation, even with our progress. I can't have the balloon fill up again. I've been good at managing it this trip. Driving with Ian toward the mall is critical and I need to keep it together. I don't know if I want her to be there or not. People who leave seem to suffer, but the people who stay likely don't have it much better.

Instead of thinking about it more, I look down at my phone displaying our route. "We're getting close, apparently. Time to pay attention. This is our exit."

Soon we're driving along a sleepy main street that links two dozen stores together. Most of the stores have papered over their windows because they're permanently closed and probably have been for years. Several small *For Sale* signs on the outside of the windows are yellowing and look like they could crumble if touched. In between those empty storefronts, is a faded insurance place, a barber shop, a liquor store, and a post office that have somehow managed to keep the lights on. That's it. I understand now why Matt would order his members to travel an hour outside of town to run errands. Shop owners might talk, ask questions, and Matt wouldn't want that. The people around here might get too curious about the mall, especially since the mall is what likely started the slow decay of this street originally. Not that the mall's demise reinvigorated business down here in any way. Perhaps the damage was too foundational to recover from without serious support.

Once we leave the dismal business area, we enter a residential neighbourhood. Aging houses are painted from the same restricted colour palette: avocado green, robin's egg blue, and golden yellow. The trim paint on most of these houses has chipped almost clear off. They look vacant, but it's hard to tell. Could Matt own these too? He has the means to buy them and it would make strategic sense to isolate the mall from others.

I ask Ian what he thinks.

He scoffs. "Wouldn't doubt it."

A man pops his head out his front window. So there's people here in this quasi-ghost town. "I wonder when most people left."

"This town used to be home to the Bumble Cleaner. Do you remember those?"

Before I can tell him I don't, we see a mom and her kids walking up the sidewalk. She uses one hand to hold onto her toddler and the other to push a cumbersome stroller. She stops and watches us as we pass. I smile at her, but she doesn't acknowledge me. She looks to be zoning out, like she's losing her focus, then she covers her ears in pain.

Suddenly the soft whir of a buzzing sound reaches the car. I recognize it as the sound I heard yesterday when I was in the car alone. I lean back in my seat, so I don't accidentally look in my mirrors or see my reflection in my window. I'm afraid of the state I'll see myself in.

I roll up the crack in my window while keeping my eyes closed.

We should help her. We should help her, but I'm determined not to fall apart right now. If I turn around, I might see something, that greying version of me from the rearview mirror.

"Bumble Cleaner made a type of mop that had this honeycomb pattern in it," Ian continues. He must not hear anything or else he would make a comment. How do I explain to him that my brain feels like it is going to start oozing out of my ears? I can't tune it out.

"You've probably seen one sometime in your life. There was a large manufacturing plant here for decades. It eventually closed when the owners sent the manufacturing offshore and ninety percent of the town lost their livelihood, but that's where most of this housing came from. This place is kind of like a failed company town. Almost everyone who lived here was associated with Bumble Cleaner in some way. You either worked for it or you served it, like so many of those one-trick pony towns. Now the town is virtually empty, and, as you're aware, the main shopping mall closed. The town's now trying to make a go at transforming itself into a tourist destination."

The sound fades, and I slowly open my eyes. My heart is pounding and I'm worried Ian might hear it. I concentrate on what he's saying, something about tourists.

His voice is a welcome distraction from my thoughts. We cuddled way into the night and he gave me the sweetest kiss before he went to bed. Thinking of his soft, warm lips and intoxicating aftershave helps bring me back to the moment.

"Tourists?" I glance out at the town, trying to distract myself. There is nothing about this place that would attract willing tourists. I look in the passenger-side mirror. The woman is gone, and most importantly, it's my own face as I know it reflected. Whatever was going on is over now.

"How do you know so much about this place?" I watch the old houses pass outside my window and, for just a moment, a memory of watching the scenery from the back of my parent's car with Jennifer beside me attempts to pull me in. Our last drive together into the woods. She was mad at dad. She wouldn't open her new book and I was feeling anxious about this animosity because I always had a twin-like sense of things with her. It's something I've missed the most. It was a level of love and understanding that transcended everything.

Not right now. I close my eyes and listen to the sound of Ian's engine.

"It's all research for my article," Ian says, appearing to not notice I'm gripping the door handle to steady myself. "I couldn't sleep last night after I looked at your letters again. I was up all night looking stuff up on my phone about the guy they found in the woods, then I found some interesting information on Bumble Cleaner, and I went down a rabbit hole. That's when I thought I heard you muttering about this Ben character. Want to talk about it? More importantly, should I be worried your boyfriend is going to come here looking for us?"

He takes his eyes off the road and gives me a cheeky grin. My cheeks are definitely red now.

I try to pass it off with a laugh because there is no way I'm going to get into Jennifer with him right now. "I don't talk in my sleep. Seriously. Rebecca would have told me. We lived together for years and our place had horrible soundproofing."

He shrugs, returning his eyes to the road. I hope that's all on the topic of Jennifer for now.

At the end of main street, we see a massive mustard yellow beehive jutting out high among the rest of the single-level buildings. It has to be over three stories high. "So that's the tourist draw, I'm guessing? It certainly is big." It's also tacky and, despite its size compared to anything else we've seen, underwhelming as a tourist draw. My online review, if I did those, would be: *Don't waste your gas*.

He nods in agreement, "I'll pull over so I can get a photo of it. The thing's ridiculous and will make a good illustration for my article. Imagine going out of your way to see this? Worst family road trip ever. It's like something my grandpa would have wanted to see because he thought it made him more Canadian."

An anecdote about his grandpa intrigues me because Ian hasn't talked much about his family, not that I have either, but still it's interesting. "You're going to have to explain that one."

He sighs, a more resigned one than normal, and I sense a shift in him. Maybe this topic is too personal. I get it. I didn't want to tell him about Jennifer. There's pain here.

"My grandpa was, I guess you would say, very competitive," he says slowly. "Everything he did was a chance to one up his perceived enemies. He was in manufacturing for decades and he took pride that he did it all in the same country he lived in."

"Construction with dad and manufacturing with grandpa. You were a busy kid."

Ian shakes his head. "It got…interesting, especially when my uncle started importing from places with very little in the way of labour laws behind my grandpa's back. Anyway, we're here. Let's check it out."

We park on the street and walk up to the hive. As we get closer, we hear the rhythmic buzzing of bees crackle from an overhead speaker. Was this what I heard earlier? It wasn't as high-pitched as I thought, but the sound might have distorted as it travelled. It's settled. I've been hearing a recording. I can accept that. A tourist trap of this calibre probably isn't subtle with their marketing tactics, even if it's creepy as hell.

"Why would a town pay homage in this way to the product that sank them in the first place? It doesn't make sense. Where is the imagination for something different?" Ian takes a photo with his phone. "It's as if we can't let go of what is clearly gone. Everything I've seen in this town so far should be let go of. Matt probably sees this too and that's exactly what drew him here. There are few obstacles in a scheme like Matt's, and just imagine how many towns like this there are across Canada."

I wonder what Rebecca thought about this place when she saw it for the first time. Was she struck by its shabbiness as well? Did it remind her of our apartment? The very apartment Steve of all people will soon be selling from underneath me? Something else I want to avoid thinking about.

We walk through the entrance and approach the hive at eye level. I can see right away the hive is poorly made and falling apart like so much of this town, but there is an earthy earnestness to its obvious shape that draws me in. The hive doesn't make sense as a monument. I agree with Ian on that. It's a testament to a forgotten era in a town that refuses to move on or can't move on because it has little else to offer.

I get as close as I can to the honeycomb. Ian's around the corner taking photos or something. A short fence surrounds the hive, but I can still reach through and touch the honeycombs, which are made of large semi-truck tires spray painted a spectrum of gold. The tires are flaking and fading so drastically I would expect to be standing in a landfill if not for the context of the tourism signage. Still, I want to get closer. I step around the fence and kneel by a small hole to look inside. It's dark in there and much, much smaller than it looks from the outside. A whiff of something sour saturates the air. I cover my nose and look closer to see there's a carpet of dark mould growing along the back of the honeycomb rotting this tourist trap from within.

It really is quite the disgusting place. I need to get Ian back onto the road.

Before I can step away from it, a sudden movement catches my eye. There's something in there. Maybe a raccoon or a rat. I catch something else, like a glimmer out of the corner of my eye. Past the edge of the honeycomb toward the centre of the hive, I'm almost certain I see the shadow of a person, but I can't be. I lean in closer and see the shadow move. It's a child. There must be a family here and somehow the kid wandered off to see inside the hive. I look over my shoulder, but no one is here, even Ian wandered off.

I lean in closer and suddenly feel lightheaded from the sharp stench of rot. The kid cannot stay there. "Hello? Are you okay there?" My voice echoes back to me.

The child, who looks to be a girl, slowly gets up from the ground and walks toward me. She's wearing a thick coat and it's hard to tell the exact colour in the low light but it looks pink. As she gets closer, I try to get a good look at her but the closer she gets the more it looks like her face is missing. My stomach drops. I can't be seeing right. As I watch her, the area where her face should be has started glitching. I don't understand what's happening. Humans don't glitch. I need to get her out of this hive. The rot is impacting my brain.

I try to get away from the small space, but the sound of shuffling inside the hive draws my attention back. She approaches the thick strip of mould and drags her arms through it, from hands to elbows. The smell is now one hundred times worse. I fall back on the cement and try to stop myself from gagging.

"Are you okay?" I say between coughs. "Can you talk to me? Please come out of there."

The sound of footsteps approaching breaks my concentration. "What are you doing," a voice asks. I turn to see a woman standing in front of me. So there is someone here besides me and Ian. Her daughter must be the one inside.

Before I can tell her that her daughter is playing in mould, she motions me back. "I wouldn't get too close to that thing if I was you," the woman says. "There's a fence around it for a reason, to keep looky-loos out. It's fragile and complicated." Her brown eyes dart past me toward the hive then back at me again in a way that doesn't give me comfort. The locals here are as strange as their downtown.

"Someone's in there. I saw a girl. Is that your daughter?"

I step over the fence again because I want to see where the person is, but before I see inside the hive, the woman grabs my shoulder, pulling me back.

"Stay on this side of the fence please. There's no one in there, at least not in reality. I accepted a special assignment out here, but that doesn't mean I need to understand it."

She's not making sense. "I need to see if she's okay." I have to look again. I need to see her face. The light must have been too dim to see it clearly the first time. The woman takes my elbow again and I immediately pull it away. "Don't touch me."

Ian runs up to us. "Carolyn, is everything okay here? It sounded like you were yelling. I was around back." He has his voice recorder in his hand.

"I looked inside the hive and I saw someone in there. I need to know if she's okay. No one should be in there. Certainly not a child."

A child without a face. It doesn't make sense. I couldn't have been seeing right.

Ian looks at the woman. "Who are you? I'm Ian and this is my friend Carolyn. Do you work here?"

"Nice to meet you, Ian." She says with disinterest, then she lets go of me and extends her hand to shake his. Unlike her impeccably clean clothing, her hands are filthy, like she's been messing around in dirt all morning. She doesn't say her name or if she works here, but I have a hunch she works for Matt.

After she is finished shaking Ian's hand, she returns her attention to me. "Carolyn, I wouldn't get that close to the hive." Her comfort repeating my name like she didn't just learn it a second ago is unsettling. "It's not what you think it is. Are you sure you saw someone in the hive?"

Without saying anything, Ian fiddles with his voice recorder and presses the red button.

I hesitate. I haven't trusted my eyes many times this trip, but I saw someone. "Yes, I'm sure. It was a girl. She was walking toward me and then…"

Her face glitched out. I can't say it. Doubt fills me and suddenly being wedged between this strange woman and this rotting hive is making me feel claustrophobic. I brush a bead of sweat from my forehead.

Ian steps in front of me and faces the woman. "Would you mind if I interviewed you right now? It will only take five minutes, tops. I'm working on a story about your town. I'd love to ask you a few questions about this place. Have you lived here long?"

"A story about here?" The woman laughs. "This isn't my town. This isn't my community. You should find a local, if you can find one of them since they all tried to leave the network for the most part. I wonder how well that worked out for them. He offered to pay all their property taxes. If something is too good to be true, it probably is. I have nothing to tell you for your story."

She looks at Ian and then at me. "Fine, I'll say this: nothing is free, and no one is truly in control even if they think they are. I'll be gone from here someday. I'm doing what I'm told until then, which these days is keeping random looky-loos from getting too close to the fence hence my approaching you two. Sad as it sounds." She kicks her boot on the hive and a chunk falls off. "This isn't the worst way I've spent my time."

"Okay…" Ian nods slowly and pushes his recorder closer to her. "Can I ask you some questions? Like, I'm really interested in…"

She ignores his question with a wave of her hand. "I just wanted to warn your friend about touching the hive, that's all. If you're already seeing something in there, hun, brace yourself."

"Wait a second," Ian follows her for a few steps. "What's with the hive? My friend saw a kid in there."

"There's mould in it. Apparently City Council cheaped out when they built it eight years ago as a last ditch effort to drum up interest in the town. Typical. It's now falling apart like everything else. So much for building a tourist destination that doesn't make you physically ill."

I gently push myself away from the hive and will myself to get closer to her. "Why do I need to brace myself?"

She sighs. "You should *brace* yourself for more is all I'm saying. If it's already starting here, this far out, I'd be worried. But then again, I don't really know how things are progressing anymore. Clearly I'm on the outside, and you know, I'm fine with it. I was offered this gig and I accepted it. I'm paying how I need to pay."

Her words rattle me. How much of what I've been experiencing is related to all this? "Can you tell me what is happening? Things haven't been feeling right…"

She shakes her head. "You'll find out on your own. I wouldn't be able to explain it if I tried. Lots of people here have been feeling what you're feeling. It's a shame what happened in the forest and what that dog walker witnessed. The challenge is keeping the visions at bay. I know I've had to work very hard. I didn't fully understand what I consented to, what I was truly giving up, but that's how it goes. Isn't that what all those tech gurus make bank on? That we sign off on the terms of use without fully understanding the extent of what we are giving up. Luckily there are other ways. Good luck."

She walks away and disappears around a corner. I take a step to follow after her, but Ian grabs my elbow. His hand grazes the wound on my forearm, and the pain pulses through my body like a jolt of electricity. The wound is fresh again. What is going on?

Ian puts his phone in his pocket and stops his recorder. "We should get going. It's starting to rain."

"Did you see the person in there when you looked in? She had on a pink coat. I'm sure of it." It was pink, it was dirty. Her face, well, her face wasn't there.

"You're tired. My couch is not comfortable. I know from many nights of falling asleep on it. I don't know what you saw, but there's no one in there. I looked and it was empty. There's not much room in there. You probably saw the movement of a rat, which would be on brand for this town. I'm sorry." Ian takes my hand and gently pulls me toward him. He's probably right. We walk back to where we parked.

Inside the truck, Ian plugs in his phone. I should have done that last night. My phone's almost dead.

"Let's go to the mall," I say, numbly looking back at the hive. "We'll find Rebecca then get out of here." The mountains can't save this place. They feel so jagged. Rebecca said they felt like they could close in on her. To me they feel like they could crush me down into the dirt.

Ian starts his truck and pulls out of the gravel parking lot and we're back on the road. We're only minutes away from the mall, which means we're close to the community, to Rebecca, to ending this.

It's now late morning and the dark clouds look full of rain just waiting to escape.

The road is faded and pockmarked like it hasn't been touched in years let alone driven on. Ian swerves one pothole and then another. I haven't seen another driver since we left the beehive. The road is empty, not even delivery drivers are using the street. The quiet here isn't just silent; it feels thick and rancid, like it could slowly turn to poison. If Rebecca left the mall without a ride, she'd have a tough walk into town. I can't think of her walking that far alone. I edge forward in my seat and look up, there's no streetlights anywhere. Even if there were lights further up, I'm betting they'll be burnt out. The town gave up. This road will be pitch black as soon as the sun goes down.

We take a few right turns and pass a small cemetery with a gate that hangs open, looking like it's barely holding on to its rusting hinges. Up ahead, a rain-soaked couch sits along the shoulder of the road with all the old cushions perfectly intact as if it's been waiting for decades for someone to come back and sit. Bags of garbage, torn with whatever filled them, are spilling out into the street like guts. A pile of broken gypsum board sits on the road and Ian must swerve to miss this too. The grass along the crumbling street is tall enough to shroud anyone who stood behind it. My stomach falls with this realization sending a shiver down my spine. I don't like it here and it's not even night.

We approach a big fenced off building. Tall, blue security fencing surrounds the property to the edge of the road like a punctured shield. A thick weave of wild morning glory vines and blackberry bushes grow along the fencing making it hard to see directly through. A taller barrier of faded construction hoarding pops up behind the fence with long fraying strips that flap in the mid-morning breeze like a pennant banner announcing a used car lot off a highway. Razor wire twists around the top of the fence for a welcoming touch. I can just imagine Matt greeting his people here, telling them how special they are to be chosen to help him reach his goals in this isolated hell hole.

We drive past a hand painted sign strung to the fence that reads *trespassers will be executed*. A typo, I tell myself. I've seen that kind of typo before. It's nothing and I shouldn't read into it. I don't see security guards. The site looks abandoned, except we know it's not. Hundreds of people live here, working off their student loan debt forgiveness. What kind of word is *forgiveness* anyway?

Raindrops trickle down on Ian's windshield, and he pulls up the lever for the wipers. I listen to the rhythmic clack of the wipers to distract me from the silence. Without the faint buzzing sounds, I realize how the city is never quiet like this. Natural settings are. Forests are.

Didn't you hear anything? What's wrong with your ears? Think! I'm not going there with that memory.

"This is it." Ian drives past the mall. "There's a playground around one kilometre from here. I saw a sign for it a few minutes ago. We'll park around there to avoid suspicion."

As if that's possible in a town that has cut off one entire area. It makes me wonder if Matt owns not just the mall and some of those old houses, but the whole town.

We pull into the parking lot of a playground that has withered and bleached. All that's left of the swing set are the drooping chains where the seats once were. I feel the balloon start to inflate in my lungs. I'm not going to be able to leave this truck. I touch the door lightly with my fingertips. This place could be something completely different than Matt's community. Ian might be wrong. How did Ian even know this address?

"Before we get out there, I've been thinking." Ian turns off the engine and puts the keys in his backpack. He looks at me. "If we draw attention to ourselves when we get there, Matt will send us away. They're not going to let us just ask for Rebecca. Matt is greedy. I need to trust my intuition…"

Perhaps his gut is smarter than mine because mine is sounding the alarms and telling me to go back home. My feet feel like lead. I won't be able to get up. I breathe in and out. Ian might still be talking but I can't hear his voice anymore. I close my eyes, willing the balloon that has lingered in me for over twenty years to deflate.

"So what does that mean?" I snap back into the conversation. "How will we get Rebecca? This place is a fortress." Only my decades of experience shopping in malls can help me now and that's not feeling practical enough. The mall is fully fenced, and the entrance is gone. The whole area is lined in shiny razor wire. Ian takes my hand as if sensing my anxiety just at the right moment. It's a small comfort but what I need is to keep the balloon from filling.

"We'll find our own way in and look around first, just us. That will allow us to understand how the mall is laid out and being used. Then we can confront Matt, once we get a sightline of Rebecca. It's important for us to see her first. We don't want to attract attention."

I'd imagined walking up to the mall and knocking on the door. *Didn't you wonder where she went? Didn't you hear anything? What's wrong with your ears? Think! She's your twin ferchristsakes!*

Ian's outside before I can respond. I take a moment to breathe and before I muster up the strength to push the door open Ian's already doing it for me.

"You coming?" His eyes are twinkly and at this moment his handsome face calms me just enough to lift my legs out of the truck and onto the street. I look over my shoulder to see if anyone is around. We're alone.

"Jumpy, are you?" he says, shooting me another one of his cheeky grins. "Don't worry, it's just a mall. You've been to plenty in your life, I'm sure."

"True, but never one openly masquerading as a cult."

We walk from the park and past the cemetery. The rain isn't bad yet, but I pull up my hood out of habit. We see the perimeter of the mall just up ahead. I turn around again, thinking I hear something. It might have been a buzz, like the one I heard at the beehive, but I'm not sure. I listen again, nothing. It's probably just the breeze rustling through the trees.

Now that we're on foot and I can see closer through the vines and prickles covering the security fence. The construction hoarding behind it is tagged solid with graffiti. Attempts to paint over the graffiti with beige paint are visible but whoever was doing that has given up trying. What's left behind now is a checkerboard of different beige paint covered in tags. As we continue walking, one piece of graffiti stands out among the rest. *Break me first. Help me second. Pacify me third.*

"Do you see that?" I point through the grate of the fence to the words. Ian stops and takes his phone out to snap a photo.

"Break me first. Help me second. Pacify me third?" He takes a photo. "Break 'em down then build 'em up according to their rules. The capitalist way. I don't know why Matt has not covered this up. It's obviously a direct criticism of him. The paint looks fresh enough."

He walks with such eagerness, it's like there's a spring in his step. I must have missed the memo that coming to an abandoned mall in a town where the playground swings have no seats and most of the people have vanished except for the strange ones that hover around dilapidated tourist monuments was fun.

"Last night when I was doing a bit of research, I read that this mall has been closed since 2015," Ian says. "It all happened when Target left Canada."

"I remember those stores," I say. "One big box leaving could shut the entire place down? Seriously? This property is huge. There must have been hundreds of stores here when it was functioning."

The wind is picking up and the buzzing is back. It's louder now, more distorted, like the sounds are being layered and funneled. It wraps around me and now I know I can't go in there. This place, this town, is making me dizzy. I look at Ian. "What if this is just an abandoned mall, nothing else."

"Hey, look." Ian says, as we turn the corner. "I see a place over there where we can slip through the fence."

A way in. It's now my decision to go forward to find Rebecca or go home because I'm scared.

"Are you sure?" I take a few steps and then I see it, it's a small section of the security fence that hasn't been chained shut. This is not how I imagined we'd be entering the mall. Though, I'm not sure what I thought. Maybe I didn't truly think I'd ever make it this far.

He takes my hand and gives it a small squeeze, then he pulls me close and kisses my cheek like he did the night before. I feel my face blush. I give him a kiss back and a tingle shoots through my entire body. I don't hate this progression in our partnership. "Are you ready to find Rebecca," he asks.

"Ready, sure. Scared, absolutely." What I feel is almost light-headed, like I could cry from the sudden relief of finding the mall, of the potential of helping my best friend back to reality. But I'm also scared of what we might find in there, of Matt and what he's doing at the mall.

"Let's go." His hand is soft and warm, and I let this moment distract me from the fact that we are officially standing in the parking lot of Matt's mall and there's no turning back now. Above us, the sky opens and all the rain it's been holding back comes plummeting out at once, soaking us to our cores in seconds.

14

The parking lot wraps around us in a boundless sea of grey punctured with potholes overtopping with rain. Splotches of decades old motor oil stain the spaces between the faded parking space lines. I take my foot off a thick tuft of dandelion cracking through the asphalt that has successfully crumbled the faded surface that was meant to contain it. It feels darker inside the fence and wetter like the rain is working overtime to wash this place away. Weeds and gangly bushes pop up through chunks of asphalt throughout the parking lot like the whole property will slowly be absorbed back into the earth because no one is watching.

I brush off a shiver by running to catch up with Ian who's already walking so far ahead of me. His phone is out and he's taking photos like he's part of a surveillance team. I pull my phone from my pocket just to see if I've missed anything, that call from Rebecca I've been waiting for that will make this journey here redundant and unnecessary.

No reception, and no data, either. Perfect.

Up ahead, a bank of rusting shopping carts sits clustered together, as if waiting for ghost shoppers to come grab them and take them on a ride to fulfill their eternal duty.

"Maybe I should give you a push in one of those?" Ian calls from up ahead. "There's lots of room in this parking lot for a joy ride."

I laugh but it ends up sounding more like a snort even though I'm terrified of this place and want to turn around more than anything.

The building just ahead of us looks like any mall I've seen before, but rougher and stranger, like the whole thing should have been erased a long time ago and stricken from the building record, if anyone cared enough to turn back once the lights went out for good all those years ago. It doesn't look like a place where hundreds of people are living.

Ian's closer to the building than me. "Maybe the automatic sliding doors still work," he says, turning back to flash me a smile. "I love those things. Magic."

The mall is a two-storey peach stucco building with corners jutting up into pillars to support spaces for the names of flagship stores that would have at one time drawn people in. The stained remnants of a removed Target sign spot one. This detail is a confirmation. Ian might have brought us to the right mall. Still, this space doesn't feel right. There's a smell, something I can't put my finger on. It's familiar and rotting. A thick drip of rain slides down my cheek. I wipe it away with the sleeve of my soaked sweater.

The closer to the mall we get, the clearer the perfectly boarded up fences topped with razor wire are. We won't be able to find the entrance without any tools and the thought of breaking down some door just seems too ridiculous at this point. I turn to tell Ian we should leave before we march into a building that is likely condemned, but I stop when I hear something.

Ian turns around and our eyes met. He hears it too. We're frozen. It's a vehicle and the sound of the motor is clear enough that it is on this side of the fence. My lungs seize and I feel that balloon start to fill again. Fast. This is it. Matt has sent someone to escort us out before we even got through the doors.

As the sound of a diesel engine gets louder, a dirty white van blasts out from the other end of the parking lot. We should have walked all around the property first to see if there were any other entrances. The obviousness of this realization makes me feel nauseous. A mall will have multiple entrance points from the street. This is common mall knowledge.

"Hey…" Ian says, pulling my wet hand toward him. "Get down."

We duck behind a juniper bush busting open a planter near one of the boarded-up entrances and watch the van drive straight toward us. I lean against the planter hoping to disappear. As it travels closer, a loading bay door a few feet ahead jerks up with three or four big tugs. Someone is inside that bay.

"This is our chance. We'll run in after the truck. Okay?" Ian stands up like he's going to run for it with or without me. If I don't follow, I'll be left alone to find my way back home and by the looks of that town driving in, it won't be easy.

"Are you kidding me? We can't do this. We aren't close enough and we don't know what's through those doors." My voice is shaky this time, any confidence I felt before about finding Rebecca has vanished.

"We have to. Let's go." He takes off and I instinctively follow because I don't know what else to do. I have no other choice. I came here with him and my vehicle is over an hour down the highway at his apartment. The mall is the only place for me to go.

After the truck enters through the large loading bay, the door hangs open. Ian starts running faster, splashing up pooling water as he goes. I manage to keep up even though my feet are soaking wet. We're going for it. The door lingers open. We slow down and walk through the threshold trying to make our steps as quiet as we can. We're inside. We're actually inside the mall and I'm in disbelief that we just did that. I look over at Ian and catch a look on his face. It's not a look of fear, like I feel, it's a look of satisfaction, almost smugness, and it unsettles me. My adrenaline is running so high right now, I could lose it at any second. I'm looking for any reason to fall apart, to turn us both around, to let the balloon in my lungs fill up and spill over into a toxic mess like I did with Rebecca.

Rane's words come back to me, *wouldn't you look for your sister?*

She may not be my sister, but I'm the reason she's in this old mall. I need to trust what we are doing because otherwise I'd be leaving Rebecca and, from everything I've seen so far, this is the worst mall ever.

Daylight spills in through the open door and shines on the old shipping and receiving area. We quietly move toward a shadowy spot near a wall. My lungs are heaving and I worry someone in this loading bay will hear.

The truck is far inside now, waiting for another gate to take its sweet time to open up. The door behind us rattles to a close with the same four distinct jerks as before. We're locked in and it's dark. I feel the grooves of the cool brick wall to make sure I'm really here. Rain beats down on the roof, echoing throughout the hollow loading area. I smother the sudden urge to scream as loud as I can, to turn myself in to get the inevitable confrontation over with.

Ian senses I'm losing it and pulls me close. "We're inside," he whispers close to my ear. "We did it. We're going to help your friend get out of this place. We're so close."

Under a pool of dim light near the exit, I see four people stand with dolly carts waiting for the truck to open. They will see us. They will see us any moment now. How could they not see us?

Their boots tap on the concrete floor. It sounds so close. I'm too scared to move. The balloon in my lungs has filled to an all-time full, I feel the dread spilling over the edges and dripping down my ribcage. If that happens, I won't be able to move. There will be a scene, and this whole thing will be over before it even starts. When I panic, my body turns to stone.

"Hey, come on. We need to hide," Ian whispers, grabbing my hand and pulling me further into the shadows behind a dumpster. I focus on breathing because it's the only thing that works. I try to count down from ten. I make it to seven and I peek behind the bin to where the truck is. The most I can see is the back door of the van swinging open and four people looking inside. A woman pops out from the van.

"It's all here. Our fearless leader will be relieved," she says. Was that a mock tone I detected? It's hard to tell when my mind feels like it's swimming in garbage.

She raises her arms above her head to pump the air. The people waiting with the carts cheer. She laughs and takes a dramatic bow.

I take a moment to observe them. More debt-ridden people forced to live away from family, forced to work, and forced to play Matt's game.

"Come and get it." She kicks down a narrow ramp with a thud and one of the members walks up with his dolly.

All the boxes coming off the van are the same size with a familiar red logo: Maxis Ltd.

I whisper to Ian, "What do you think is in those boxes? There are so many of them."

"It could be anything. Maxis Ltd. is a business that has enough money to get involved with whatever it wants. It's his family's company. Of course he thinks he can do whatever he wants with it, even before he takes over. He has no idea how to provide for himself, clearly."

He takes his camera out and records a few minutes of video and takes a couple photos.

I watch the small crew unload more boxes. "If those boxes are full of food that means this place has a lot of people."

"Maxis Ltd. could get anything from anywhere in the world shipped to where they want it. It could be anything. It could be food, sure. It could be gratitude journals. It could be guns. It could be something worse."

I look at him and before I can ask him what he's talking about, a box slips from a worker's stack and falls to the ground with a bang that travels through the garage.

"Ooops," the driver says, looking down at the fallen box.

"Careful everyone," the first woman says. "We can't spare any of these. Remember what Matt said. We're trying to set an example. That means no waste. You know what he says in Performance? Everything is precious."

"Everything is precious," the man repeats quietly. "I'll be more careful."

"I know you will, Josh. I won't say anything about it when we get in." She kicks the box to the side. The rest of the workers continue unloading until all four dollies are full.

"Well, you won't be able to because…" the woman pretends to zip her mouth shut with her fingers. Then she puts her hands together in a prayer pose. They all laugh.

"That's all we can fit this round," she says. "We'll drop off this load and come back for the rest right after. Great work, everyone. We're making impressive progress on our work. The world is ready for our work and our approach. Bless up and out."

The group repeats, *Bless up and out*.

Ian turns back to me, making a gagging face. One of the members pulls up a pass from the lanyard around his neck and taps it on the door in the back of the bay. He holds it open while everyone walks through with their carts. The door closes and they're gone. I breath for the first time since we entered the bay.

I turn to Ian. "We can't stay here until they get back. They'll see us. This is impossible. We need to go." Maybe in this scenario leaving is the best choice. It's still an awful feeling, even though it is the one that makes most sense.

Ian walks out from behind the dumpster.

"Where are you going?" I whisper as loud as I can, but my lungs are overwhelmed. Soon I won't be able to move. "I don't want to leave this brick wall. What does *bless up and out* mean?"

He ignores me and walks up the ramp to the other gate and rattles it, then waves me over.

"We might be able to manually open this gate by pushing it up," he says. "It happened in my condo once when the power went out. A few people pushed it up. It was permanently broken after, but they were able to get out."

I shake my head and he returns a sweet look that's all dimples. "Come one, we're here. We've made it further than I ever thought I could and that's because you're with me. It would be a shame to run away now. What about Rebecca? We need to find out what's wrong here."

He's right, I haven't gone far enough. We got inside. That's a huge feat.

I gather all my strength and grab a bar from the gate in each of my hands. Ian counts to three and we hoist it up just enough to roll under. It's heavy, but once we get it off the ground, it rises to the height of our knees without much effort.

"There we go, Carolyn. There's that star-level teamwork."

We crawl under and then Ian jumps onto the bottom of the gate to lower it back to the ground. The shipping crew might not even notice it's broken when they get back, at least for a few minutes.

Ian goes straight to the box that fell. He picks it up and shakes it. Shattered glass tinkles inside. He opens his backpack and pulls out a pocket knife. He said he wouldn't bring a knife. Even though this isn't the same one from his kitchen, it strikes me as a deception.

"Don't touch that," I whisper. "If they find an open box, they'll know someone was in here."

"Right." He drops the box where he found it. "You're right," he repeats as if he needs to convince himself. "We've got to get moving. They could be back for a second load any minute. We have no idea where they are going."

I walk over to the door and give it a small push. It doesn't budge. Ian's looking inside the delivery truck. I go over and open the driver's door and check the ignition. The keys are still in. I pull them out and there's a card attached.

"I found something." I hold the card up. "It might be like the one they used."

Ian crawls out of the truck and takes the keypass from me.

"You're amazing." He kisses my forehead, then taps the pass on the door and we hear a beep. He slowly pushes the door open. We're about to enter the community.

It doesn't feel real. In one sense I'm proud of myself for persisting and making it this far, in another sense I feel like puking from stress.

As I step through the doorway, I glance up at a concave mirror positioned to see the incoming traffic from the main bay door and my heart almost stops. Next to the dumpster where we just were, someone is standing there watching us. They saw everything we just did. A hoodie hides their face, but there's someone there. I can't move. They saw us. They watched us break in. Someone knows we don't belong here.

"Ian," I whisper, barely able to get the words out of my mouth. I pull his shoulder back. "There's someone in here. Look."

He glances back and frowns.

"I don't see anyone there. We're the only ones here. You've got to keep it together. We won't be long."

I turn back to the dumpster and the person is gone. It's so dark, Ian must not have looked fast enough. Someone was there, I know they were there. A dark hoodie and sandals. They might have been wearing jeans. Someone from the mall was watching us.

"No, there was someone right there. I saw them." I have an urge to run back to the ramp and look closer, but Ian pulls me through the doorway without acknowledging what I said and suddenly we're standing in a dark, cavernous mall corridor. The smell overpowers me, earthy and rotting, like a compost pile slowly decomposing. The tiles under my feet are cracked and the cement foundation is exposed.

Before we start walking, my phone vibrates with an incoming text message. The mall itself must be within proper cell reception range again. I better check now before I lose reception and my phone completely dies. I open my phone and see a text from an unknown number. I swipe to open it and a strike of panic almost winds me.

WELL LOOK WHO IT IS? FOUND US, YEAH? YOU'LL REGRET THIS. YOU'RE GOING VIRAL, BITCH!

15

I clench the phone until my hand hurts, loosening my grip only to reread the message. GOING VIRAL, BITCH? It must be a mistake, another spam message innocently sent by someone who has no idea who I am and managed to get through on a sliver of reception right at this exact moment. It's clearly a phishing scam threatening cyber ransom. People like me don't go viral. But the timing is too perfect and that's what scares me.

Jennifer would have called this a coincidence. She was known in our house for staying up late reading by flashlight about witches and magic and century-old letters discovered in dusty attics. To her, coincidence and happenstance were enchanting and entertaining. These occurrences didn't have to be personal, but they were special. This text wasn't for *me*, specifically. Maybe others are discovering this exact message, too. I repeat the words to myself to help them sink in: this was a coincidence.

I reread it.

WELL LOOK WHO IT IS?

My reception bars still show zero. I couldn't even make a call—to who? My brother? My cell phone provider to tell them to get it together about spam—if I tried. I check my Wi-Fi settings and see I've automatically connected to a network I've never seen before: SPREAD_AUTHENTICITY. The phone freezes when I toggle to forget the network. I can't disconnect. I try again, but nothing's working.

"Ian, what's going on? Look at this." I hold the phone up for him to read. "Did you get anything?"

He pulls out his phone and checks. No reception either. He also hasn't received a message, and his phone isn't connected to any networks.

"You need to disconnect from that network. Please. Right now."

He reaches for my phone, but I pull it closer. Maybe this isn't typical spam. I've received several messages like this over the past few days. I want to start connecting them, to see something more than just coincidence, but I don't want to open that door. Now is not the time.

"Whoever runs the network here will be able to see your phone's IP address," he continues. "The members aren't allowed phones so there won't be many people on the network. Disconnect now."

I look through my settings again and tap to forget the network. It doesn't work. I slide the Wi-Fi off but it's still connected.

"I'm trying, but nothing's working. What do they mean about going viral? I've never wanted to go viral in my life." This message was meant for me and maybe all the ones I deleted were, too. Not a coincidence, but targeted. When I freelanced, clients would joke about wanting their boring mortgage broker content to go viral or their excruciatingly detailed eight-minute project update video thinking that it would do something good for their business or reputation and I cautioned them to be careful what they wished for. The last thing I want is to go viral on the internet for breaking into an intentional community. I look around. Who's watching me?

Ian takes my phone and holds down the side button, powering it down, then hands it back to me. "It's probably best just to keep your phone off for now."

I put my phone back in my purse and zip it closed. I realize I've had my hood on this entire time and push it off. Then I remember the face I saw in the mirror out in the loading bay, the way their hood hung to hide their eyes and the look of their brown sandals and pasty white feet. Did they look wet, as if they'd been outside in the parking lot with us from the beginning?

"I saw someone back there. You have to believe me. They saw what we were doing. Someone is following us." But even I'm doubting myself. If someone was there, they would have said something, run up to us, telling us to leave the mall immediately. Matt is rich enough to have security, people who would not hesitate to kick us out.

"You've been under a lot of stress." His voice is kind and I realize how much I need his understanding right now. I want to cry, but I fight it. There's no time for tears. "I can totally empathize with you, but we're in here now and we've got to keep moving. Everything's going to be okay. Remember, we need to see Rebecca first to confirm she's here, and then we'll find Matt and talk to him, okay? That's the plan."

I look back at the door to the loading bay. It's possible my eyes were playing tricks on me. After all, when I turned back, I didn't see anything. Did I summon it all myself, making myself see what I wanted to see to sabotage my efforts of finding my best friend? Maybe Ian's right. It's stress. Stress has done upsetting things to me in the past, it could be doing the same thing now. I need to get a hold of myself to focus on what I'm doing here. Rescuing my best friend. Helping Ian with his story. Not letting my subconscious take control and sabotage our work.

I take a deep breath. "I want to find Rebecca and get out of here." I repeat this again to myself to make sure I believe it, and I think I do.

Ian nods and takes my hand, and we continue our walk into the dark and dusty mall corridor. Hunter green accents from the 1990s on the walls collide with the straight-from-the-1970s orange-brown brick floor. This place would have been bustling with people at one time. Families. Friends. Workers. All long gone. Now the space is dark, with only a few rays of light filtering in from the jagged seams between the nailed-up boards covering the windows. The ceiling has large holes where plant roots have started to grow in and hang down in curls. This mall doesn't look like anyone lives here. However, I bet there are wild animals somewhere. Rats. Racoons. Coyotes. The members with the dollies are nowhere and it's quiet again except the pounding of rain.

We sidestep puddles of rainwater leaking through the roof. For someone who can buy back thousands, if not millions, in student loan debt, Matt has kept this mall ragged. If this is the state of a mall abandoned for less than a decade, his other, older malls must look far worse. Retail spaces like this exist all across the country, left to rot when people need housing. Matt's initial idea has always appealed to me but the people who live here should not have to go no contact with their old lives to be accepted.

Small tungsten emergency pot lights hang from the ceiling providing just enough light to make out where in the mall we are. Ian has already taken dozens of photos, some with flash. When he does, the corridor momentarily fills with light, exposing dusty corners and mouldy furniture still lingering in the centre of the aisles. It's all still here for the convenience of long forgotten shoppers looking for a spot to rest. Between these benches, artificial palm trees sit perfectly preserved in decaying landscape boxes.

"Yeah, over here," says a faint voice from down the hall. "We moved it over after the last flood."

Ian and I stop. He looks at me and puts a finger to his lips. The sound of footsteps get closer. I crouch down behind one of the old couches and Ian follows me, staying close, as two of the men I recognize from the loading bay walk by with their dollies.

"Where are we taking these ones?" one of them asks. Hearing them makes my heart beat faster. They'll find us. They'll see us. They'll pull us out of this corner and demand to know what we're doing. If they let us leave, that will be a lucky outcome. I didn't tell anyone where I was going. Not even Chris and Farrah. That seems like an oversight now.

"Renovation area, I think," says a soft voice.

"It's so dirty in there. Makes me cough every time. You sure?"

"That's all I know. Let's just take it there and see. People are waiting for us there, ready to start unpacking."

Ian takes out his phone and tries to snap a photo of the men but fumbles and drops it instead. The rumble of the phone hitting the floor echoes through the corridor. Ian immediately scoops it up and mouths *sorry* to me. I'm too scared to move.

"What was that?" one of the men asks. They stop pushing their dollies and look back. A flash of light illuminates the open space, revealing an eerie outline of an abandoned food court. Chairs are tipped over on the floor and the old, plastic menus are still hanging on the walks behind the counters, prices untouched by inflation.

"I don't know. Could be anything. Maybe an animal," says the other one. "The unrenovated part of the mall creeps me out. Reminds me of when I was a teenager and worked in a popcorn stand. I can almost smell it sometimes. I'm glad I only have to come down here when the truck is in. I swear there's something living here."

"Well there are probably several things living here. Things with beady eyes and tails and wings and sharp teeth. I'm sure you've heard the stories of people disappearing."

"You're making me sick. This is the worst part of the job, but it's nice to talk out here, isn't it? When we're doing the "introspection" work, I get lonely. And this is not where people have gone missing. That is…"

"Shhhh…" the man cuts in. "I heard he has this part of the mall bugged." The light turns off.

"Oh really? Okay, YOU NEED A HAIRCUT SO BADLY. Get over yourself. You are not Steve Jobs circa 1990. But also thank you for paying $200,000 in student loan debt for me. I'd say it to your face but we can rarely talk."

The other man chuckles and they continue down the corridor until they reach a set of doors. One of them punches a code into a control panel, which opens the automatic door, and they're gone. The door closes tightly behind them. The quality of the door is out of place with the rest of what we've seen. It's the only upgrade.

I tuck out from behind the couch and wipe a mess of cobwebs from my hair. I'm covered in a thick layer of dust.

"That door down the hall where they came from will take us to where the community is. I know it will," Ian says. He's wearing the passkey lanyard around his neck. "Let's go."

Before we reach the door, a bird—or bat?—dive bombs from some dark corner in the ceiling, narrowly missing Ian's head. I feel an abrupt fan of air on my face from the swift flap of its wings. It was a close call. Whatever that was could have easily taken him down.

"What was that?" Ian brushes his head, as if something might fall from his hair.

"Are you okay?" I look up to where I heard the bird or creature come from.

"I think so. I don't think it hit me, it came close though." He keeps talking about how strange it felt to have something fly so close to him, but I've stopped listening because I notice a large chunk of the ceiling hanging open in the back of the food court. Unlike everywhere else where the ceiling has failed, rain isn't coming to this spot. It's dry and an aura of blue ambient light is coming through. I take a step forward to get a better look and then I see it, the glimmer of a large LED monitor sitting in the attic. Even from this distance, I see it's a social media feed on display. When I read it, I swallow so hard I think I might have swallowed my tongue, which might be a good thing to keep me from screaming.

The feed shows a photo of me. Me!

My eyes are big and shadowed, my head is framed in a waxy-looking hexagon. I'm not looking at the camera, but past it, as if in a daze. It takes a moment to place it, where a photo like this could have been taken, but then I see the blue t-shirt collar peek out from under my hoodie. The photo is from earlier this morning at the beehive. We were only there like an hour ago. Someone got a picture of me when I looked in to check on the girl with the glitchy face. She didn't have a camera. She didn't even have a face. The space was so small, no one could have been in there with her and that strange woman couldn't have taken it because she was standing with us the whole time. It's too crisp and composed to be a security camera shot, too deliberate.

As I stand there staring, the feed starts to scroll and it's nothing but the photo of my face repeating and repeating, and that's when I hear someone scream straight into my ears, overtaking my entire body.

16

Ian grabs me, covering my mouth to muffle the voice ringing through the empty hall.

"Be quiet," he whispers. "Seriously. Shut up. Those men might not be out of earshot yet. We still have a lot to see before we approach Matt."

The scream sounded like it came from outside of my body. I don't remember opening my mouth. I start to lower my body to sit down on the smashed tiles below, but Ian pulls me back up and looks at me like he thinks I'm losing it. I haven't. They know me. Someone at the mall knows who I am. They've been watching me, following me. Is this what Rane meant when she said someone followed her? When did it start? Ever since I got into this empty town? Before? During my drive? At the quay? Somebody is following me. I point to the screen flashing in the ceiling. Ian looks in the direction and takes a moment to study the image.

"Are you expecting us to go up there or something?" Ian says. "We can't. It's beyond the scope of the plan. Someone might be coming to get us now after that scream. I don't know what got into you."

No one's coming. The corridor is just as quiet as before. A tendril of root hanging down from the ceiling brushes the top of my head and the light touch freaks me out. I bat it away.

"What was I supposed to do? It's my face—not yours—plastered across a feed, their feed." I don't know who they are. I don't know who took that picture. "What is going on here? How did they get a photo of me from an hour ago?"

"This is clearly Matt playing around with personal space and privacy." He gently brushes the hair from my eyes. Even in the darkness of this mall, Ian's eyes are brilliant and have a calming effect on me. "You heard the woman back at the hive. Matt

owns that mouldy thing. He probably has these voyeuristic photos of everyone that dares to look in there. It's all part of his sick
process. Matt doesn't respect privacy."

"What do you mean by privacy?" My stomach twists. I
shouldn't have come. I should have listened to my brother for
once and just moved on with my life. I could have got a permanent job. I could have started dating again. I could have moved
into a basement suite deep in the suburbs and found a new best
friend. Being completely humiliated here only confirms that.

He ignores the question. "We need to keep going." He takes
my hand again and we turn a corner to enter a new part of the
mall, but I'm in a daze. Nothing about this place feels real. Before
the screen is out of sight, I glance back and watch the endless
scroll of my photo go on and on. YOU'RE GOING VIRAL,
BITCH! I couldn't have. There's no reason for that to happen. I
keep to myself. No one knows me. I don't even post on social
media.

Ian's phone rings, cutting through the silence with a shriek.

Our eyes met. "Seriously?" I say. "You left your phone on?
After telling me to be quiet?"

He gives me a sheepish look and turns the phone to silent.
We look over our shoulders, but it's quiet again, like it was in the
parking lot outside. Everything about the mall feels like we're
encased in a jar.

"It's probably my editor wondering why I'm not in the
office yet. I'll text her later."

"You're getting reception now?" My phone is still off and
tucked away in my purse. Another message could be waiting to
tell me something else. I'm tempted to turn my phone on and
look, but Ian's watching me closely like he knows what I'm
thinking so I hesitate. He frowns. He's probably right. Seeing
another odd text message wouldn't help me feel better about
what's happening anyway. Just like seeing my weird photo plastered across every social media platform right now would make
me curl up and die under the busted Orange Julius maker.

We enter a part of the mall that looks wilder and more broken
than where we came from. Thick shards of tempered glass lay in

large heaps outside the entrances of the old stores and planter boxes overflow with dusty lava rock and spider plants with twisted ends touch the floor in swoops. I watch my step, careful not to get any glass near my toes, but it's impossible not to feel unsettled by the crunch of shattered storefronts under my feet.

"The glass reminds me of snow. It's strangely beautiful," Ian says. He's right, with the limited light and the sparkle of the glass, there's something magical and special about this part of the mall and it's enough to distract me for a minute. It's fragile and dangerous, and somehow the plants in here are growing beautifully without anyone around to appreciate them. Or without anyone around to keep them small.

I walk ahead then look back at Ian and stop. There's a dull spot among the sparkle of the glass I hadn't noticed. I turn back to get a closer look then hesitate when it registers what I'm looking at. Small droplets of blood dot the glass.

"Ian, look," I whisper. He's ignoring me or he doesn't hear me. "There's blood. I see blood." At least I think it's blood. I'm not sure what else it could be, and it looks fresh.

A sudden pressure grips down on my shoulder. Ian's ahead of me. It's not a root I'm feeling this time because it's cold, like the terrifying feeling I had in the rest stop bathroom on the road here. It's happening again. I try to brush it away, but it stays and the pressure this time is too intense to ignore. This isn't an icy poke but the cold grip of two full hands. The grip is trying to hold me still, keep me from moving forward. I can't bring myself to speak or take a step.

Ian is crouching down to get a better shot of the smashed glass. He hasn't noticed I'm petrified in place. Pigeons sitting in the rafters fly out, the flapping of their wings sounding flat like a punch on a thick pillow because they're so close to us.

It takes everything in me not to turn around and run out of this mall, into the parking lot, and out onto the street. But I can't bring myself to move one step. If I leave now, when I'm so close to finding her, I'll never know yet again and that could destroy me this time.

I force myself to step forward and the grip is gone.

Jennifer was lost because we turned around and I will probably never know what happened to her. It destroyed my parents. Something wild like a bear or a cougar could have hunted her, swiped her with sharp claws. Was there a person? A man who found her on the path and led her out? Or did she fall down a ravine and twist her ankle, eventually dying of starvation? I've watched countless evening news stories about skiers, confident in their abilities to manage the backcountry, glide off the edges of cliffs to their deaths within minutes of setting out. People have tried taking selfies on the edge of the most beautiful natural landscape they've ever seen in their lives, only to fall moments later. Jennifer might have been walking and reading, something she enjoyed doing, especially when she was absorbed in the story. She often was. She said she felt more comfortable in worlds other than her own. She was midway through a new series, and she had the next three books with her in her camping bag. These books were special and she protected them after what happened earlier with dad. If she was walking and reading, it means she wasn't paying attention. Bears, cougars, cliffs. Someone in the woods, waiting. I can't blame her. She needed to distract herself and sometimes it's hard to stay alive when nothing makes sense.

Her relationship with our parents hit an all-time low that spring. They wanted her to put the books down and be more social. They were worried she didn't have any friends. But she had me and she said that's all she needed. I had a couple friends from karate, but Jennifer was all I needed too.

"I want you to join a club. Any kind of club," dad said a few days before we left on our trip. We were all sitting at the kitchen table eating dinner.

"Way ahead of you," she said, barely looking up from her plate. "I'm in a book club."

"Do you meet them in person?"

"We do it through a chain letter we send in the mail. I'm really enjoying it."

Mom poured another glass of wine. She said she was allowed wine on Sundays because she needed to do a final bit of unwinding before she had to go back to work as a paralegal.

"That's not good enough," dad boomed, throwing his fork back onto his plate. "You need to meet with real people otherwise everyone will think you're the weird one your entire life."

"How come you don't get Chris or Carolyn to join a club? Why is it always me?"

Chris looked down at his food and shrunk, which was unusual for him because he liked to take the spotlight whenever he could, often at the expense of his twin sisters. But tonight he closed his eyes like he wanted to disappear.

"Because they are both in a sport. Chris plays basketball and Carolyn is doing that kicking thing. You need to meet people. Your mother and I are worried. Reading can only take you so far."

Jennifer stood up at the table and pushed her chair in.

"Reading will get me further than anything you've ever done in your life." She walked away.

"What did you say to me?" His voice was loud and scary. "Get back here."

But Jennifer kept walking and when she got to her room, she shut the door. Dad followed and banged like he was trying to smash through.

"Open up. Now!"

But Jennifer didn't open the door. I could only imagine how scary it would have been for her to watch that door pulse and vibrate from inside her room.

"I'll take every book you own and throw them away." He pounded the door, shaking the door and the rest of the house with it.

Mom finally clued into what was happening and looked up from her glass. "Dave, Dave, reading is good. Remember you tried to read that book that time? It's just the way she is," she said. Already her words were slurring.

Dad pushed on the door, but it must have been blocked by something. I later found out she had moved her desk in front of it to protect it. Encountering resistance would have only angered him more, so he pushed his large, rolling body against the door until it finally flew open with a crash.

I closed my eyes, just like Chris had. I couldn't watch any-more, but I could hear him pull her books off the shelf and throw them into the hallway, each book landed with a thud against the wall before falling on the carpet. One by one, all her books came off. Jennifer yelled and screamed and tried to stop him. The rest of us sat at the table like we were incapable of stepping in and helping her. I've replayed this thousands of times. I should have done something. Leaving her in the forest wasn't the only time I failed her.

When all the books were in the hall, he put them into a garbage bag. He grabbed his old jean jacket, went outside and slammed the door. We heard his car start and drive away.

On our camping trip, the three books she had were brand new. Dad had cooled off by then and said she could bring them, but that's all she had. Books were everything to her and now her collection was destroyed. She was heartbroken.

That's why she wanted to read alone, in the forest, where no one would bother her or interrupt the world she was living in at that moment. It was much better than her reality in our family.

Suddenly, it's hours later and I'm with my dad in the forest looking for Jennifer. I didn't understand what was happening, how she could really be missing. I expected her to step out of the woods any second, allowing our lives to go back to its imperfect normal.

"Jennifer! Jennifer, where are you?" It's my voice but it sounds like it's coming from somewhere else, like my scream from earlier. The voice echoes. "Jen, Jen come back! We're waiting for you. We're all looking for you."

Glass crunches under my feet. Ian catches up to me.

He looks scared. "Are you okay? You're screaming again. What if someone hears you? We need to be as quiet as possible."

Before I say anything, the tiny amount of emergency lighting the mall still has goes out and we're standing in complete dark-ness. The cold grip on my shoulder is back and feels tighter. I reach back. No one is there. I feel the pressure of the grip inten-sify and my knees begin to buckle. Before I hit the ground, last night's dream comes back to me in vivid and chaotic flashes.

In the dream, I'm walking through each room of my childhood home, opening and closing doors and closets. I keep going until it feels like I've looked everywhere, and then I go through them all again. When I reach the closet in mom and dad's room, I find something new. It's my sister's hat, the one she was wearing when she went into the woods. Where did they get it? How long have they had it without telling me? Who found it? I take the hat to the kitchen table they're sitting at. I look to my dad in hopes of tearing off his ear. He told me money was not allowed in the bathroom. I had a bucket of change and led him back into the kitchen. I take a wooden spoon out of the drawer that should have contained the chef's knife and hold the old piece of wood close to my body, like I could feel safe in this world with nothing but a spoon close to me as protection. Dad's bleeding by his ears now. Blood oozes from his head, and he paws at the wound with his hand. His hands slip through the blood. I could stop to help him, but I kept going, kept looking through the rooms and then the kitchen drawers. I look again at his ears and see now that there is a thrash of claw marks starting from his ear and ending on the little butt of his chin. He was following me, asking me to stop, wondering what's wrong? He asks me why I'm bleeding. I tell him I'm looking for the person from the parkade, that he's the one who's bleeding. Someone's watching me. My dad takes me by the shoulders and asks if I ever think about Jennifer anymore, if she's still with me on this earth. Yes, I tell him, in everything I do I feel her. That's when I see Jennifer. She's not nine anymore, she's aged twenty-two years like me, only she's warmer and softer. She has a spiral-bound book in her hands. We weren't identical twins, but we always looked similar. She takes me by the shoulder now and I roll my head back and back until I'm back here in the mall and the touch I feel on my shoulder now is Ian shaking me, snapping me out of the dream and back into the impossible reality of the mall.

"Carolyn? Hello, earth to Carolyn. You're bleeding. Why are you bleeding? Are you feeling okay? What happened?"

Ian has his reporter notebook in hand, ready to write everything down.

I look down at my arm and the same spot from before is pooling blood, more blood than when it first started. I cover it with my hand. I feel more light-headed than before. The speckles of blood I saw on the glass earlier are from me.

"I've been dealing with this cut on my arm since I caught my arm on something in my trunk on the way here. It's nothing." The lies come easier and easier. "I just haven't had a chance to let it fully heal since I've been on the road."

If he doesn't believe me, he doesn't show it because he keeps walking ahead. He's pushing doors and kicking shards of glass with his boots.

"I think I found the entrance to the garden," he says, tucking his notebook back into his pocket. "This is what we've come for. We're so close."

I look at the stream of buttery light shining through the door. It's stopped raining. Before he can swipe our pass and open the door, I feel my phone vibrate from inside my purse. I hadn't realized I turned it back on. The notification was quieter this time, only I know it happened. Ian doesn't look at me when I think this, he doesn't even frown when I think of fishing out my phone and joining the network and checking in. Of course, this is because he doesn't know I'm thinking about it. I wonder if Jennifer knew what the opposite of a coincidence was called? Maybe it's reality. Nothing whimsy, just the cold truth of our everyday life and all the things that can go wrong.

"Are you ready?" he asks. I smile and he pushes the door open.

As soon as he opens it, the sound of buzzing almost knocks me down.

17

As we rush into the garden, my eyes immediately land on someone I never wanted to see again.

Diamond. I didn't think she ever left that quay. Yet here she is standing with a group of members and pointing her fancy camera at them as they work in a garden plot, the rain falling on their heads.

I can't let Diamond see me. Diamond out of everyone here knows I don't belong and have no right to be in this garden. I'd rather wait on the crunched up broken glass than be confronted by her.

I turn back to the door and yank on the handle. It's locked and Ian has the pass.

The buzzing stops and it's quiet.

"*Lynnie.*"

The name stops me in my tracks. I turn around to see where the voice came from. "*Lynnie.*" I hear it again. I'm sure this time. Someone is whispering *Lynnie*. The voice was breathless and unmistakable. I feel the balloon in my lungs start to fill in overtime.

No. Not now.

I put my hand out to get the pass from Ian. It's time to get out of here.

"You aren't going back in there," he says. "We have to keep going. We're finally in the actual community. It won't be long now until we've seen everything and we're ready to approach Matt."

"You don't understand." I crouch behind Ian, using his body to hide me from Diamond's view. I don't hear *Lynnie* again. No one here would know what that name means to me. Not even Rebecca. Hearing it now moments after reliving my dream in the mall is enough to send me over the deep end.

I watch over Ian's shoulder as she puts her camera down and starts walking toward us. But maybe she's not. She stops and engages silently with members. Maybe she didn't recognize me. My interview was months ago now. She has probably talked to hundreds of women like me since then. I'm not remarkable. She will have forgotten me.

Ian takes my hand. His touch takes my mind off Diamond and the voice for a moment.

"We don't know what they're planting," he whispers. "It might be significant to understand what this community is about. We need to investigate further." He turns back to the open area.

I follow his glance and my eyes go directly to Diamond again. I watch her stop to take more photos of the members working. She's gesturing to them, it's all very casual and I think she really won't recognize me until she glances at me in a way that sends a shiver through every part of my body.

"Give me the pass and put your phone away. Our cover is blown. They know we're here."

Ian looks around. "How? It's loud in here and people are working. We don't look different from them. In fact, we could totally pass as community members. I hate that on a moral level, but it's in our favour now. We need to keep going."

I'm not going to explain Diamond to him. I reach for his lanyard to grab the pass, but he puts his arm out to stop me and I feel the weight of his palm on my chest. "We're going to keep going. You and I are in this together, and as long as we're together we'll be fine. We're not turning back now. It's too late."

Ian's attitude is frustrating but making a scene could be worse. I look around and this time I don't see Diamond.

"Can you believe this place," he says with a scoff. "Why not just move to a farm? Matt always has to go overboard. I have yet to see anything special here or inspired. Matt, as usual, has totally bored me. I knew he didn't have the vision he said he had. This is textbook cult leader shit and very boring."

It's getting darker now, probably late afternoon. I'm too scared to look at my phone to check the time. We probably have a couple hours before the sun goes down completely. "You included a series of quotes from Matt himself in your article," I say. "How did you get the quotes? Did you have a sit-down interview with him? You included details about his mannerisms. What do you remember about him? It could help us now."

There are way more people here than I thought there would be, but still no sign of Rebecca. This is making me worried. I came to find her, not have a nervous breakdown in the middle of a faux country garden.

Ian straightens his back and adjusts the straps on his backpack. "I'm a journalist. I'm responsible for telling an accurate story. Details are important. I seek them out. That's how you tell a good story."

"Was there anything more you talked about? Something that didn't make the article?"

Before he can reply, a bell rings. The members put down what they're doing in their garden plots and make their way toward a door.

"Come on," Ian says. "We need to follow them."

We hurry up to join the group as they make their way to a large dining hall inside. Large thermal coffee dispensers sit on tables with platters of muffins and cut fruit. Members take their snacks; some sit down, and others stand in groups and chat. They're talking, so I have no idea what's going on. Is the silence over with? They were quiet outside, but on break they are chatting and joking like any lunchroom I've ever been in. There must be parameters around the silence.

Because we're trying to fit in or maybe because we're just plain hungry at this point, Ian takes a coffee and a muffin and I shifty follow suit. Ian shoves a chunk of bran in his mouth. I take a bite and the deliciousness and flavour catches me off guard.

"I remember you," says a voice behind me. I don't have to turn around to know it's Diamond. Ian looks at me. I look up at her and my eyes must betray how horrified I am that she's found us. "It's okay, don't worry," she adds.

I don't reply.

"The last time we spoke, I was worried about you," she continues, sipping a mug of tea. "I have thought about you several times since. You seemed so fragile. You were hiding something from me. If only you had been more honest with yourself and with me. Outcomes may have been different, but you are helping us in your own way."

Ian puts down his coffee, but, remarkably, keeps his mouth shut.

"The last time I saw you, I was going through a hard time." I didn't realize how hard it actually was. "I wasn't myself."

"I'm sorry I couldn't have helped you more. Most times I can only follow the rules. It's not the easiest part of the job." Her face softens. I notice her camera again. Did she take the photo of me looking into the beehive? She doesn't seem upset to see me, or surprised. We have broken into their community and she's being nice to me. Is she the one I have felt following us here?

"I get it," I lie. I wanted anything to be invited. When Rebecca packed her bags, I wanted to do the same. I was tired of our place. I wanted a change too. I wanted to join Matt's community and have student loans paid off, but I wasn't accepted. I failed the interview for the mall.

Ian tries to interject by waving his hand, but Diamond ignores him.

"How much do you remember of her?" She looks at me with interest. "Is it helping?"

I shake my head. "I haven't seen Rebecca yet. Can you tell me where she is? I just need to speak with her."

"This isn't about Rebecca. You need to listen. You're connected to this place, even if you're not a member. Have you figured that out yet? I can't say I like how Matt runs his technology, but his genius is remarkable." She blushes.

"Can I interview you?" Ian jumps in. "It won't take long."

She looks from me to Ian and sighs. "I will never talk to a reporter. Especially when that reporter is you." She picks up her phone and checks a message, then walks away without another word.

The entire interaction with her troubles me. What is my connection to this place beyond Rebecca? I don't have one. I've never been here before, even when it was a real mall. And why didn't she kick us out? But everything has been so strange since we got here. Maybe even before.

"Ian, I think we should leave. This place is not right, and I don't think it's good for us to be here anymore."

"That's exactly why we need to stay." He loosens the collar of his shirt and wipes away beads of sweat from his forehead despite the chill in the air.

"Are you okay?" It never occurred to me that this place could be affecting him in unsettling ways as well. The colour from his cheeks has drained away.

"I'm fine," he mutters. "Look, they're going back to the garden now." We watch them quietly exit the dining hall and it's just us again. Then he faces me. "What was that? You didn't tell me you wanted to join the mall with Rebecca?"

"That was Diamond." I may as well tell him the whole thing. "She interviewed me for the mall when Rebecca was interviewed. I was disappointed when they didn't want me, but that's how it went down."

Shock spreads across his face, and maybe a bit of hurt. "You're only telling me now that you applied to become a member of the mall community? You had an *interview* with one of their recruiters, seriously?"

"It didn't cross my mind to tell you." The truth is, I'm embarrassed to talk about it. It was yet another rejection. Another thing I wasn't good enough to do.

"What happened? What was the interview process like?"

"They asked me some questions about myself and how I feel about things. She didn't want to call it a personality test, but that's what it was." I leave out the part about doing it for twenty bucks to save myself some dignity.

When I got the follow up email, I was disappointed by the rejection. Rebecca had already received her invitation and accepted it a few days before. Acceptances always go out first. I know we lead with celebration, not failure. When I heard how excited she was about going, about not having any debt, about taking on a communal way of life, I wanted more than anything to get invited too. It wasn't something I knew I wanted at the

time, but when I saw Rebecca making the leap, I wanted to follow along with her. If the change was good for her, it would be
good for me, too.

One afternoon when I saw her sorting through her things in
the kitchen in the lead up to the move, I sat on the couch and
said something to myself under my breath. "That Matt guy probably is into the whole sister-wife thing."

I thought I said it to myself, only she heard me loud and
clear.

"It's nothing like that. Besides, they know what I'm going
through right now, there's no way I would be up for it." She
tried to smile, like it was a joke she was making for the first time
in months. I instantly felt sorry that I said anything.

"I know, of course. I'm glad they understand and can be
there for you." Even if I couldn't.

She nodded and continued wrapping each of her knives in
newspaper. She would be donating them to a hospice thrift store
later that afternoon, which was fine by me because I couldn't
stomach handling one of those again. They were too sharp.

Now, seeing Diamond at the mall, I don't want to think
about how I overshared with her or how she analyzed me and
knew I was all wrong for this place. I told her about my sister and
that's a social embarrassment I don't want to face again. She
knows about the part of me that will always hurt.

"I want to talk about this later, but we need to keep going.
There's more of the mall to explore."

He's about to charge forward then he hesitates. "There's
actually something…" He stops. "There's something… they're
hiding here. Let's look for another way out of here that isn't back
to the garden."

We split up and circle the dining hall. I try a door and it's
locked. My heart beats faster thinking I'm going to see Diamond
again. Any minute she could bust open a door with a big security
team waiting to roughly escort us out.

"Over here," Ian says. "I think I found something."

We open the door to a small hallway. This hallway is different from anything we've seen so far. It's bright with LED lighting

that fills the space. The floor is a buffed cement that looks clean and new. At the end of the hall is another door. Ian marches toward it, swiping our pass and barging through like he's part of a SWAT team. I follow close behind him, but snooping through this part of the mall feels different than being in the garden where the others are. We've lost the benefit of a wide-open space and that feels risky. If someone comes, Diamond, anyone, we'll be trapped.

"Well look at all this," Ian whispers.

The room is lined with computers and flat screen monitors. This is the only other sign of technology I've noticed here besides the pass keys and the lovely screen endlessly scrolling my face. I push the reminder of that out of my head now. Rebecca said she was programming again in one of the letters. She may work here. I look around for signs of her.

I approach a whiteboard with words that read: *Product Prototype.* Scribbles of hand-drawn phone screens lay underneath. They remind me of the (para)normal work Rebecca used to do when she was a grad student. She'd make these prototypes to share with her class as a way to discuss the work before she started programming to know if it was a good idea or not.

"They're designing some sort of app," I say, pointing to the whiteboard. Ian is too busy shuffling between keyboards trying to fluke a correct password to listen to what I'm saying.

A note below the whiteboard on a table says *Product Goal: To Make a Connection with a Loved One Passed On.*

"I found one that turns on without a password," he announces. One of the screens is on, showing a start-up screen photo of the back garden in full bloom, behind it is what looks to be the entire community. There are hundreds of members, smiling at the camera. Many are kids. We haven't seen a single child in this place. Ian takes another picture. A couple members are holding babies.

He tries to move the cursor and it's frozen. "Dead end." He looks at me and I point to the whiteboard.

"It's all right here." I look back at the board. "They're trying to get the (para)normal technology to actually work."

He gets up from the desk and stands close to me. "And what is (para)normal?" He takes his notebook out and starts writing.

"It's a programming language that can connect with the dead." Rebecca told me about it so many times that it doesn't feel impossible, but the look on Ian's face makes me unsure. "Apparently it can be done. She studied it in grad school. She got close, but never made a connection."

"Connect with the dead?" Ian sneers. "Matt wouldn't care about that because the thing is, Matt Maxis doesn't *need* to do that. He can buy whatever he wants. What would talking to a dead person mean to someone like him? Life means nothing to him, look what he's doing to all the people that live here. He'll inherit Maxis Ltd. one day soon and become one of the richest Canadians in history. Matt is not nostalgic for people who have passed on. He's playing everyone here. He's a liar and needs to be exposed. That's what I'm here to do. The world must know."

He takes a picture of the whiteboard and then takes his sleeve and erases everything that's there.

"Hey, come on now." I place my hand on his shoulder. "Honestly, Rebecca could never get (para)normal to work. It's theoretical."

Ian turns back from the board. "Nothing is theoretical for Matt. If he wants it, he'll get it. That's just how life works for him. I got that from my research."

He marches back to the desk and pulls open each drawer until he stops and lifts up a huge stack of paper. Why is Ian acting like such a jerk now? After I told him about my interview with Diamond, this isn't how I expected him to be.

"What do we have here?" he says. He peers down on the papers and a smirk forms at the corners of his lips. "Oh, this is good. Really, really good."

I take a step closer and see it's the draft of a manuscript. The title reads: *Living Intentionally Haunted. A Workbook by Matt Maxis. Draft 1.*

I reach for the pages, but Ian's already ripping through them, scanning the table of contents like it's a menu full of gourmet food he's allergic too.

"He thinks he can be a writer now?" He laughs. "He's always had to do everything. Business success, then yoga, then leader of a cult, and now *a writer*? I've studied writing and research for years. It's not easy to put good sentences together. The ego on this guy. I wish I was surprised, but the more I see of this place, I'm not. He can have whatever he wants."

I look around the room. There's a small bookshelf neatly lined with books. I scan the spines, there's some on philosophy, a couple on modern art, and at the very bottom of the shelf there is a modest spiral-bound book that sticks out from the rest. I pull it out, but I already know what it is. It's Rebecca's thesis from her computer science degree, "The Future of Community Wellness with (para)normal."

Did Rebecca bring this here? She said I had her only copy. An image of the notecard he sent her before she left comes back to me. It was all planned. He knew exactly what Rebecca was capable of. He sought her out because of her talents with (para)normal. When they flagged us down to do the personality test, it felt random. But she received her acceptance immediately. They wanted her. Everything about our encounter on the quay was strategic to help Matt get what he needed, Rebecca. His brilliant (para)normal programmer. The gifted woman who could make Matt's wishes come true. This realization should relieve me from my guilt, but it doesn't. I made it too easy for them by suggesting we take the test.

Ian interrupts my thoughts. "This manuscript is so terrible it's good," he says. "Actually, it's hilarious. What was he thinking writing all this junk down? Vanity project!" He takes a photo.

"Let's put it away and keep going. We're getting close to Rebecca. I can feel it." I shove the rest of Rebecca's thesis back onto the shelf before Ian sees and takes a million photos of it too. "Also, your anonymous source, did they say anything about what was in this mall? Maybe that will give us a sense of where to go so we're not wandering around aimlessly."

Ian collects the pages of the manuscript and puts them into his backpack.

"You should put it back."

He zips up his bag and swings it over his shoulder. "He'll have a digital copy. This manuscript is full of his so-called philosophy or, as he calls it, *Performance*. Anyone with time and resources could write it. This is totally an act of the privileged. What guidance can he give someone who hasn't been handed everything their whole lives? On what grounds is he relating to all the people here? What the hell does he mean about living intentionally haunted? It doesn't even make sense."

He walks to the door and motions me to follow him, but I don't move.

"Your source, did they say anything about the operation going on here? How come no one's in the computer lab in the middle of the day? Everyone seems to be in the garden."

He stops and puts his hand on the doorknob but doesn't pull it open. "A lot of this stuff wasn't mentioned" he says, without looking at me. "I'm discovering it all in real time with you. I didn't have much time with him. People don't want to risk upsetting anyone from the Maxis family. Come on, there's more to see."

He opens the door and disappears into the hallway.

I stay behind. I need a moment away from Ian to think. I turn around and take another look at the space and Rebecca's work on the whiteboard. She found an opportunity to code here, but (para)normal can't possibly work how they claim it will. Ian's right, what does *intentionally haunted* even mean?

Before I can think about it anymore, the door behind me clicks. I look back expecting to see Ian's face popping in wondering why I haven't followed him yet, but instead a dog-eared paperback lies in a thick puddle of mud at the foot of the door. It looks so out of place, but with all the rain a leak must have sprung somewhere in the mall. I take a step closer and flinch. The book is thumping like it's trying to resurrect itself from the mud, then it starts glitching. This can't be happening again. I'm dehydrated, exhausted, and this is my imagination. The mud puddle grows larger and runnier like soon it will cover half the office. The book, though. I'd recognize that cover anywhere. It's the book Jennifer took with her when she walked into the forest. Just as I take another step toward the book, the door flies open, and Ian is standing in the frame looking concerned.

"I'm sorry if I've been abrupt," he says gently. "It's just this place. Everything that Matt is doing here is wrong. Please come with me. It's not safe for us to separate. We've made a great team so far. More importantly, please don't leave me alone in this creepy mall."

I look at his feet where the book and mud should be, but there's nothing but a clean floor.

"Are you okay? You look pale?"

I touch my forehead. It's damp and cold. "I'm fine. Let's get going."

We leave the room and continue our way down the hall and find a door that leads to a main corridor of the mall. I do everything I can to keep my mind off what happened in the office and focus on following Ian through another corridor that looks like all the other ones.

This corridor, however, has been renovated and looks more modern than the food court area we passed through earlier. Instead of dusty couches in the middle of the halls for resting, there are long benches off-set by small pods. The space, again, is empty. I walk over to a pod and see a docking station set up with a screen.

"Over here. This must be where the workshops take place," he says, walking through a large doorway into a massive space.

I recognize it instantly from Rane's video. Yoga mats lean against the wall and meditation pillows are piled up in the corner. The space is ready for tonight's Performance.

"Take a look at this," Ian whispers. I join him at a low table near a podium where he's looking through a binder with headshots of people. "These must be members."

I flip through until I see Rebecca. It's her. There are notes under everyone's photo. Rebecca's profile says, *gifted and heartbroken.* I rip her page out and put it in my pocket. I will slowly dissolve this place of her.

Ian continues looking through the book, flipping the pages like he's either repulsed or ready to devour them.

"Look at all these people," he says, not looking up. "I almost feel sorry for them, to be caught up in this scam. They have taken Matt at face value, which can only be to their peril."

I lean in close to him. At the end of the book is some sort of monthly schedule. Names are everywhere. I scan until I see Rebecca's name. Her scheduled time is tomorrow.

"Is this his schedule of sister-wives and husbands? Is this how he keeps everyone on track?" Ian snorts. "What kind of place is this guy running? And he claimed to be so loyal to Barb. Even after she died, he went on about how he would never forget her. Please."

A wave of sickness washes over me. Behind the schedule is a ledger with dates, numbers and years noted for each person. He flips through the pages, but I look away trying to calm myself.

"These are the student loans he's bought. Why wouldn't he keep all this together digitally? It's like these are part of his teaching notes. He knows everyone's status with him while he talks. Hey, look at this." Ian holds out the book toward me and I glance down. The words send a shiver down my spine: "Consent: Yes or No." Everyone is ticked *yes*. Our eyes meet, the coolness of his gaze startles me, then he snatches the book back.

"This is quite the total," he scoffs. "He's bought back millions of student loan debt. If all these people bail before their agreed exit date, he is set to make back millions more in interest. He's abusing them with his scam. I knew it. It was about getting rich." He takes his phone out to take more photos. "This is my proof. He is making money off them, forcing them to leave early due to humiliating living conditions."

The coolness I saw flickering in his eyes moments earlier has dissolved into a daze. "I don't know how I'm going to get this into one story. It will have to be a podcast. I'll need to contact my editor to see if she will sponsor one. This is bigger than us now. People will be interested. The public will be interested. I'll need your help piecing it all together of course. It's important that you lend your voice to what we're seeing."

He puts his phone away and jots down some notes in his notebook. I pick up the binder and flip through the pages of people and study their smiling faces, then I turn to see how much time they are committed to living in the community. Alice Yu will be here for close to ten years. Another person, Christina Len, will be here for nine and a half years. The time-lines seem like forever to me, but something about the debt forgiveness made it all worthwhile for them to accept his offer. On the last page of the book, there is a list of members who've left. Eight names are listed. One person's reason for leaving was a "change of heart" and another was "deceased." There is no mention of how the person died. I don't see Aria's name so this can't be the official record.

"Ian, someone died here." I point to the entry, trying to keep my hand from shaking. "It would have been around the time of Rebecca's last letter to me. She said her roommate disappeared."

"Does it give any more details? This could be a crime scene." He takes a closer look and starts to rip the page out of the book.

"Shouldn't you leave that the way it was? That could be evidence."

"Yeah, I guess you're right," he shrugs then flips through more pages before slamming it shut and pushing it aside. He continues his way across the room and opens the closet. I pull the book toward me, close it, and put it back where we found it. Maybe Matt won't notice anything is wrong when he gets here for his Performance.

"Wait," Ian whispers. "There's a door in the back of this closet."

He's standing in front of a closet with the doors wide open. He turns the knob.

"It's not locked." He pushes the door open and looks inside. I walk closer. "What do you see?"

"It looks like a maintenance route. It probably goes around the periphery of the mall. When I was in construction, I'd see these all the time. I'm going in. It's time we found Matt. I've found more for my story than I could have imagined."

Without looking back at me, he takes a step through the door and looks around. He walks further and it's as if the darkness of the hall swallows him and I don't see him anymore, even with the residual light from this room cascading through the door.

"Ian?" I'm careful to keep my voice low in case someone is nearby. I take a cautious step forward. "Why are you going in there right now? I don't think that's the best way to find Matt. Let's go back to the garden and start talking, that will get their attention."

That's when the maintenance hall door swings shut.

18

I listen for Ian's footsteps on the other side of the door. He wouldn't leave me like this. He said it himself that he didn't want to be alone in this creepy mall.

I cup my ear to the door, nothing.

"Ian? Where are you? Come back in here. Let's go back to the garden and find someone who will bring us directly to Matt. We've seen enough." I wait and listen, still not even a footstep in response.

"What's happening, Ian?" My voice is louder than it should be if I'm trying to be careful, which I should be. I look back at the massive room. Members will be here to set up for Performance soon. If someone comes to set up the yoga mats or whatever they use, I don't know how I'll explain why I'm in the closet.

Suddenly the lights turn off and I hear the faint echo of footsteps from the other side of the room. The footsteps stopped but it was undeniable. Someone is here with me. I glance back and see the soupy glow of a shadowy face looking down at a phone. I can't run into anyone from the mall without Ian, not even Diamond. I open the door to see if Ian's there. The hallway is long, dark, and empty of Ian.

The only place left to go is inside that maintenance hall. I step in and close the door behind me. Once my eyes adjust to the darkness, I scan the hallway again. Ian couldn't have gotten out of sight so quickly, unless he was running and he wouldn't run off on me like this. At least I don't think so. Besides, I would have heard his feet.

I stop and listen. The quiet in this hallway is so intense it hurts my ears. It's starkly different than the buzzing, but almost as disorientating. I look over my shoulder to see if the door I just walked through bursts open and Diamond marches through to haul me away without ever seeing Rebecca again. I face the door and a chill runs down my spine. Something is happening with it. The door rattles and pulses like at any moment it will tear away from its hinges and reveal a nightmare. A small emergency light above the door sheds just enough to illuminate the space in a grey haze and that's when I see it. The mud from the office has followed me here. Dark mud oozes out from underneath the door to pool across the threshold. Only it's not mud. The emergency light bounces off the surface of the pool just enough to give me a new perspective. It's blood. Dark, dark blood.

"Ian! Come on," I whisper. "We've got to find another way out. We can't turn back. Something's happening. We won't be able to get back into the main part of the mall the way we came."

The walls in this hallway feel so narrow I sense my claustrophobia coming full on. Earlier my phone had less than a quarter of its battery left when I shut it off. Now I need the light or I'm not getting far. I reach into my purse and pull it out. The phone has been on this whole time. No, no. When Ian turned it off, did he do it wrong? I did hear a message when I thought I did. I read it.

I'M UPSTAIRS. JOIN ME. STAY OUT OF THE GARDEN. I NEED TO TALK TO YOU. IT'S NOT GOING TO WORK. NONE OF THIS WILL WORK LIKE HE WANTS. YOU ARE ALL IN DANGER.

It's been Diamond sending these, I'm sure of it. She saw me in the garden and she didn't want to make a scene. This is her way of messing with me or telling me something important without out Matt knowing.

Ian's not here to stop me, so I reply: *How do I get up there?* The message is sending but I can't tell if it's gone through on the network.

I hold my phone up to shine the shred of light I have on this so-called maintenance route and see light coming from underneath a door ahead. I slowly walk toward it. It's so cold here and I can't see anything further than I can stretch my arm.

When I reach the door, I pull the handle. Nothing. It won't budge, but there's a light on. This brings some relief. Ian probably found another office and he's inside frantically taking pictures and notes for his podcast.

"Ian? Are you in there? You left me."

I listen for movement inside, then knock. It's quiet and the sound of my knock echoes down the hall. I don't know if I should continue along or turn back. Panic sweeps over me. The pulsing door leading back inside the Performance space, was it real?

"Where are you?" As soon as I say this, a slight breeze crosses my face. I look for a vent but it's too dark; I bang the door again, but my hands barely make a sound on the heavy door. No one inside could hear me. If Ian is gone, then no one knows I'm here except Diamond. The darkness of the hall feels thicker like it's wrapping around me, pushing air out of my lungs.

No, no, no.

I kick the door and bang it with my knuckles. The door is so heavy that my knuckles start throbbing. I knock and knock until I feel blood on my hands. Then I start to kick with my feet again. "Help. I'm in the hallway. I think it's a maintenance hallway. Please help me. I just want to get out of here."

But it's no use. No one will hear me. I yell as loud as I can, only stopping when I start coughing from the strain. Tears run down my cheeks. I pick up my phone and try to call, I don't know, 911, my brother who is hours away? It's no use, I have no reception anyway. Before I put my phone down, I hear my phone vibrate with a new message.

FOLLOW THE BUZZING. FOLLOW.

I haven't heard buzzing since we were in the garden. It's so quiet in here I can hear the pounding of my own heart. I reply: *I know I shouldn't be here. I'm stuck somewhere behind one of your offices and I can't get out. Please help me.*

I step back from the door and try to breathe in and out to steady myself.

"Ian," I scream again. Each sound I make sounds more desperate than the last.

I look down at my phone again. Diamond has not replied yet. I try to knock one more time, but it hurts my hand too much. My knuckles are red and bulging. I can't. I bang the palms of my hands, but the sound is dull and useless. I put my phone back in my pocket, to save what little battery I have left, and sit in the almost pitch dark. The cold in this hallway is vicious. I wrap my arms around myself to keep the cold from getting in me. I sit down and lean against a cold wall. I don't know where to go. Walking further could be riskier than staying still.

Right now, I would like nothing more than to be filing papers away at the lawyer's office, or standing on a cramped, stuffy train at rush hour, or buying vegetables I can barely afford. I could be talking to Chris on the phone about my incredible nieces. Leaving Rebecca alone was always an option, but I came all this way for my own selfish reasons and now I'm stranded. Ian's gone. I count to soothe my anxiety, but my eyes fill with tears and briefly lose focus, then I get up and start walking. Ian left or got lost in this hall. It's so dark I can barely see the floor in front of me, but I can't sit still in the cold.

It has been a long time since I felt so truly alone. The day we lost Jennifer we were heading west into Pemberton. Jennifer and I were in the back of the car. My brother was off at some high school science camp at the university that he managed to get accepted to for free. When we arrived at our site, dad tried to set up the tent in the rain.

"Damn it," he said. "Goddamn it!" Then he slammed the trunk closed. The pole we needed to finish the set up was not there, which meant no tent for us. We'd need to somehow sleep in the car, all of us. Dad stomped over to mom and tore a strip off her. Had she seen it? Wasn't she supposed to double check his rushed packing job like she always did? Jennifer started to cry. She could never handle hearing them fight, and this was a big one. I kept my mouth shut. It was easier if they forgot I was there. She took one of her new novels out of her small duffle bag. She zipped it inside her jacket. She didn't want anyone to see, but I did.

With nothing but the book, she marched into the woods. It didn't feel so dangerous. It was daytime and we both had done it many times before.

Mom and dad hadn't noticed she left. Mom was sitting on her camping chair in the rain with a tall can of warm beer. She always had a drink close by, no matter where we were. Dad was in the driver's seat with his head in his hands. I decided to sit in the dilapidated tent because there was nowhere else to go, and I ended up falling asleep.

"Carolyn?" I woke up when I heard my name. "Carolyn?"

"I'm in the tent, mom." How long had I been sleeping?

"Is your sister with you?" Her voice was sharp. All these years later, I still remember how those words sliced through me. *Is your sister with you?*

"Nope." I could see from the mesh ceiling of the tent that it was dark out now. I must have slept for two hours.

"She's not there," she yelled back to my dad, her voice was already slowing down from the alcohol, but even the booze could not hide the panic. I'd seen her pour some of her whiskey into her coffee travel mug for the drive up here. If I'd been counting how much she was drinking, I'd have lost track by now. "Weren't you watching her?"

"You're the one who was sitting right there!" he barked back, then stomped off to the car to grab a flashlight.

"Jennifer!" she yelled out into the woods behind the campsite. "Jennifer! Where are you?"

I crawled out of the tent and called her name, not quite knowing what was happening yet. Dad joined in. Soon the campground warden was there asking us what the problem was. Dad explained how Jennifer had been gone for over two hours and we were all worried. It wasn't like her to leave for long periods of time by herself. My chest seized up when I registered what my dad was saying and I felt the balloon grow and take up space in my lungs for the first time in my life. It would happen a few more times before I understood what it felt like to have dread well up inside me. At first I thought I was going to die when I felt that balloon. When it happened the second time at Jennifer's funeral, I didn't mind that I was dying. I couldn't believe my parents would hold a funeral for my sister who we never found. I never thought of her as dead. She was lost.

"Jennifer!" I screamed. "Jennifer, where are you?"

"Jennifer."

"Jenn…"

And the rest, is just the rest. I put my hood back on for some warmth. This time at the mall is the most I've reflected on what happened in years. It doesn't feel good.

I check my phone. Still no reception. It's past 8PM now, which means I've been separated from Ian for almost two hours. That's enough time to never see him again.

The only way out of here is the muddy entrance. It's my only option. I turn around and start my walk back to where I think the door is but it quickly becomes clear I took a wrong turn. I turn around. *We're turning around. Get going.* I'm just like my dad, turning around, giving up. I came this far, only to turn around alone.

I stop, thinking I hear a bang but it's the thumping of my own nervous heart. I swallow.

"Where are you?"

Did I hear someone? It was a whisper, so faint I don't trust my ears.

"Where. Are. Youuuuu…"

It sounds glitchy, like a recording from a bad connection. It can't be. I'm anxious and my mind is past the point of exhaustion.

"Ian?" I say. "Is that you? Are you here?"

No response. I'm not waiting around here to find out more. I turn the corner and see an emergency exit sign up above a door ahead, the red light brightening up the area around me just enough that when I look down at my hands, I see blood from my split knuckles dripping down my fingers.

"Rebecca!" I scream one last time. "Rebecca, come get me. I'm here looking for you. It's me."

The battery on my phone is almost dead. I still don't have a response from the last message.

I'm leaving. Ian can look me up later. I'll figure out a way to get back to town, but I'll do it. I have no other choice. No one is coming to get me. I place my hand on the push bar of the emergency exit, and to my relief it opens.

19

Once I walk through this door, I'll be officially giving up on finding Rebecca and proving to myself that I'm no better than my parents, that I also just turn around when it gets too hard. I'm beginning to understand that sometimes it makes zero sense to go on, and I hate that this is another failure I need to live with.

We could have kept looking. You just gave up! She'll be alone forever. Those are the words I hurled at my dad the last time I saw him.

I step back, collect my breath, then push the door open just enough to step through, only I'm not outside. This isn't an exit. My stomach drops with another disappointment. I'm in another small room now. No windows. No other doors that I can see. I reach for the light switch and flick it on. I'm standing in a freshly painted room with a pink yoga ball on a mat in the corner. Great, I'm in another meditation room, a personal one. How many of these does Matt need?

I don't want to close the door in case it locks and I'm stuck in here. With my foot on the door, I lean toward a bookshelf and grab the first thick book I see. I glance at the title. *What to Expect When You're Expecting.* I drop it on the floor and let the door close. It manages to hold just enough.

So there's a bookshelf, a yoga ball. Reminds me of my guest room, except much nicer and less musty. Here the emptiness manages to look modern instead of lonely.

A wooden privacy screen hides a large, updated version of the old clawfoot tub. Near the edge of the room, two overstuffed armchairs are angled together as if in conversation. I sit in one and lean back into the comfort of the cushions. Instead of feeling the back of the chair, I glide back, and then forward. I push back again, and I glide back and forth. A rocking chair.

"What is this place?" I whisper to no one. Hearing something, even my own voice, is helping me manage my claustrophobia. If someone walks through that door, I'll be forced to confront them by myself. It's hard accepting that Ian just left me. I don't want to think about it. I stay in the chair and look around the room. Near the tub is a bed. I get up from the chair and lay down on it. I'm exhausted. All the sleep I've been missing these past months since Rebecca left for this so-called community has caught up with me. I pull the thin sheets over my head.

I don't know if I nodded off but I jerk awake when the door clicks shut. I sit up and look at the door and my makeshift door stop is gone.

"Hello?" I say, hoping to hear Ian. I don't want to be alone anymore. I'm not good at being alone. I walk to the door and push it. It doesn't budge. "Ian? Is that you?"

Nothing. Absolute silence. It's another heavy, fire-resistant door so maybe the book wasn't enough to keep it open and it swung shut on its own. I check my phone and still no response to my text. Come on, Diamond! You, out of everyone here, know how much I don't belong in a place like this.

I sit back on the bed. On the small table beside me, I see a small notebook and a tablet. I pull the charger from the tablet, and stick it in my phone. I may be stuck in some egomaniac's private meditation room with no way out, but at least my phone will be fully charged soon. I grab the notebook and flip open the cover.

On the first page, I see it. Rebecca's handwriting. Her loops, the irregular spacing of each letter she writes. This is her journal. I study the cover. She wouldn't be happy if I snooped in here. That's how I got into this situation in the first place, but maybe this is an extenuating circumstance that she will understand? I crack open the cover.

Reflection. How I feel. I don't think it's that easy. My wounds have been bleeding, sometimes physically. This is how I know I'm getting the para(normal) script right. I'm connecting. How do I feel? I'm scared. I want to get it right. She should be one year old, but I wanted to see her as a newborn. I want every minute I should have had with her. I've left comments in my code to describe her. When the time comes, and it could be soon, I want her to look as she should have looked if she were alive. Then we will finally be together.

I put the book down and look around. Near the bookcase there is a small bassinet. I had thought it was just a basket. On the other bedside table is a pink box. I should have recognized that box. It was the only thing she brought with her from the apartment. This is Rebecca's nursery.

Matt thinks I should acknowledge my loss before things get too complicated with the app. He should talk! I was twelve weeks along when it happened. I had never wanted anything more. My midwife said it was common to lose a pregnancy in those early weeks. Still, I think about what I could have done differently so my daughter would be alive. With this pregnancy, I'm trying to stay calm. I don't want anything to happen to my daughter, and things are going great. But I want my children to be together. Somehow.

That's where it ends. This is her only entry but what she's written here crushes me. Shame floods my body. I did not fully recognize how much she was grieving when she had her miscarriage. Like my handling of Steve, being an empathetic and supportive friend for her after a miscarriage was not my finest moment.

I put the book down. We never talked about motherhood. I was unprepared when I found out how much being a mother meant to her.

"Chris asked me when I was thinking of having kids," I said one night. We were sitting in our balcony on our folding chairs, these awful blue things that a neighbour in our building left propped against the dumpster in the underground parking lot, but they worked. "He just annoys me so much. No, I'm not like him and Farrah who've been together forever and have done everything right since day one. And, no, I haven't had a burning desire to be a mother ever, so it's not really on my radar. He thinks I'm in denial, as usual."

Rebecca is quiet at first. "I thought I'd have a kid by now," she said, after a pause. "When I was a kid, I wanted three kids. I thought it would just, you know, happen. One day I would be a mother."

"You'll have your kids. There's lots of time." If only I would have chosen my words more carefully, but I was projecting how I thought about kids, that they could be put off and off until it was too late and eventually another part of life I let pass me by.

She winced. "I've been single for years. Ever since Steve."

I laugh. "God. Realtor Steve! Imagine the greedy little kids you could have had with him." Again, more harmful, thoughtless words.

She snorted. She only snorted when she thought something was beyond funny, so funny that she could start crying any second. "I'd have loved them all the same. And, besides, they'd be half me so maybe they would have been okay, in the end."

"Your children will be amazing. And very smart and kind."

Then the tears came, but these were not her usual tears that followed a snort. These tears were real and they were sad.

"Oh, hey, are you okay?" I hadn't realized how important being a mother was to her. She loved it when we looked after my nieces, but I hadn't known how devoted to the idea of motherhood she was.

She looked up to me with red eyes. "I'm going to tell you something," she sniffed. "Maybe I should have told you earlier, but it was too hard."

I nodded. "Okay…"

"I," she paused, taking a deep breath. "I miscarried last month."

"You did?" I was shocked. "Why didn't you tell me?" Me, me, it was always about me. If I could relive that moment, I would have asked how she was feeling, I would have focused on her.

"It was early and I wanted to keep it a surprise until I was sure everything was okay." I could hear in her voice that she was holding back tears, but it was impossible. They flowed down her cheeks like they had been waiting, accumulating in her for days.

"I didn't know you were even seeing anyone." Again, I made it about me.

She tried to wipe some of her tears away with the back of her hand. She sighed. "I'm not, technically. Steve was the dad."

I jumped on this, launching into logistics instead of being there for her in her grief. "Steve! Did he at least take you to the hospital when you miscarried?"

She looked so unhappy. It broke my heart looking at her. "No," she said. "I went by myself. He had an important viewing, and…"

Steve, that weasel! I knew I was right about him. "Don't tell me you've been dealing with all this alone?"

"No," she said slowly. "Not at all. I've been doing okay, really."

We looked out into the courtyard where a couple toddlers played on an old playground set. They were laughing at the top of the slide and taking turns going down on their stomachs. It was cute. Then they both started crying because one of them wanted to go down first. The mom started asking "Claire" to give her sister the space she needed to go down the slide first.

"More wine?" I asked, and she pulled up her glass. We didn't talk about it again for weeks, but the miscarriage came up again later. In the meantime, I never checked in on her. Not once. I moved on with my little life and the whole time she was grieving. I didn't realize she was processing everything that happened to her, how she was healing mentally and physically and how that took time. I didn't understand what that loss meant to her. This was when she stopped going into her job at the tech kiosk, and she stopped even calling in sick. She stayed in her room alone most of the time. I thought it was because she was sick of the customers.

Weeks after she told me what happened, I decided to pick on Steve. It happened out of habit because Steve was my favourite target. When we talked about him before, she laughed along with me.

"You dodged a bullet with Steve," I said. "Now you don't need that guy in your life forever." As soon as the words left my mouth, I knew it was a mistake. I knew I didn't mean what I said, but it was too late.

She was at the counter making herself something for lunch. I can't remember what. Seeing her in the kitchen was a rare sighting those days. I thought she must have been feeling better. She was chopping, something like carrots. Her face looked like my words had torn through her. She took a deep breath, gripping the chef's knife she was using tight.

"I don't think you really understand. I asked Steve to help me get pregnant. It wasn't about being in a relationship or being together. I *wanted* a baby. It was our arrangement. He was helping me."

Arrangement? I tried to recover from the shock of hearing this and suggested she try again with Steve, that things could be different the second time. Words like that kept spewing out of my mouth until she put a stop to it.

"I can't go through all that again. I can't go through with the pain of losing someone, not in this environment."

I should have taken this as a signal to back off, but I kept going. "You won't. Everything will be fine." I stepped toward her to show I cared, and I came in close, too close. "You can do it." The words sounded hollow even to me.

"That's what you say about everything. That everything will be fine. I don't believe it anymore. It took me years to get pregnant. Years. I saw him once a month exactly when I was ovulating."

I was having trouble seeing straight. I thought my text message had ended it between them. She would have known about that message, but never said anything to me because her goal was to get pregnant. The balloon in my lungs quickly filled to a near breaking point.

Okay, so I'd been wrong about her relationship with Steve. That was in the past. I switched up my strategy and tried keeping it light. We always kept it light and it worked for our friendship. We didn't talk about Jennifer and we really didn't talk about babies. Apparently we didn't talk about Steve. "Lucky for you it's my job as your best friend to believe everything will be fine for you. You will be a mother one day."

She rolled her eyes and began lowering the knife back onto the counter, only it slipped out of her hand and sliced my arm. It was my fault; I was hovering too close. The pain shot through me. She didn't mean to stab me. I glanced down at the cut. Blood was everywhere. It was deeper than it felt, much deeper. As soon as I saw the blood, I held my arm, speechless at what had just happened. I reached for the tea towel hanging on the oven handle to soak up the blood. All she did was stare at me numbly, then she said she was sorry about my arm and took her food to her room. Days later, she left for the mall. The time leading up to her departure, we acted like nothing happened, she helped with a grocery shop, and we tried to pretend we still had our friendship like it was before. But the damage was done. I hadn't supported her when she needed me the most and I couldn't undo that.

But now, at the mall, she's pregnant again. Did she know when she wrote me the letters? It's possible that she didn't know, but more likely she was hesitant to tell me. I'd ask too many questions, like who is the father? Is she in a relationship with someone here? But, these questions can wait, I need to apologize, to make things right with her.

I scan the room, taking it in all over again knowing that this is Rebecca's nursery. I pick up a book on her bedside table about hypnobirthing. I flip to an earmarked page, glance at the words, then put the book down on my lap. Every aspect of this space has been tailored for Rebecca. It has her essence in here, same as her room did back at our apartment, but only more thoughtful and refined. There were babies in that picture I saw on the computer we opened. Rebecca will have her family in this community, this awful, claustrophobic community. I couldn't, but something about the mall made her feel safe, safe enough to try again for motherhood.

I lean over to open each of the drawers in her bedside table. A few more books, a tube of Chapstick, a vanilla-scented candle.

The sound of the door creaking open stops me from snooping further. Ian must have found me. I push the drawer shut and stand up; the book on my lap lands on the hardwood floor with a slap.

I am suddenly standing face-to-face with someone I never thought I'd see again. It's Jennifer. Jennifer is standing at the door watching me.

Jennifer. I can't believe my eyes. My sister is in this room with me. She's not nine years old, but it's her. She looks like me, just a little different, like she always did. It's overwhelming to see her like this, a fully grown adult, but it's her. It's as if she's lived the last 22 years like she should have. I've waited for this moment since the day we lost her. It's as if all the years I've been without her have been erased. She has lived her life without me.

"I've been looking for you." My voice is quivering. I walk closer to her. She doesn't say anything. Her eyes are still so sad and fragile, as if everything she's seen these last decades has slid off them like water. "I never stopped, Jennifer. Never."

She puts her hands up, still not saying anything. She knows I'm lying. She always knew when I was lying. I could never keep it straight around her.

She knows I never went back to the woods after the search party was called off. I could have found a way to keep looking, but the backwoods are too dense, too dark. While I couldn't face them again, that darkness has followed me and cloaked my memories of walking through them with our dad. I was worried I'd never find my way out if I went into the woods again, but I could have tried. Chris once said our parents go camping to that exact site every summer because they feel they are with her that way. They said they felt her presence in the wind. I could never.

But here she is. She survived. She survived without any help from me or her family.

"You found me," I say. She had to find me because I wasn't brave enough to find her like I should have.

She reaches out and I step closer. "I've missed you so much." My voice catches in my throat and I do everything I can not to cry. I was the one who didn't go back. I stopped on the path. I let our dad leave her there. "Jennifer, where have you been? How did you get to the mall?"

A small grin spreads across her pale lips. All I want is to hear her voice after all these years, to hear her talk to me. I need to know what happened out there.

I bring my hands to hers and pull them back immediately. She's ice cold. So cold that it stings my skin. She grips my hands again and the cold starts to wash over me, making me nauseous. As I steady myself, I notice her clothes. A black hoodie, jeans, and sandals. I recognize this outfit. I saw it earlier. It was Jennifer in the garage when we first got here. It was her I saw in the concave mirror. She's been with me the whole time. She's been watching over me. I pull away, my hands are too cold now and it's spreading up my wrists. I'm losing my ability to move them. She takes another step toward me, her eyes locked on mine. She pulls me into a hug and it feels like falling into a bank of thick, fresh snow.

I step back, managing to break away from her grasp. "You need to understand, I would have gone back if I could. It wasn't up to me. I wanted to keep looking. I didn't want to go. Dad, he just gave up. He wouldn't listen."

Stop, just stop right there. We're turning around. Get going. His words have rattled around in my head ever since.

The woods were dark and large, but that shouldn't have stopped us. Could I have left him and gone on my own? I was a kid. A nine-year-old kid. It's what I've told myself for years.

She lunges toward me, taking my hands again. They're colder than before, wetter, like I could sink into them and stay with her as a one person. I buckle toward her. I missed her.

"What are you doing?"

Our fingers melt into one. I feel the cold from her body enter mine and drip down to my toes. It's like walking into a glacier-fed lake.

"Carolyn, what are you doing?"

I barely hear the question. Jennifer turns her head to look back and a set of thick claw marks have slashed her grey cheek. Fresh and dripping blood. How hadn't I seen this when I noticed her in the doorway? I reach up to wipe the blood away, to help her the best I can. I've wanted nothing more than to be there for her. I look down. My hands are covered in red moss. I try to shake it off, but I've lost all feeling in my fingers. The moss is growing higher up my wrists.

"Stop touching that."

I hear a splash and feel myself get yanked backward by my shoulders.

"Carolyn, what are you doing?" The voice is firm.

I'm being pushed down into a chair. I can't feel Jennifer's touch anymore. The cold feeling is gone. I want it back. I want to be with my twin.

"What's happening?" It's Ian. I realize it's his voice I've been hearing. I look around the room. Jennifer's gone. I look at my hands and the moss has disappeared. I bring my fingers up to my cheeks. They're still ice cold.

"Ian, you're back." I push myself up from the chair and curl up in his arms. His warmth is so different from the icy grip of Jennifer. It's welcoming, but all I want is to be with Jennifer again. "Did you see her?"

"Her?" He looks confused. "When I came in here, you were in this, like, transfixed state and standing in a bathtub with the cold water running. Did you find some ice or something? You're soaked. Look at you."

I hadn't noticed I was wet until now. I look down at my wet jeans clinging to my legs and fight off a shiver.

"You need to tell me what you were doing. I saw the way you were holding your hands out. It was weird. I didn't like it." He hugs me tight and kisses the top of my head. "We need to get out of here. I've seen enough and I'm getting worried about you."

If Ian saw me acting this way, then it means Jennifer was here. She lives here. I can't stop my hands from shaking. I need to know how she found me. Is she really one of Matt's community members?

"Did you see her?"

He gives me another confused look, so I ask again. "Did you see my sister?"

"Your sister? Your sister lives at the mall too?"

Ian doesn't know about my sister yet. I shake my head. "Never mind. It's nothing. Where did you go? I went looking for you but it's like you vanished."

"I'm sorry," he says. "I didn't mean to leave you. The door closed and I must have taken a wrong turn in the dark. I was trying to catch up the whole time."

"Catch up with who?"

A look for pity overcomes Ian's face. "You. I was following you. You led me here."

20

Ian couldn't have followed me because he left before I did. "*You* left me in that huge room. You're the one who went ahead. The door closed moments later. I couldn't have been in front of you to follow."

He saw Jennifer. She's here. I saw her and so did he. It's real. My stomach sinks thinking that she has been looking for me this whole time. She never stopped looking for me. Where did she go? I felt her. Somehow this place has brought us together, but how?

"It's so dark. I thought it was you, but then you did this, this thing and I had to get away from you." His face is pale and he frantically runs his hand over his hair.

Something is happening in this mall and maybe outside of it. The reflection I saw of myself when I was driving. I thought it was me, a version of me conjured from my overtired mind, but it was connected to Matt somehow. The girl in the hive might have been too. I've been seeing things and they have been real.

"You need to tell me what happened, exactly. Step by step."

"Why? What's going on?"

"I don't know, but that was not me you were following. I think it was... someone else." I tell him about my sister, everything comes out.

Instead of trying to deny what I'm saying, like I expect because anyone who heard this would, he nods. "I can't believe I'm saying this, but that makes sense. As I was following her, I kept calling your name, but she wasn't answering. I ran up beside her. Honestly, I thought you were upset with me for leaving you behind in that room for so long." He stops to give me an assessing look.

"Keep going." I'm trying to keep my composure, but chills were running up and down the side of my body. Is it possible that

Jennifer has been alive all these years and my family didn't know? I dismiss the idea. It's more painful to think about this possibility and to think about what she must have gone through to survive than to assume she was dead, and this makes me the most selfish twin alive.

"Just before I could reach her, she turned around and…" He stops and shakes his head. "Maybe my eyes weren't adjusting to the light properly. I might not have seen anything. I haven't been sleeping well. I want to get the story here. Matt is such scum for creating this place."

"What do you see?" I press.

"It's not what I saw," he says, slower. "It's what I heard."

"What do you mean?"

"When she opened her mouth, the entire hallway filled with severe, like, buzzing. It sounded as if there were millions of honeybees all around us, but all mechanical and malfunctioning. I froze. I didn't know what to do, the sound was overwhelming. I couldn't see straight. I might have even passed out. I'm not sure."

"You've heard the buzzing then. I've been hearing a low rumble for days now, following me like it's attached to me. What does it mean?"

"I don't know." His eyes widened. "As soon as I snapped out of it, she was gone. I retraced our steps and tried to find my way back to you. I thought I might have imagined the whole thing. And when I found you in the tub…" He shakes his head.

"I saw her, too, but she didn't say anything to me. She just stood there looking at me."

"We need to get moving. I have enough for my story. Let's find Rebecca. She needs to get out of here. When I was trying to find my way back, I tried one of the doors and I found a staircase leading to an upper level. Maybe it will bring us back to the main part of the mall."

After telling him everything about Jennifer, I feel raw but I also feel more connected to him right now. He takes my hand, and we walk out into the darkness of the hall.

He stops. "When we were apart, I was really worried about you," he says. "When we leave today, I don't want this to end."

"Neither do I."

Our eyes meet, but within a moment something dark comes over them. He looks like he's about to say something, but then hesitates.

"What is it?"

He shakes his head and starts walking. "It's nothing. Let's go."

Ian opens the door to a staircase and I follow him up the narrow stairs.

"Hello?" It's a child's voice.

I look around Ian and see a young girl, maybe ten years old, standing in the doorway. This is the first kid I've seen the whole time we've been here. She's wearing a bright pink dress with purple runners. Her dark brown hair is pulled back with a unicorn headband. She reminds me of my nieces.

The girl looks at Ian and then looks over at me. I wave to her. "Hi there, we are trying to get out of here. We haven't seen many people here since we left the garden."

She doesn't move. "Do you want to see my bedroom before you leave?" she says. "It could be your last chance. Dad will want to see you soon."

Ian and I look at each other. We haven't even asked her what her name is. Her parents are probably working in the garden. She should be in school at least.

"Who is your dad?" I ask.

"We really should be going," Ian says, pushing me back toward the door. He pushes it and it's locked. "It's been a long day and we have a long drive home tonight. Can you let us out?"

She shrugs. "It will only take a minute." The crinoline lining under her dress bounces up and down as she walks. "I want to show you something."

"How do you like living in a mall?" Ian asks. He has his notebook and recorder in hand.

"It's fine. I haven't been here too long. After my mom died, I was sent here. It's been under construction for a long time, but now it's starting to feel like home. Kind of."

Ian looks back at me, then turns off his recorder and puts it back in his pocket. He's quiet.

"I'm sorry to hear about your mom," I say. Ian echoes my words in a mumble. I've seen this look on him before, he's processing something. He's far away, absorbed.

"It happened five years ago," she says matter-of-factly, like she is stating something obvious, like her favourite colour clearly being pink. "It's not so bad because dad is working on it. He's excited because he's getting all these investors. He thinks he's going to change the world."

"Change the world how?" Ian sneers. "What's your dad really doing here?"

"She got very sick," the girl says, ignoring him. She opens a door and we follow her into her bedroom. Old white racks left over from the store that used to be here line the walls. A butterfly poster and twinkly lights help make the space feel a little cozier. "So sick that she couldn't leave her bed anymore."

"That sounds tough," I say. "I'm sorry you had to go through that."

"It was," the girl says as she pulls a book out and flips through the pages. "I didn't see daddy again after she died until I had to move here."

Ian looks down at his feet.

"This place is nice. I like how you've decorated your room," I say. She looks up at me and beams. Ian repeats what I said, but she barely looks at him. Her eyes are fixed on me. I smile back, feeling my cheeks grow red from her intense attention.

"You look familiar," she says to me. "I see my mom, you know." She picks up a tablet from her desk. She unlocks it by pressing her thumb.

"I thought you said your mother passed away. Do you see her in your dreams or in photos?" I take a step closer to her, but she's now fixated on Ian.

"Have you seen her yet, Uncle Ian? I bet she would love to see you. She used to ask about you when she was earth side. She wanted everyone in the family to get along. She can't talk yet, but dad says it's coming."

"Uncle Ian?" I look at him, taking a step away. "Her mom wanted "the family" to get along?" I can't believe what I'm hearing.

He reaches for my hand, but I pull away. "I can explain. Seriously. I can explain everything, but we need to go now."

"This girl is your niece, which means, what then, you are…?"

Before he can confirm anything, footsteps shuffle outside the door.

"Ian…" A voice booms from the hall. Moments later the door swings open. At this exact moment, my phone vibrates in my purse. It must be a response at last. I open my phone and read the message.

YOU'RE GOING TO WISH YOU LISTENED TO ME AND FOLLOWED THE BUZZING WHEN I SAID. IT'S ALL ABOUT TO CHANGE. BE WELL, LYNNIE.

My hands shake. Only one person in the world has ever called me by that name. I haven't heard that nickname in 22 years before coming to the mall. These texts haven't been from Diamond.

The door bursts open and Matt Maxis is standing there. He found us.

"Welcome," Matt says. His voice is softer than I imagined it would be, not at all like the confident voice I heard in Rane's video. He comes closer to me. "You're very special to us here, Carolyn. The data you have been providing us has been good because your memories are pure. You haven't forgotten them. Solid data is one of the most important parts of building an app like we are. Rebecca taught me that. She is so brilliant. Of course, I don't need to tell you that." Matt takes a breath and looks me up and down, then smiles cooly. "Come with me. I want to learn how you've been enjoying our prototype so far and how you feel your first experience at my community has been. We're chatting user-to-user, though I'm thinking a retreat here could be considered an upgrade for the most devoted so they can see where the magic happens." He chuckles. "I'd love your thoughts. And, Ian, great to see you, but you're staying put. It's for the best. You've always been so sneaky. I'm sorry but this is just another Maxis project you aren't invited to be a part of."

I look at Matt in confusion. I haven't consented to giving him any data. I haven't been using a prototype. "What are you talking about? What have I been using?"

"Haunt Me," he says. "I'm working on a patent for a revolutionary technology that will rightfully reunite us with our loved ones who have passed. It's all so very exciting." He looks me up and down again, and smiles. "Yes, I believe our investors will just love you."

21

Not only did Matt plan to recruit Rebecca, but he also led us here. He prepared this whole experience. He wanted us to walk through the mall, to discover the space for ourselves, to get deeper into his world until he was ready to pull the puppet strings harder. He knew we were here and that's why Diamond never did anything when she saw us. She was following his orders. The realization feels like a cold slap in the face. Of course she was.

"When did you start following me? Why did you let us just walk around?"

He doesn't have to answer, the look of sympathy flickering across his face is all I need. I feel weak and lightheaded. I turn toward the door, but one of his crew is quick to stand in front of it, trapping us in.

Matt approaches me slowly. "You're not quite getting it yet. Come with me and I'll show you. You haven't finished seeing everything. The mall is a good place."

"I can't follow you without Ian." I cross my arms. "I know we shouldn't be here, that we weren't invited, but I need to find Rebecca. I came here to make sure she is okay. Whatever it is you say I've been testing, I don't want to be a part of it. Please take me to her and then I will leave your mall."

He looks at Ian and scoffs. "Carolyn, you've seen everything here except one special area we are working on. I think you would be particularly interested in this work. It will speak to your wounds, and I know how important they are to you. I want your feedback on how it's been working for you. Have you seen her yet? Are you remembering more? Are the messages helping you feel engaged with her?"

Diamond's question in the dining area comes back to me. *How much do you remember of her?*

I shake my head. I can't talk about my visions, the bleeding arm, or what I experienced in the nursery, all these vivid dreams. Matt has invaded my life, my memories, my grief, all so his machines could learn from me. "The only person I'll talk to here is Rebecca."

Matt walks toward me. He holds himself casually, as if he also expected me to resist him. I try to stand as strongly as I can. I'm not going anywhere with him, not until I see Rebecca.

"When you see what I want to show you, I'll take you to your friend," he says. "You can trust me. Everyone who lives here trusts me. I don't take that lightly."

He turns to Ian. "You can stay right there. Also, how rude of me, how have you been? It's been a while since I saw you last. What was it, grandma's 80th at her favourite steakhouse on the beach?" He leans into the doorframe and folds his arms like he's getting ready for a chat.

Ian looks up at him and their cool blue eyes seem to lock together. "I've been making a living, on my own, providing for myself, which is more than you could ever do. Clearly. Why are you forcing all these people to live with you like this? It's disgusting."

I take a step away from Ian. I don't know how I could be so foolish. I should have realized the connection much sooner. All his jabs at Matt. It was personal. It had to be. There's even a family resemblance I didn't pick up on.

"So you're related to Matt?" It's humiliating to have to ask at this point, but I need him to say it. "You've been using me this whole time." Hot tears sting my eyes. Matt is quick to hand me a linen handkerchief from his pocket, but I brush it away.

"No," Ian says, trying to grab my hand but I avoid him. "I wanted to tell you many times, but it was never the right time. I wasn't using you. Everything I said I felt about Matt is true and you can see that, can't you? He needs to be exposed. Everything I feel about you is real. I meant what I said."

I can't listen to him. I don't trust what he says anymore. So much for making a good team. Any feelings I might have felt toward him were built on lies.

"The first step toward radical self-care is accepting where you've come from and how that came to be," Matt interrupts. "It's up to you, as a *journalist*, to use your own words to tell your own original story. Tell her where you're from. It's not right to deceive people, especially someone you spend so much time with."

Ian's face turns red. "This has nothing to do with you. You've been ruining my life since you were old enough to realize you could."

Matt looks at him, his lips pressed into a thin line. Ian takes a deep breath and continues, "Okay, fine. I'm Matt's cousin. My mom is his dad's sister. Are you happy now, Matt? Please forgive me. I wanted to tell you so many times but I just couldn't. It's hard for me to admit I'm related to this monster."

I turn away from him. He takes another step toward me but backs off immediately. Ian's been lying to me this whole time and he's been using me. I told him about Jennifer. My sister. I feel gross. This is all too much. Decent people don't deceive others like this.

"I'm sorry for not coming clean with you earlier," he says in a low voice. "I wanted to tell you on the drive here and other times, I really did, but I couldn't bring myself to do it. I hate that I'm related to this abuser. I didn't want you to think I was like him."

"Watch it," Matt says sharply.

"Is that how you could write about Matt's mannerisms in your article, because you knew him personally?" I can barely speak. Out of the corner of my eye, I see a shadow of a smirk forming on Matt's face. He's enjoying that this rift is forming between us.

"Not exactly," Ian says, sitting back down in the chair. "I made the interview up. Matt never said those things. I thought he owed me an interview at least that. I'm related to him, I should be the one to break the story around this sham. What's family for?"

Another blow. "Did you make up the anonymous sources, too?" He doesn't need to say anything. I already know he did. The quotes were just enough to make Matt sound like he was doing something sinister and to gather world-wide attention, and for Ian to get noticed for his writing. It was just enough for me to think I had a shared goal with him. All the times he tried to interview me, that's what this was about. He needed real quotes from someone involved, someone like me, to legitimize his story. He withheld the location of the mall from me until he needed to use it as a carrot to keep me going.

"So coming here was all about money!" Everything is always about money.

"No, it's not like that. I didn't set out to lie, but a few made up quotes here and there got people interested in what Matt was doing here. No one would believe me otherwise. Sources are necessary otherwise it's aimless blogging and no one cares about that. Why else would Matt be stepping away from everything and buying back student loans? It's ludicrous and now you've seen it, right? This place is messed up."

Matt raises his hand to silence him. "You know, I've missed you, cousin. You could have kept in touch in more conventional ways, like phone or email, but I suppose a pop in never hurt anyone."

"Okay, we should have knocked," Ian says. "But you left me no other choice. I have been trying to get a meeting with you for years. You are impossible to get a hold of. We're family, man."

Matt's face darkens. He swiftly pulls Ian out of the chair he's sitting in and kicks the chair across the room. It slams into the wall. The violence of his sudden action reminds me of the part of Rane's video when he jumped into the audience after being confronted about missing members.

"I've been grieving. Maybe you are one of so many on this earth that don't understand that. My grief is not a switch that can turn off and on. It had nothing to do with you. I needed to start my new path. It led me to create Haunt Me. It hasn't been easy. Finding the right coder, no, the perfect coder is near impossible, but now I have her and there is incredible interest in my project. We have very committed investors now, people who see the possibilities of what we are building. Once Carolyn talks to me about her experiences, I will reunite her with Rebecca."

They both look at me, Ian with pleading eyes and Matt with that unsettling curiosity I noticed before. Coming here hasn't been about them. It's been about Rebecca.

"Okay. I'll talk." If that's what I have to do, I'll do it.

"Are you sure you don't want me to go with you?" He's frantic. "You don't know what you're walking into."

Not a chance. "You've lied to me since the moment I met you."

I walk toward Matt. He nods and I follow him out into the hall.

Out in the hall, we walk in silence. My mind is going in a million directions, but I manage to keep my calm.

"I understand from Diamond that you wanted to join the mall as well at one point."

"Not exactly. I took the personality test for the cash." It's a humiliating thing to admit to someone with unfathomable wealth. "Anyway, what is Haunt Me and why's it so important to you?"

"It's important to you, too."

"How could it be important to me? I don't even know what it is."

He stops right in front of me and turns around. "But what about your sister? You want to know more about her, right? Don't you want to see her again? Hear her voice? Know what happened and how she feels about it now? Don't you want to tell her you are sorry."

My knees weaken and I almost fall to the floor. "You don't know Jennifer. She's been gone a long time. She was nine when she went missing. She's dead." This is the first time I have ever said she is dead. I've said she is gone or lost, but never dead. But after twenty-two years of being missing, maybe it's time for me to accept the reality of the situation. She's dead. She couldn't have survived without making contact until now.

"But you saw her here, no? And you've felt something, some-one, with you for a while now. Maybe others have seen her too?"

My nieces said I was watching them from the street. Then there was that recruiter on the promenade when I first tried to find the address of the mall. "No. It's impossible. I don't see dead people."

"Maybe you saw a ghost," Matt whispers. He's looking at me carefully, like he's trying to gauge something about me. "Maybe you didn't. Maybe you saw a digital representation of a ghost manifested from your real memories. Maybe you didn't! I love this game. I will say sometimes the ghosts have a hard time finding the person they are trying to unite with and that's why there will be encounters with more peripheral people from time-to-time. Come, I want to show you what we're doing here."

Before I can get him to clarify what he's saying so I understand, he turns on his heel and leads me into another room.

"You've been making connections so far. Don't doubt the work. You're doing a great job. I couldn't be happier." He says over his shoulder. "(para)normal is incredible technology."

Everything he is saying is impossible. Rebecca tried to do this close to a decade ago and couldn't figure it out. Her professors had no idea either. (para)normal is a concept, not actual applied technology. It doesn't work. It's one of those things people go to grad school for to *think* about something rather than do anything real with it.

We stand in the doorway and he gestures toward a leather couch and I sit down, too tired to keep standing. I could fall asleep right now. All the adrenaline I felt moments ago has drained from my body.

"I connected to a network here on my phone automatically," I say. Another wash of tiredness comes over me. "I've had text messages from someone. At first, I thought they were spam, then I thought it was Diamond…"

"It's not Diamond, but you do know the person sending them, and you've been expecting them this whole time. Everything you've been giving us through your experience with Haunt Me, brought them to you when you needed it. There are glitches Rebecca is working out, as I'm sure you noticed. But those texts are real and they were all meant for you. They were written by your sister."

I pull out my phone and it vibrates just as I do. There's a new message. I open my messages and there's a new one: I KNOW YOU TRIED. I KNOW YOU TRIED. I KNOW YOU TRIED. I KNOW YOU'RE TIRED. SLEEP WILL GET EASIER. MOM AND DAD NEVER CARED AS MUCH AS YOUUUUUUUuuuuuuu.

I drop my phone to the floor. "I want you to disconnect me from this network. Ian wasn't connected, only me. There's nothing I can do to get away from it. I turn my phone off and the messages still come. It needs to stop."

Matt picks my phone up, looks it over for cracks and passes it back to me. "You know what's happening, Carolyn. This is Jennifer. This is how she can communicate now, through the app. It's connected to your memories through (para)normal. She is texting. That will all change soon. It will be better." He rubs his hands together. "Everything is advancing better than I could have hoped."

Matt gets up from his seat and walks to a small kitchen where he takes an electric kettle out of the cupboard and fills it with water. He plugs it in and as the water boils, he pulls open another cupboard above his head and retrieves a small tin. As soon as he carefully twists off the top of a tin and gives the contents a sniff.

"I'm making us tea. Lavender, I think. You need something to soothe you, calm you, as we talk about your experiences."

"So I've been seeing a ghost of my sister?" *A digital ghost*? It sounds absurd.

He laughs. "We haven't figured out a name yet. I'm not sure calling them ghosts will resonate in the market how I want. I call mine my dear. Maybe that's where you can help us if you join since you have that underutilized marketing background. I was thinking of *Twin Spectral*, after seeing the bond between you and Jennifer."

He plops a homemade tea bag into each of the mugs. "This is important work. The (para)normal technology opens so many possibilities. We can literally connect with anyone. Anyone in history. That's appealing to many venture capitalists who have their eyes on bringing back certain people, but for

me it's more personal," he continues, not looking up at me.
"Even with a small amount of personal data, the app can create
depth and authenticity through artificial intelligence. It *is* the
person you want it to be, it really is. We're also working on a
feature that manifests physical wounds that may have superfi-
cially healed in an effort to urge the person to re-evaluate how
they got the injury in the first place. This feature is about
growth. Reflection is so important for vitality. It's powerful
stuff. We are trying to help people here. Your arm's been hurting you, correct?"

I cover my cut. I think it stopped bleeding when I was in
Rebecca's birthing room. I'm not sure because it comes and goes.
The kettle clicks off and he pours steaming water into our mugs
and watches the tea steep a moment then he places a white mug
in front of me and sits down. It smells good, but I won't drink it.
I don't trust him. Nothing he is saying is making sense. Even my
cut is related to Haunt Me? My cut has nothing to do with
Jennifer.

He blows on his cup and his lips settle into a position of satisfaction. "Your sister was your first best friend, you understood
each other like no one else. Don't you want to hear what happened to her, know where she's been all these years? These are
the conversations you can have with her. This level of healing is
possible."

Over the last decades since Jennifer went missing, I have
wanted more than anything to talk to her, to understand what she
went through and how she was feeling when she went missing.
To be together again, like we used to be.

Haunt Me can do this? It doesn't seem real. The thought of
engaging with it terrifies and attracts me at the same time. I don't
know how to feel, but, more importantly, I don't know if I can
trust it.

I look at Matt. "I need to see Rebecca."

He gulps his tea and he winces from the scalding water.
"Soon. But first we're having tea together. Food and drink are
central to our life here. I'm told you and Ian gobbled up our coffee break spread out near the garden? A future Haunt Me

upgrade will include eating and drinking with your… ghost. But that's after they can speak. The voice is special and it's…"

His words fade off and he shakes his head, then he gestures to me to drink and I pull the mug back in front of me and decide to take a sip. I haven't had anything to drink since that coffee. I feel the warm liquid reach every part of me.

I put the mug down. "Why did I get a text saying I was going viral? Why was there a photo of my face repeating on some sort of feed on a screen? Jennifer wouldn't have sent those. She wouldn't have the reference. She died in the 1990s."

"Did you like that? I think it's quite the touch," he says, tucking his chair in closer. "It's important to me that Haunt Me digital ghosts keep up with technology so they can be relevant with their contemporaries, so yes, Jennifer does understand social media, maybe even better than you."

I think of my photo on the social media feed and the caption. Is it possible Jennifer meant it as a joke and not the threat I first interpreted it as?

"What are you doing with the bees? There's been this buzzing…"

"What aren't we doing with the bees? We need to help replenish the earth's supply because someone must do it. I just love them. They are cute up close, like little fuzzy teddy bears." He pinches his fingers to mime holding a bee.

"So I have been hearing a buzzing bee. It's not just my imagination."

"Imagination has nothing to do with what we're doing here."

"What does then?"

"Engineering." He slaps his hand on the table like he's this clever person. Tea sloshes out of his mug onto the table; he uses his sleeve to wipe it up.

I push my mug away again and stand up. This conversation is over. "Have you heard enough about my experiences? I would like to see Rebecca now."

"You might want to start listening more. It will help you see what's right in front of you. You are already connected to our network after all. You've been experiencing our prototype app since the minute you connected to our Wi-Fi network on the quay. You remember our suitability test, right? You connected to our free Wi-Fi. I want to know what you think, to get your first impressions. Rebecca is always talking about getting feedback from real users. She says it's how we make things better."

"I haven't been testing anything." I bring my phone out and swipe to the settings again. The network I connected earlier to SPREAD_AUTHENTICITY is still strong. I try once again to disconnect without success.

"Not everyone here knows what we're doing. The app is something I'm making outside of regular community programming, with only a handful of people I can truly trust invited to contribute. You'd be surprised how many computer science grads we have here at the mall. And, of course, the English grads come in handy for writing. Those degrees are extremely useful and appreciated, despite what the job market will make you believe. Everyone will soon be supporting Haunt Me, especially at the beginning as we work out certain bugs."

"Are you telling me this mall is some kind of… tech campus?" So much for his altruistic ways. He's just another Jobs-Zuckerberg-Musk wanna-be.

He shakes his head. "If only. Truly, I'm the biggest luddite. I still like a hardcopy."

I can hardly hear him anymore. I'm tired, more tired than I've felt in a while. He's nodding and saying something about life expectancy and good health and morning yoga stretches. I can barely hold myself straight enough to see him anymore.

The buzzing is back in my ears and the power this time overwhelms me. I see Matt's mouth moving, but I can't make out what he's saying over the buzz. He takes his cup of tea up to his lips and takes a big gulp. I look at my tea and knock the mug over, spilling the liquid everywhere. It's all happening slower than it should, like my mind can't keep up with what's really going on. He must have mixed something into my tea. I knew I shouldn't have trusted it. I'm suddenly very weak, I stand up and start walking toward the door, but I stumble and find myself sitting back down again. I try to push myself up from the chair but my strength is gone.

"Oh no," he says. "Must have been too…" That much I make out. I try to tell him again to take me to Rebecca, but the words come out garbled and I worry I might swallow my tongue if I keep talking.

Matt rises from his seat and joins me by my side. He towers over me. Am I shrinking? What's happening? I flinch when he takes my shoulder and pulls me to my feet. I stagger forward and slip out of his hands. I manage to keep myself standing, for just a moment before falling to the ground.

22

The next thing I realize, I'm lying in a strange bed, staring up at a yellowing, water-stained popcorn ceiling. Time has passed from my tea with Matt, but I don't know how much. The buzzing is gone, but my head is pounding, and I need to go easy. I reach around the bed for my phone to figure out how long I've been out, but it's not here. I slowly hoist my body up to look around but stop when I hear someone flipping through papers nearby.

"I think you're ready now, Carolyn. We need to get back on schedule for the investors."

It's Diamond's voice. I pull myself up enough to see she's watching me from a small desk in the corner. She drops her pen in her notebook and picks up her phone.

"Ready for what?" My head is cloudy and any details about what happened after I collapsed have not come back to me. "How long have I been here? Where's Ian? I need to see Rebecca. I still haven't seen her. How do I know she is even here anymore."

Diamond ignores me, busy typing something on her phone. I've seen traces of Rebecca. Her thesis. Her notes. Her nursery, but not her. Matt praised her for developing Haunt Me, why hasn't she come and found me yet?

"Did Matt put something in that tea?" I push myself up on the bed and lean against the wall to steady my dizziness. I need to collect myself if I'm going to make it out of here. The room is feeling smaller. I push off an old quilt that had been draped over me.

"Absolutely not." She doesn't look up. "He would never." Her voice trails off either because she's distracted or can't bring herself to finish the lie.

I don't believe anything she says. She gave me the credentials for free Wi-Fi that turned out to be anything but free.

"You passed out because there was a glitch in the network," she continues. "The signal from the app was too strong. You heard a lot of that awful buzzing, right?"

It was loud. The loudest I've heard it.

I must look like I'm confirming things for her because she nods. "Right. *That* was a bug in the technology. It's all worked out now. Sorry for that. Even his precious Rebecca makes mistakes." Her apology sounded about as sympathetic as a customer service chatbot, but I can't help but sense her jealousy over Rebecca's status with Matt.

"I withdraw my consent for the network. I can do that. That's my right." I move to kick off the rest of the blankets but my leg movement is restricted. I grab the blanket and pull it off. My ankles are bound to the bed with ties. Panic floods through me. I look around. I don't even know if I'm still in the mall or somewhere else.

I pull my legs harder and the binding gets tighter. "Take these off immediately."

Diamond finally looks up from her phone and glances at me. "Relax. It's not what you think. I tied you because I was worried you would walk off when I left the room and get lost again. You can untie them yourself. It's not a fancy knot or anything."

I slide down to the foot of the bed and untie the knot as quickly as I can and step down. As soon as my feet reach the ground, my knees buckle with weakness. I grab the edge of the mattress to sturdy myself, then I face Diamond. "Can you show me the way out please? I'm not staying here another minute."

"Don't you want to see your sister again?" She gives me a questioning look, like she's genuinely puzzled why I wouldn't want anything to do with an app using (para)normal and whatever Matt is orchestrating. "You will after the upgrade. You will hear her, too. Imagine how that will feel. It'll be incredible. Soon she will have memories, too, from the years she was gone until now, when you were reunited. It's all on the Haunt Me roadmap. You will get to experience the upgrade first. It's important that you stay the course and see this through. Matt has been working hard to bring this to reality and you doing anything stupid right now would really ruin it for him."

"Where's Rebecca? I need to hear it from her." Diamond could say whatever she wants. I'm not believing anything she says.

Before I can get any further with Diamond, there's a quick knock at the door and Matt enters the room with a smile so big my skin prickles with fear. "How are you feeling? You gave us a scare back there."

Diamond comes over and takes my hand, suddenly shows all this interest in me, as if she has been providing me amazing patient care this entire time.

"Slow down," she cautions. "Sometimes the glitch can make you weak. Best to take it nice and easy."

I pull my hand away. Thanks, Diamond. It's not like I haven't been struggling since the moment I woke up.

"I need to see Rebecca. You need to tell me, is she even here anymore or did she leave?"

Matt shakes his head. "We got carried away. Yes, yes, you need to see Rebecca. I think she'll be able to explain her work better than I can. I'll take you to her right now."

Out in the hall, we passed through the halls I walked through when I was lost. The lights are on now. We pass the pods we found in the old Target. Community members are sitting behind tablets connected with microphones and auxiliary keyboards.

"What's going on there?" I stop and watch them.

"Oh that?" Matt says. "It's nothing. Just some of the background work we are doing with Haunt Me right now as we work through some, uh, kinks in the software. We'll get there, and it will happen soon."

He continues walking ahead. Before I move to follow him, I catch the eye of one of the people working in the pod. It's a man in his thirties, maybe a couple years older than Ian. He's hunched over his keyboard and looks so tired.

"Come on, Carolyn. Rebecca is expecting us."

I catch up with Matt and we walk in silence until he stops in front of a door. He knocks. He could use his pass, but he knocks.

This time there's a familiar voice inviting us to come in. Rebecca. It's her. She's here.

Matt opens the door and there's Rebecca sitting in front of a large computer with lines and lines of code on the screen. It's hard to tell in the darkness of the room, but she looks different. Paler. When she pushes her chair away from her desk, I see her round belly.

"Carolyn, it's you!" She gives me a big hug and it fills me with warmth. She holds on tight. "I'm glad to see you. I've missed you. When I heard you were here, I couldn't wait to see you." She looks at me intently and everything feels so weird. I can't believe it's her.

Tears well up in my eye and I wipe them away. "I hadn't heard from you when you said I would. Are you okay? What is going on here?"

"I'm doing okay," she says, pausing to look at Matt. He raises his eyebrow and she nods. I sense her tone change. She is more subdued than a moment ago. "I'm doing good. I love my work. Really."

Matt points to her screen. "Why don't you show us what you've been doing from the backend? Carolyn seems to be a "details" person. It's very exciting. Rebecca is a genius. I wouldn't have been able to do any of this without her. The software developer who started this for me could never strike the proper balance. Another failure was that he used himself as a prototype user. He got too close, too fast. It messed with him."

As soon as Matt turns his back, Rebecca opens her eyes wide and mouths the words, "be careful."

Be careful. The words cut through my core. I was right. This isn't working. Rebecca's not okay here.

Before Matt has a chance to notice, Rebecca swivels her chair around to face her screens and takes a deep breath. There it is: her typical breath that means something's worrying her. I'd know it from anywhere. "The team here is making an app. It's called Haunt Me." She stops abruptly, then to Matt she says, "I can't add any more simulations until I complete the update I told you about, which I can't do until midnight when the system goes offline."

He pulls Rebecca's chair toward him. "What about Barbara?" His voice is sharp. Rebecca flinches and forces a strained smile.

You feel. You understand grief. The words from his notecard to her come back to me. This is all deeply personal for Matt. Matt wants to hear Barbara's voice again. Everything he's doing, all the work on (para)normal is for him and him alone. What has he got Rebecca doing that is terrifying her so much? Why can't she walk away?

I know what it's like to want to see someone again, to hear someone again, to live each day as if this person, this dead person, is with you. Diamond said I'd be able to hear Jennifer. She said I'd be the first. I haven't had a moment to let this sink in. Shouldn't Matt be the first since Haunt Me is his app? Seeing Jennifer, hearing her, it's what I've wanted for twenty-two years. I've daydreamed about this moment and never thought it would happen, but it doesn't feel right. It doesn't feel real. If only I could speak with Rebecca without Matt around.

"She will go offline for a couple hours," Rebecca says slowly, like she's talking down a raging toddler to prevent him from having a tantrum. "She'll be back and better than before. I promise. Diamond has our plan on the roadmap. It's all documented, just how you like it. You know exactly what me and the team are working on."

Matt doesn't respond directly, but he seems to accept this because he lets go of her chair and takes a step back to give her more room.

"Anyway, this is the code," she says, pointing to the screen. "It's not super exciting. Just (para)normal code."

"Oh but it is," Matt chimes. "Remember what we talked about? Mindset is important. You need to remember that your brilliance is attracting investment from people all over the world. Remember, you are the most brilliant coder in the entire world."

"I know. I'm excited." She turns to me again and stands up from her desk. Her eyes tell me everything I need to know. She's absolutely exhausted. I watch as she blinks hard as if to wake herself up. Maybe it's the pregnancy hormones, but maybe it's more.

Rebecca gets up from her desk slowly and approaches me. "Can I get you something to drink or eat? You must be hungry after all that. The glitches can be hard. At least, that's what I've heard. I haven't experienced Haunt Me myself."

She would have every ground to experience the app given her loss. The fact I'm testing the latest update first nags at me more. Why me?

"Soon you will, my dear. Once we roll it out to our exclusive early users, you will have a chance." Matt approaches her again and puts his thin hands on her shoulders to rub them. She backs away.

"Food?" she repeats.

"Umm..." I'm still not sure what happened to me after I drank the lavender tea and I'm not sure if I believe it was a glitch. "That's okay. I'm fine. Besides, I should be getting you something. You should have your feet up."

"I insist. I'll make you a plate. I could use a snack as well." She walks toward the door and as she does, she steps on my foot. It's an accident. At least, I think it is.

"Oh sorry," she says. "I wasn't looking. Silly me."

With these words, I instantly fall back into our old script. "No worries. Happens to the best of us." We've done this exchange countless times before. If she says what I think she's going to say, it means she's in trouble and she wants to get out of here.

"I'm always so clumsy." There it is. She's looking at me like she wants me to remember. I could never forget. It's time to go home. "Should we get going now?"

I turn to follow her out the door.

Matt lunges forward to pull me back. "You're our esteemed guest Carolyn." His voice has more of an edge that wasn't there before. "Rebecca will go to the kitchen and you can wait with me. I'm not finished hearing about your initial experiences yet. I want to learn more about you. Our investors will want to know the details."

Rebecca gives me one backward glance and that's all I need. She's not saying what she needs to say, but we need to get out of here.

I sit across from him. "What is Haunt Me, really?" My voice is shaky, but I keep going. "Why are you selling it? What happened to Ian and where did you put my phone?"

"See, talking is fun," he chuckles. "But I couldn't possibly answer all those questions."

I centre myself. I'll need to be more selective. "Have you been watching me the whole time? I felt like I was being watched the moment we drove into town."

"It's not watching like you think we are watching. Haunt Me is more about simulating an authentic experience than surveillance."

"How is it possible that Jennifer can text?"

He shakes his hand. "During our last development sprint, the focus was conjuring the voice of the loved one. The texts are derived from memories and thoughts of the one being intentionally haunted. Artificial Intelligence helps keep it generative. They are learning from you. You think of your sister often. Please tell me, were the messages getting more accurate as they went on?"

Lynnie.

I shake my head. I can't talk to him about this. I glance at the door. Rebecca should be coming back soon. I listen for her steps, but I don't hear anything. Being without her again, and even Ian, is making me nervous.

"I heard a whisper too. How?"

Matt stares at me. "Impossible. The update hasn't happened yet. You must be mistaken. The upgrade hasn't happened yet," he says firmly.

There is no point arguing with him like this. I'll ask Rebecca about it later. I heard it. I know I did. "I thought this place was about creating an intentional living community? Why even get involved with (para)normal here?"

Matt sits down in Rebecca's chair. "My work is about creating community, yes. Most of the members here are strictly here to work in the garden and enjoy a communal life together, free from debt. But I also wanted to create a service for people that would release them from their grief. Haunt Me is an app that empowers the user to connect with a beloved person in their lives who passed away. We think the conversation doesn't need to stop just because the person is dead. Ultimately, I will make a community of those alive and those unalive. Death is so sad." He frowns.

My cheeks burn red. "I didn't give you permission to use my questionnaire to make a ghost to haunt me."

"We didn't *make* a ghost. Your sister is visiting you, that's an important feat. The figure you are seeing is really her. Besides, you signed off on the terms when Diamond interviewed you. Are you saying that you didn't read them before signing off?" He grins at me.

Of course I didn't read the terms. No one does. People like Matt know this and use it to slip into my privacy.

I glance again at the door. Rebecca still isn't back yet. If she had to walk all the way to the kitchen Ian and I saw when we first got here, she'll be gone awhile. Each minute that goes by that I'm not with Rebecca feels like forever. I need to get us out of here.

"Fine," I say, putting my hands up. "But why bother making this? Death is a part of life."

"I lost someone, and I needed them again in my life. Somehow. I wasn't finished. There wasn't enough time. I wanted to spend the rest of my life with her. The technology was all there to make it work. We've been able to get the data. Even the most hardened person will start talking about their wounds if you ask gently enough."

He swivels the chair around to look at Rebecca's screens. "Rebecca is just so brilliant. There's nothing I want more than to hear Barbara's voice again." He looks off for a minute, distracted by a memory. "Our network can make it happen. I know it can."

Even the most hardened person will start talking about their wounds if you ask gently enough. It's time to start playing his way. "What do you miss most about Barbara's voice?"

He smiles and his face softens. "She was the most amazing person. Creative. Generous. Absolutely stunning. In her voice, I miss her optimism. They say the voice is the first thing we forget when someone dies and I can't let that happen."

"But it won't be her. This is just an app. It's not real."

All the light from his face disappears and he straightens his back, looks me in the eye. "It is real. This app isn't just a bot we've trained to mimic the living. Anyone with an internet connection could do that. Haunt Me *conjures* the dead. The technology we've developed taps into the natural manifestations that happen around us all the time. We have found a way to connect our networks, which is like connecting life to the after-life. It's like making a video call to someone in another city, except…"

I'm quiet for a moment. "But I saw her physically."

"That is what makes Haunt Me truly special. Rebecca need-ed some coaxing to do it, sure. She still has some, some reserva-tions, let's put it that way. But I heard about her master's thesis in (para)normal coding through my network and sought her out. I can be quite convincing when I want to." He brushes back his hair.

The note I found in her room. *The pain will stop when you see her.* "Was she trying to…"

"Yes," he interrupts. "Wouldn't you? She was crushed from the loss. She had no one in her life that understood. I figured that out quickly from the transcript and video of her personality."

The notes on the paper were all for show. It was being recorded the whole time.

"But she said she hasn't used Haunt Me."

He sucks his teeth. "Absolutely not. Once it is launched and out on the market, which it will be soon, she will be permitted. Until then, Haunt Me must remain pure. Developers who see themselves as the edge case make mistakes and when we make mistakes we risk the success of the entire project. We've had tragedies, but I cannot dwell on them. I need to protect my mindset as the leader of his community and this product."

"Why not just hire her and pay her what she's worth, which is a lot. Why embed her in this mall collective?"

Before Matt can continue talking, Rebecca walks into the room with a plate of food. She sets it on the table. "Here you go, fresh from the garden."

She gestures toward the carrots and I take one. She watches me take a slow bite. Matt watches me, too. Do I really believe that the tea he gave me wasn't dosed with something?

"Thank you," I say, setting the rest of the carrot on my plate. Rebecca wouldn't tamper with my food, but I can't take a chance right now.

"I was filling in Carolyn on Haunt Me and our exciting new update," Matt says, walking up to her to pat her on the back. I watch her recoil. "You've made so much progress. I am impressed and grateful for your talents. Bless up and out to you and your child."

I can almost feel her shudder from where I stand, then she closes her eyes slowly and finds a smile. "That's what I'm here for."

"Since it will be a few hours until I can start deploying the code for the enhancement, can I take Carolyn to my room and brief her on what will happen with the update?" Rebecca keeps that smile going. "She needs to understand that she will be the first to hear a voice and what we need from her in order to know the upgrade is safe enough to deploy for everyone." Her voice is deliberate, every word that comes out of her mouth is so clear. Jennifer and I would talk like this when dad was in one of his volatile moods. One wrong word and his anger would be unleashed.

He looks at us both. "Fine. But please join us tonight in the workshop before you start deploying. I am making a big announcement tonight to the greater community. One I have been hoping to make for many years. You really shouldn't miss it. In fact, it's mandatory for everyone here, including you Carolyn. You are one of us now."

Rebecca thanks him and guides me to the door.

Before she can open it, Matt moves in front of us.

"Remember, the update must happen on schedule, and it will be safe for everyone. I can't wait any longer. If it doesn't go as planned, well."

She reaches past him to open the door. "It will," she says, and pushes me into the hall.

23

I follow behind her into the staircase. She doesn't stop until we reach a part of the mall Ian and I hadn't seen. It's a newer area where large stores have been repurposed into private residences. So this is where the members live. We reach her unit, and she swipes the pad with her pass and pushes the door open. Inside is the partially converted RadioShack store she told me about.

I look around. It's cold and sterile here, like the woman's room from the promo video I watched.

"Where's your roommate? Is it safe to talk?" I think about the recording that took place in the trailer with Diamond back in the quay.

"She'll be gone for a few more hours. The gardeners work until six and then they have dinner together. She'll be here to wash up before going down to the dining hall. We're okay."

We sit on a small, thin couch. Rebecca puts her feet up on the coffee table, in what looks like an attempt to get into a comfortable position before she readjusts herself again. Once she is settled, she rests on hands on her belly.

My heart is racing. "What is going on here? Are you really conjuring the dead with your code? You said it yourself that it couldn't work. What about the garden? How is it connected to all this? What's this about me being the first to try the upgrade?"

She looks at me and nods. "I've made the technology work; it's hard to explain. It all clicked for me while I was here because Matt had so much, I don't know, faith in me and my predecessor was on the right track so I had a solid foundation to work from. But it's gotten out of control. The direction he wants to go… it scares me."

"So he's forcing you to do this?"

"Not exactly, no." She hesitates. "He approached me about my coding skills a few weeks before I arrived. I didn't think much of it. We had a few conversations about the potential of his vision. I have only ever done things that were theoretical. I joined this team a little over a month ago after my other guy… fled. Unlike most people here, I have an internet connection. The police found my predecessor dead in the park. I know what's happening on the outside. Collective living doesn't need to be like this."

The timing of her joining the team lines up with when I stopped hearing from her. "Why did you stop sending your letters?"

"It was starting to feel too dangerous. I couldn't risk getting caught. I was getting in far too deep with Haunt Me." She looks down at her hands. "Since you know about it, he's not going to let you leave. You know that by now, right? He'll find a way to parade you around the world as one of our first full users. I wish you would have stayed home, to protect yourself."

I slouch into the couch. "Does this mean I've really been seeing Jennifer. Like, that was actually her?" It feels too strange to process.

She nods. "It's not how I want to use the technology. You can't bring back the dead like this. In my theories, (para)normal is better utilized to connect with those who have passed on in small and meaningful ways. What Matt is pushing me to do is essentially bring them back for good, and no matter how many times I tell him we shouldn't mess with life and death like this, he won't listen. He's rich, so in his mind that translates to know-ing the best."

"Where's Ian?" I haven't seen him since before I passed out. Matt must have told him the details about Haunt Me by now. Being a reporter, it might have been more dangerous for him to learn about this app. I'm still mad at him for lying to me, but I don't want him to get hurt.

"He's alone. He's still here at the mall, but Matt felt he need-ed isolation so he could reflect."

I'm not ready to see him yet anyway. But he was right, something was going on here. Matt is up to something and he's using Rebecca to do it. "We should go home now. I can help you pack."

"You don't understand. I can't just leave."

"You have more power than most here. You have an internet connection!"

"I can't leave because I can't let him continue with Haunt Me in the full capacity he wants. It's not only unethical; it's dangerous. He doesn't care about what this app will do to people. He isn't satisfied with just using it personally to contact Barbara. He's obsessed with scaling and so-called "helping" as many people as he can. The experience is better with more people online, the connections become stronger. The power of the (para)normal coding comes in connecting with as many manifestations as we can as a group. The more crowd power we can tap into, the better the connection is overall. Matt wants the best experience there can be, no matter the sacrifice. It means the digital ghosts can stay around longer, which is essentially bringing them back to life permanently."

I pause. "So you figured it out then? You got (para)normal to work when no one else could."

"He's going about it the wrong way. This is not how it should be used."

I stand up and pace around her small living room. "Rebecca, he won't be able to do the update without you so he can't move forward with the project once you leave. You don't believe in the path Matt wants to take. Pack your bag and let's go."

"No, listen. I can't go without his permission because there's enough to the app that if I leave it in the wrong hands, the mistakes that could happen might be deadly. The update he wants just shouldn't happen; it can't happen. The ghosts cannot talk."

"What's going to happen when the ghosts start to talk?"

She glances over her shoulder.

"You can trust me. I'm here for you." I may not have been before, but I sure am now. I look down at the old cut on my arm and it's finally almost healed.

She closes her eyes. "The feature will give these manifestations their *original* voices back. They will be able to talk and function as if they are still alive."

I think of Jennifer and our encounters so far. She's been quiet, not saying a word. What would she even sound like after all these years?

Her eyes meet mine. "Their voices are not like they were when they were living. Their voices have been dead for some time, some have been dead for decades. With this update, we are not just working with digital manifestations—we are melding together the organic matter of the original person."

She stops and studies my face, as if trying to gauge if I'm still following her. I'm not fully understanding but a decomposing or cremated larynx coming back to life doesn't sound good.

"Don't you understand what I'm getting at?"

I shrug. "I'm getting zombie vibes."

She nods. "Well, in a way, it's like that."

"So if he continues down this path without you, what's the problem? We'll be long gone by then. It's Matt's infrastructure supporting it. He can find someone else who can code in this language. He found you. You can't be the only one who knows what to do."

She sighs deeply again. "It's the voices themselves. They are deadly. When we hear the manifestation's voice, they let out the toxins they've absorbed through their daily life and all the years they've been dead. The toxins have been sitting dormant in their body since they died, but it's like they've been steeping and getting stronger and more potent. That's how I understand it from the modeling I've run, at least. When they talk, this concentrated gas evaporates into the atmosphere and no one can escape it. It will start here in the mall and then spread out into the community. There will be no way to contain it and by the time the public realizes what's going on. We'll all be gone. As I said, the more manifestations Haunt Me has on the network, the more power this program has. The upgrade can't happen. We will be unleashing something that cannot be stopped."

Matt's plans are worse than I could have ever guessed. If he has investors interested at this early stage, I can only imagine who they are eager to get back. It makes my stomach sick. Rebecca is right. This upgrade cannot happen.

"Can you get them to talk without the toxins? Like just make a simulation of talking."

A simulation would work. If the purpose is truly to hear a late loved one's voice, this would work. I would listen to a simulated voice if it was supposed to be Jennifer if it meant I would finally learn what happened to her.

She shakes her head. "There's no way. I have tried to add a synthetic voice function to (para)normal but it either kept glitching or sounded like Siri. It doesn't work. There is no workaround to deliver the authentic experience Matt demands. He thinks he will hear Barbara like she didn't die. He wants everything back and he's not letting anything stand in his way. I've told him about the toxins but he thinks there's a chance it won't happen. He doesn't understand the science. To him, it's worth the risk. And with you here and experiencing such a strong connection with Jennifer, he decided that you will go first in case anything catastrophic happens immediately."

So that's what this whole thing has been about, luring me here so I can be Matt's experimental subject.

"Did Ian know about the upgrade?"

"No, I don't think he did. Matt wasn't happy when he showed up with you, but I don't think he was surprised since he read his articles."

Knowing that Ian wasn't involved in getting me through the doors makes me feel a little better. "Well, we've got to run. That's the only way forward." We need to be anywhere but here.

She looks at me with sympathy and I know in my heart she will not leave while Haunt Me is still operating. It's the same look she gave me when she told me she was leaving our life to come here. Her mind is made up. She's committed to making sure this upgrade never happens. "You know I can't just do that. I won't be able to live with myself. He will find someone else, someone he can easily buy off. Maybe someone who doesn't fully understand what they are facilitating. He offered me all the money in the world to do this work, but I said no."

She looks like she hasn't slept in days. I hadn't noticed the dark circles under her eyes when I first saw her in the computer lab. This isn't the vibrant Rebecca I know. This work is killing her.

"How can I help?" I ask.

"The thing is, Matt wants to make Haunt Me big and common. He thinks there is a market for this and, honestly, he might be right. And the real problem is, he knows so many of the giants in tech that it would be easy for him to scale our work and make SPREAD_AUTHENTICITY a mandatory network. I can guarantee that the infrastructure to run (para)normal is already on most smartphones out there. It wouldn't be too hard to get this going. People don't read the Terms and Conditions. He has lots of friends who can sneak some wording in about this app that will fly over everyone's head."

"Doesn't he understand how hard it can be for people?" The trauma of someone opening their phone one day only to be connecting to a network they didn't know they were connected to. I have no words. I wouldn't wish this on anyone. Diamond gave me a Wi-Fi password and I took it without a second thought. It can happen so fast.

She waves her hand. "We must get ready for the workshop. If we're late, he'll suspect something. He is so anxious to hear Barbara again that he's on edge. If he perceives there's anything that might be getting in the way of the plan, he will lose it. I'm scared how he might escalate it. He could devastate everything around here and fast."

"You can't be serious about this."

She looks at me and sighs. "Very serious. He doesn't care. He thinks he'll be able to clean up the mess or that someone else will do it for it. It's a terrible perspective. He won't back down. There's only one option to get out of this."

"And what's that?"

"We need to destroy Haunt Me. There can be nothing left." I nod and she gives me a relieved smile.

"I'm so glad you're here, Carolyn. Matt kept me away from virtually everyone in the community except during Performance because those are quiet. He was worried I might say something. It has killed me to keep this going."

I smile. "I knew you hated malls."

"Yup, never cared for them at all. I think this community could be very leading edge if it was run as an actual collective, in the truest sense of the word. People supporting people, living together. Matt is holding this place back. Even with all his work with meditation, what we are doing here is still just about investors and line items in a budget." She sits up slowly. "Ugh, I have to go pee. Again. When they say pregnant women pee like twenty times a day, they aren't lying."

Rebecca pushes herself up from the couch.

"Oh," she says and reaches into her pocket. "You should have this back. I think he took it back because he didn't want to give you a chance of engaging with Haunt Me until after the upgrade, but it's not happening so it's okay."

She places my cell phone back into my hands and walks out of the room.

I look at my phone with the screen facing down in my palm. If I open it, there might be a text message from my sister. I study the phone for a moment. All those texts were from her. And, yes, Matt, they had become more specific as time went on. Haunt Me may not have been ethical, but it was working.

I slowly turn it over and see there's another text waiting for me. I open it and feel as if I've been winded.

LYNNIE, PLEASE COME FIND ME IN THE FOOD COURT. I WANT YOU TO KNOW WHAT HAPPENED OUT THERE, SISTER. I'VE WAITED 22 YEARS FOR THIS AND I KNOW YOU HAVE TOO. I WANT YOU TO KNOW THE TRUTH OF WHAT HAPPENED TO ME.

After everything Rebecca has told me, it breaks me that I still have such a strong urge to know what happened to her. Regret has followed me my whole life. To look like Jennifer but not quite has been a constant reminder that the better version of me got lost in the woods and was never found.

Her last message feels like a jolt to the heart.

I WANT YOU TO KNOW THE TRUTH.

I have always wanted to know the truth, no matter how brutal it was. Matt said the messages are enhanced with AI learning.

Maybe none of this is real. But what if there is a nugget of truth in it? Haunt Me might be my only chance to know for sure what I've agonized about for the last two decades. If the plan is to destroy Haunt Me tonight instead of doing the update, then maybe a quick trip back into the abandoned part of the mall to see Jennifer one last time couldn't hurt. She's only a digital ghost after all, not a real one, and this will be my last chance to see her ever again.

But first I need to fix my hair because we're heading to community Performance.

24

Rebecca and I make our way to the old Target to hear Matt's announcement. Jennifer's last text about meeting her in the food court feels like it's beating in my pocket. Before we left Rebecca's room, she told me how serious Matt takes the prescription of silence during Performance. There would be no talking once we got close to the old Target store.

"You okay?" Rebecca mouths. I nod, then I take a deep breath trying to keep it all together.

The closer we get, the more people we walk among. Soon hundreds of people are walking in the same direction. I'm shocked by the size of the crowd. This is much more than we saw in the garden. The crowd moves without a sound.

I whisper to Rebecca, "Where did all these people come from? There was a fraction of this many people in the garden."

"The garden is the backbone," she whispers. "Matt wants everyone here to sign up for Haunt Me as prototype users. Right now, most of them are on the network but they haven't experienced anything yet. I've been trying to delay this. It's his next milestone after the upgrade. He will do anything to get more ghosts on the network."

"That's why he gave everyone tablets."

Rebecca stops. "How did you know that?"

"I connected with a woman online who was searching for her sister here. Rane."

She pulls me toward the side of the room. Everyone is very quiet as they walk in, but there is still enough padding of feet on the cement floor that nobody looks our way. "Rane came here looking for her sister. Matt said he took care of it. I don't know what happened. I don't know who her sister is."

"How do you know Rane was here?"

"It happened when I first arrived. Everyone was acting really weird. Diamond was here, which I now know was odd because she runs recruitment and is rarely here. She told me there had been a leak of confidential information and Matt was certain it came from her team. She's ambitious. She wants him to trust her enough to run a separate community in one of the other malls he owns."

"When I spoke with Rane," I say. "She said she still hadn't found her sister and that she felt like she was being watched." She also told me she didn't know where the mall actually was.

Rebecca nods. "It's entirely possible. She had probably connected to the network and was put in the Haunt Me application in the early days. The early days of this app were bad and traumatizing for everyone with a connection. I have a hard time sleeping because of it, even though it was the previous programmer who did it. He didn't understand (para)normal as much as me. Just because people do not read about what they are signing up for, doesn't mean a person should be forced into traumatizing situations. We had early community members volunteer to help, loyal ones too, and all but one escaped the mall in hopes they would break the network and be free. Now Matt keeps the project locked down."

"Why didn't you remove them from the app?"

She takes a long blink and I'm not sure if she's trying to hold back tears. "Matt made me grant him full profile administration rights. That means he's in complete control over who is or isn't registered in the app, and since he knows that the more people in the network makes the manifestations stronger, he leaves everyone in simply for the power. There is no physical way to get far enough from the network, even if you toss your phone. Once you are connected, it transcends phones. I wish I could reverse all this damage, but in many cases, it's too late. That's why it needs to be destroyed. Fully. We may not be able to truly right our wrongs, but we can put a stop to something that could become unstoppable very soon."

We move from the wall and continue walking toward the stage area. It's a long shot, but I scan the crowd for Ian. I don't see him, but I see his niece I met in the hallway. She's alone.

"That's the girl I saw earlier. She said she saw her mom? I'm guessing she was using Haunt Me?"

"That's Violet. A sweet girl. He even has kids on the network, his own included. I worry about them the most. They might not understand what they are experiencing."

"Is she wanting to hear Barbara's voice?"

"I don't think she really understands. If anything, she wants to be with her dad doing normal kid stuff. Haunt Me has consumed all his time and energy."

Just then, the crowd quiets down. The overhead lights dim on the crowd and stage lights shine on Matt.

"Some people in the community," he says as he looks across the audience back and forth, "have started to ask some questions about our work here, and rightfully so. This is an intelligent group of people, and I wouldn't expect anything less. That is why you were carefully chosen to live in this community."

Suddenly a low buzzing sound fills the space. A couple people next to me start whispering to each other, and then others start talking amongst themselves too.

"It's the buzzing. You're wondering how our little bees can *be* so loud." He laughs to himself, trying to squint over the stage lights. "Well, it's time for me to tell you all what we've been doing here, in addition to the good and important work you've been doing outside for us all. You are sustaining us physically and I want to start helping you emotionally. It's time for you all to connect with your pasts so you can heal."

He motions to someone off stage. Ian comes walking out, his head hangs low.

"But first. This is my esteemed cousin. Say hi, Ian."

Ian looks at the crowd and gives a weak wave. He won't be able to see me with the stage lights glaring in his eyes. His shoulders are slouched and he looks tired as he brushes a piece of his hair out of his eyes.

"Ian was trying to shut us down, and many people were trying to figure out why anyone would do such a thing. You see, he's a journalist and a good one, I'll admit. It's time he start using his talents for good. He is writing my memoir, and he will also moderate us in a community-wide dialogue. I want to know how everyone feels about seeing someone special who has passed on. Let's talk, everyone!"

Matt gestures to him to approach the microphone. Ian steps up to it but doesn't say anything. He looks back at Matt, who motions him to go forward again. "That's right," Ian says slowly. "I'll be here to help with the conversation."

I nudge Rebecca. "His mandatory meeting is a community dialogue?"

She shrugs. From all I've learned about Matt, it could have been worse.

"What's with the buzzing? It's all I hear," someone shouts from the audience. "It's creeping me out. I can't sleep. I can't think. It's painful."

People in the crowd agree. Matt looks at Ian, then slowly nods his head with his eyes tightly shut. After a long pause he opens his eyes and breathes deeply. "It's time I told you all. You have been hearing the hum of our network. It's getting more powerful because we've all been contributing to it," he says. "If you are really quiet, you can hear it working in the background, creating important linkages to sustain us. You will all be added to Haunt Me, an app that creates authentic and long-term connections with a person who passed away. Eventually there will be a subscription option, but everyone here will be registered for free."

People around us start whispering.

"I didn't give you permission for that." Someone else yells, this is also followed by echoes of others saying the same thing. A shoe flies from the audience onto the stage, narrowly missing Ian in the face.

"I can't do this, Matt. It's on you. I don't care anymore. Do with me what you will." Ian walks off stage.

"I want to leave, but I can't because my debt is owed to you." Someone yells. "I'm committed to you and I don't want to be anymore. I'd like to go home. I miss my family."

"There is no time-debt here," Matt says, his face darkening. "When I pay off the loans for all of you here, it's a gift. You are free of your loans and can leave here whenever you want. I choose who comes here carefully. If you want to leave, you are free to pack your things and go, but…"

Matt stops talking and tries again to peer over the stage lights into the audience. He scans until his eyes land on Rebecca. "We're doing a major feature upgrade to the network tonight. Just watch, you'll all see. You may also begin to see an important person from your past. It could be a sibling, a parent, or any figure in history. Conjure them and they will come. I have investors coming this weekend to see it in action. They are interested in bringing back the heroes, the defining leaders of our past, back to life. They understand that Haunt Me is a legacy in the making."

I look at Rebecca. "Haunt Me can bring back people that a person doesn't even know personally?"

Any remaining colour she had drains from her face. "No, no, that isn't on the roadmap. I would have never agreed to that. This was supposed to be about making connections with loved ones. There needs to be authentic experiences with the person for the AI to work in real and meaningful ways. It generates meaning from authentic memories deep in a person's subconscious. If there aren't real memories, the ghosts could become anything the person imagines. It's not how the technology is ethically used."

The whole crowd starts talking to each other and their conversations take over the buzzing sound. It's a relief to hear people's voices instead of the artificial buzzing of the network.

"No, no," Matt says, pacing the stage. "Please, I ask all of you to be quiet so the network can do good work. You'll see. This is important. We can talk one at a time."

Instead, the crowd gets louder. I feel a tap on my shoulder and turn around. Ian is behind me.

"We need to get out of here," he says. "I'm sorry I lied to you, I shouldn't have. This is not how I imagined things working out. I honestly thought my terrible cousin was simply laundering money like his dad did and this community was a front for a billion-dollar operation. I had no idea he was this out of it. He has told me way too much. This place is not safe for anyone. His deal with the investors is shocking. They want to bring back some truly disturbing people and Matt is about to lay out the red carpet to make it happen."

"We have a plan," Rebecca says. "Come with us."

Ian and I follow Rebecca out of the old Target and back to her room.

She sits down at her small dinette table. She's trembling. I'm worried how all this stress will impact her. She rubs her belly again and it hits me. Is Matt the dad? Could her child be his eleventh? Is that another reason why Diamond was jealous? I can't ask. It's none of my business how she chooses to get pregnant. I have learned that after what happened with Steve.

Ian sits across from her. "He wants me to continue writing his memoir, a "history-in-the-making-take," as he called it, on what he's been able to accomplish with this community. The debt he has freed people from, the communal life, living well with the dead, and Haunt Me. Of course, he wants me to write it with a traditional Hero's Journey Arch because that's how he sees himself."

When he says this, I'm overwhelmed with an image of Jennifer's face from earlier in Rebecca's nursery, her torn cheek oozing with fresh blood.

COME FIND ME IN THE FOOD COURT.

If she can't talk yet, why does her digital ghost want to meet me? Why does she want to see me again?

"I'm not doing the update," Rebecca says. "But he can't know this is happening. If I don't do the upgrade, he is threatening to pull the plug on the whole mall and there are so many people here who have sacrificed a lot to join and believe in what they are doing by working together."

I roll up my sleeve and feel for my cut. I feel the ridges of a healing scab. "Why include old wounds in Haunt Me? He said it was about getting people to re-evaluate why they got them? It doesn't seem to fit. The wound that I have, well, that was connected to you and not Jennifer."

She looks at her hands. "Yeah, I'm sorry you've had to relive that one."

"It's okay now, but I wonder why include it? If the purpose behind Haunt Me is to connect the living with digital ghosts, then reopening a random wound seems more painful and distracting than productive."

"Matt thinks he knows better, that he can facilitate better people by forcing them into situations where they need to learn. As if he should talk. He is the least adjusted person I know."

"So it was all about mindset and reflection?"

"It was about power," she says firmly. "He knew (para)normal could do this, so he included it on the roadmap. The all-important roadmap that dear Sergeant Diamond manages."

It seems the tone I sensed when Diamond called Rebecca precious is mutual. Before I can ask her anything further, the door bursts open and Matt strides in followed by a man I haven't seen before.

"That did not go as planned," Matt wallows. "I thought they would have been inspired by the plans for Haunt Me. Not everyone gets an opportunity to see a major historic moment happen right before their eyes. And to be part of it, well, it's like nothing else."

I glance at Rebecca. She managed to sneak to the other side of the room, as far away from Matt as she can be without him noticing.

"Ian, are you getting all this down? I am facing challenges, but as a leader I will pull through with my leadership. I know what I need to do." He straightens his posture like he's getting ready to pose for a photoshoot for another business magazine.

Ian flips open his notebook and takes his pen out but doesn't take the lid off. He taps the butt of the pen on his page. "And what's that?"

"Change of plans. We're doing the update as soon as possible. We don't need to wait until midnight for the system to go offline. Rebecca, you can do it now. I give you permission to take Haunt Me into maintenance mode right away. Barb hasn't presented herself to me in a while anyway. The connection is not strong enough to bring us together like I need it to be."

Rebecca waves her hand into a stop sign as if this simple gesture would be enough to change his mind. "Now's not going to work. I need longer to prepare. There are things I need to do before the update can happen the way it needs to happen. The time between now and midnight is what it takes to make sure everything goes smoothly."

Matt steps toward us and grabs one of the chairs at her dinette and flings it toward one of the bedroom doors. It lands with a crash that reverberates through the room. Nobody moves. The violence of his action transports me back to my childhood home when dad was mad and wanted everyone to know it.

"I don't think you're listening to what I'm saying, Rebecca. You *will* do it now. I expect you back in your office doing whatever it is you need to do right away. I will not have the people in this community go without seeing their late loved ones any longer. We owe it to them. We owe it to our future investors and, most of all, we owe it to the world. Once the community sees it, they will transform into believers. Everyone deserves hope and that's what we'll provide for them."

Ian tosses his notebook on the table and crosses his arms. "Are you listening to yourself right now?"

Matt goes still. His gaze moves from Rebecca to Ian. "James?"

The man who came in with Matt joins him.

"James, I need you to bring Ian back to his special quarters. He can't be trusted out and about when Rebecca needs to concentrate on the update. Mindset is important and my cousin here is a poison with the ability to kill all the positive work we've accomplished so far. Always has been, always will be. It's a shame really, but that's how it goes for some people. And they wonder why they can't get ahead?"

James clears his throat. He's around the same age as us and has a chestnut brown beard that matches his brown eyes. "I'll make sure he gets there."

"Perfect. Now I must leave. I need to reschedule all the video calls I had with the investors to witness Carolyn hear her long-lost sister after twenty-two years. It will happen in two hours." He stops and walks over to Rebecca. He places his hands on her belly. "I believe in you. You won't disappoint me because you know the consequences if you do. Remember, I keep my word. Always."

25

The moment Matt closes the door behind him, I let the prickling feeling of dread I'd been holding back while he was talking to us wash over me. I'm going to hear Jennifer talk in two hours and simultaneously become exposed to a concoction of the most damaging toxins this earth has yet to experience. It's too overwhelming to comprehend.

"Ian, you've got to come with me now. Let's make this easy for everyone." James casually gestures to the door. It's like he's gone from Matt's hired gun to a relaxed usher at a discount movie theatre in a matter of seconds.

Something about the way he's acting now that Matt is gone puts me at ease, just a little. Maybe he's one of us. Someone forced to play the caricature Matt wants.

"How much debt did he buy back for you?" I can't help myself. I must know.

He hesitates then answers flatly, "Almost $250,000."

I'm too stunned to ask anything further. That is an incredible amount of money.

"I almost finished my medical degree and had to stop when my dad got sick with cancer. When he died, there was too much going on to pick it up again. Believe it or not, an almost finished medical degree doesn't mean much out there. With the modest job I managed to get, I couldn't keep up with my bills."

Before I can ask another question, I feel a tug at my hand. I turn around and Ian's starring at me.

"I need to talk to you." He's giving me puppy dog eyes and for a moment it has the power to make me forget why I'm mad at him. "I'm sorry I lied about knowing Matt."

"You didn't just know him. You're related to him. A cousin is a close family member."

He frowns. "My feelings for you are real. When this is over, I hope you'll stay in my life. I want to get to know you more. I don't want this to end. We have a spark. You can't deny that."

James takes Ian by the elbow and guides him to the door, and they're gone.

Ian's words touch something within me that I hadn't wanted to think about since I found out he was Matt's cousin. I felt that spark too. When I found out he lied about knowing Matt, it hurt more than I thought it would. I hadn't felt a spark like that with anyone for some time, but I don't know if I can ever trust him again. He could have told me he knew Matt and I probably still would have come here with him. Lying was totally unnecessary. It was his feelings of not measuring up that I resonated with as well. That at least he seemed sincere about.

I hear a sniffle behind me. Rebecca is sitting on her little couch with her head in her hands. I join her.

"It's going to be okay." I don't think I believe it myself but maybe she will.

"No, it won't." She sits up and wipes away tears from one of her red eyes. "With this change in timeline, there won't be enough time to destroy everything. Haunt Me is backed up on various cloud-based servers all over the country. I have remote login access to them all, but he'll know I'm up to something when I can't start the demo on time."

The demo for the investors. I sit back and look up at the ceiling. What will Jennifer say to me? What will a decomposed voice sound like? I've always wanted to know what happened to her, but not like this.

"I'll do the demo and then you can destroy the code."

She sits up. "I'm not letting you sacrifice yourself like that. As I told you, there is no turning back once I start this update. I can't make it work."

We sit in silence for a moment then an idea comes to me.

"What if I'm not around for the demo. What if I leave the mall."

She sighs. "You can't leave the mall. He let you in when you and Ian first got here, but there is no way he will let you out.

People only leave if he lets them leave. That's the truth of it." She looks at her Smartwatch. "I'm going to have to get going soon. I don't want him coming back here and snooping around." She rubs her belly.

Matt mentioned he hadn't seen Barbara's ghost in a while. The last text I received from Jennifer asked me to meet her in the old food court.

"If he won't let me leave, what if I hide? He can't do a demo with me if he can't find me. I'll go into the old part of the mall. He can't watch that part of the mall as easily."

She takes a deep breath. "He has some surveillance over there, but yes, you are right, it's not as refined as it is over on this side. It could work, but when he finds you, he is going to be angry. Like really angry."

"I'll be fine. It's nothing I can't handle." I get up from the couch. "Text me when it's time to destroy the code."

She shakes her head. "Be careful over there. If you see her, remember things are different now. The system needed a major patch, but I didn't do it so I could further weaken the connections. That's one of the reasons for the glitches. If you get too close to Jennifer, the glitch could hurt. If you see her, turn the other way. She won't follow you. She doesn't have enough of a signal right now. I will work as quickly as I can on ditching the code." She pushes a passkey into my hand, hugs me, and then she walks to her room.

I take off down the hallway. If I remember correctly, I need to walk through the garden again and then swipe the pass to get back where the food court is. If I'm fast, I should be able to get there without anyone noticing me.

At the end of the hallway, I reach a door and swipe the pass. I'm back in the dining area where Ian and I first entered the renovated part of the mall. It's empty. I see the door we went through first, the one that led us to the offices and then to the Performance space and beyond. How might our experience here have been different if we chose the door that led straight to the residences? A chill runs through me just thinking about my first encounter with Jennifer in the bathtub of Rebecca's nursery.

I quickly make my way across the floor to the door I know will bring me right back to the garden. Before I take another step, a loud whistle pieces the air.

"Where do you think you're going?"

I don't even need to turn around to know Diamond is standing there.

"Matt changed the roadmap. The timelines have shifted. We need you back in the offices. Get ready for your close up. You're not ruining our chance to impress the investors with any games."

I turn to face her. Instead of her usual overalls and linen shirts, she's wearing a well-fitted black suit and her hair is pulled back into a slick bun. "Matt is busy with the reschedule but it is happening so you must get ready. You're going to talk to your sister." She claps with an eager joy I find repulsive. If I had more time, I would slap this woman.

But perhaps she doesn't know what the consequences are. It's clear that Rebecca and Diamond have some sort of rivalry. Maybe Rebecca hasn't enlightened her about the problem.

"You know that can't happen, Diamond."

She crosses her arms. "Both you and Rebecca are so difficult. I have said this the entire time. Rebecca may be "gifted," but it comes at a price, and the price is her pious attitude. We are trying to bring an important service to people. It's pure. People can do with it what they want."

"When people are in the midst of grief, I agree, it's hard to say goodbye. Trust me, I've been there, but you can't bring people who have passed on back to life in this aggressive way. They should not be able to talk. Their voices are dead and toxic. The upgrade will be catastrophic. Rebecca has informed the team about this."

She shakes her head. "It's what Matt wants. He built all of this, and I don't think people really understand how great he is. He is amazing. A true visionary. He can change the world."

"The update will unleash a toxic chemical into the environment that would wipe everyone in its path out. That is far from visionary. It's selfish."

Suddenly Diamond runs up and grabs me, attempting to pull me back to the other side of the room. I pull away and sprint back to the door. Before I make it, my legs are knocked out from under me and I fall. My body hits the floor with a thud and the pain shoots through me fast, but I manage to scramble back to my feet.

"What was that? A tackle?"

"You need to come with me. Rebecca is back there getting everything ready. What kind of friend would make a run for it when she has everything riding on this?"

Matt's final words to us come back to me. *I keep my word. Always.*

"What is their deal? How does he keep her tethered to this project?"

She sighs. "I don't like it, but he says she can run the mall the way she wants if Haunt Me is developed exactly as he asks. I'm not happy about it because Rebecca doesn't even have an interest in the mall aspect of the business, but she gets her own mall anyway. It's all because…" She stops.

"Because what?" I think I know what she's going to say, but I want her to confirm it. "Because?"

"Oh, nothing. Matt's private. It's none of your business. What you need to do is come with me back to the office so you can get ready to hear your sister. Onward."

She reaches for my arm again, but I dodge her. "I'm not going anywhere with you. You will let me leave the dining room and go my own way."

Diamond moves in closer to me, this time trying to grab my hand. "You're not getting this. I'm not the one with the control. I am doing what he asks of me."

"Then let me go. You don't have to let him know you saw me. Turn around and go back to the office and let me take this lead."

She studies my face and when I think she's going to let me continue on my way, she swipes toward me again. Before she can latch her fingers into me, she stoops down and clutches her ears in pain. I turn back to see what is happening because I don't hear anything. I feel the balloon in my lungs start to fill up once again, but I'm quick to diffuse it. When I look at the door out to the garden, the door I need to go through, I see that it's vibrating just like the door back to the Performance space had when I was in the maintenance hall. Mud gushes through the bottom of the door, cascading its way over to us. Diamond is writhing on the floor in pain. The mud will reach us any moment. She's too distracted by whatever is going on in her head to notice what's coming our way.

Rebecca had said the connections are weak right now and glitches were possible. Painful glitches. I hadn't thought of Diamond as someone grieving or that she might be experiencing a digital ghost prototype of her passed loved one as well, but perhaps she is. Even still, it's not enough for me to feel sympathy for her.

Before the mud gets closer, I look at her on the floor and the glimmer of her diamond-studded cheek catches the light. She wasn't going to let me leave this dining hall on my own. She isn't like the rest of us, she strived to please Matt, no matter who she had to step over to make it happen.

"Make it stop," she cries. "Please make it stop."

I step over her and stomp through the bubbling layer of mud that is now moments from washing over Diamond. I swipe my pass and enter the garden.

The garden is empty. Did the members leave when they saw the mud? Or is the heavy rain keeping them from working today? I pull my hoodie over my head. Mud covers the entire surface. I follow a stream of it all the way to the door that leads back to the old part of the mall.

I WANT YOU TO KNOW THE TRUTH.

How can Jennifer tell me the truth when she hasn't had the update and never will? She can't speak and something is keeping her from telling me in a text. But didn't I hear her call out to me. *Lynnie.* That was her. It had to have been.

I tread through the mud, feeling the coldness of it slip between the toes of my sandals. I rest my hand on the doorknob that will bring me back to the food court. This is it. I swipe the pass and open the heavy door. I'm back in the crumbling wing of the mall.

Inside, the mud is gone. It's dry and everything looks like it did when I was here with Ian. Maybe Diamond didn't see the mud. Maybe she was asking me to stop the buzzing in her ears but had no idea about the mud. Glitches could be different for everyone.

Rain wails on the foggy skylights above, providing me with just enough light to see where I am. I move quietly. The food court area is just around the corner. Jennifer is just around the corner. It's happening.

I walk through the mall, careful never to get too close to the piles of glass. Then I stop. I hear something. I listen closer. It's laughter. I turn to see who it's coming from and out of the corner of my eye I see the flash of a pink jacket on a small girl.

"Violet?" I whisper. "Are you here? Does your dad know you are here?"

I wait for her to come out but stop when I hear a huge crash behind me. A large storage rack from one of the old stores has been pushed over into the middle of the corridor.

Jennifer is standing on the other side of it in the doorway of a shop; a thick layer of mud reaches the knees of her torn jeans. Did she slip off a mountain? Is that how she died? Is mud to blame?

She turns and walks into the store, and I follow. I walk over thick piles of broken glass and shreds of an old banner that reads, *LAST CHANCE CLEARANCE.* I enter the store and what I see, where she has led me, takes my breath away. We're in a bookstore together. One more time. Yellowing paperbacks still line old wire shelves. Posters for author events curl off the walls. A long vine falls from a duct in the ceiling all the way down to brush the old brown carpet. A stuffed chair is faded and worn but reminds me immediately of going to the bookstore with Jennifer and waiting as she sat on a chair just like this one while she read a page or two from the stack of books in front of her. She only had enough money to buy one or two so her decision on which book to buy had to be perfect. I wipe a tear away as the memory feels so vivid.

I look up and she's in front of me. The mud is gone from her jeans now. Her face doesn't have the claw marks from before.

She gestures to me to go with her. I follow her down a narrow aisle until she stops, then she takes a book off the shelf, opens it and scans the page. She points to a word. I nod, and then she points to another word and another. I look up at her and take in her kind eyes. This could be the last time I see her.

"Carolyn." A voice butts into my moment with Jennifer, interrupting our connection. I turn around and see Matt peering at us from the end of the aisle. "That wasn't very nice of you to wander off when I need you to do the demo for the investors. There's a lot riding on this. Don't worry, Jennifer will be able to tell you everything soon. You'll get to hear her say it. It will be a better experience that way. Dialogue is key to any healthy relationship."

When I turn back, Jennifer is gone and the book she was showing me is lying in a puddle of rain on the floor.

26

"I found her. Our little runaway, Carolyn," he says as he pushes me into the office. Rebecca and Ian are sitting at a table. The dark circles under Rebecca's eyes look worse than before.

"Now that we are almost ready, I'm going to get Diamond who will help me set up the call with the investors. I can never figure out how to let them into the "room." I never had to work in the modern office. Some of these tools are not easy." Before he leaves, he turns around and glares at me. "Don't go anywhere. I mean it." Then he leaves.

"What happened? I thought you were hiding."

I can't talk about what happened with Jennifer, not yet.

Ian throws his hands up. "So we're doing it? We're letting Carolyn go through with this, seriously? Matt is going to be back any minute. It's not safe for her. If I could go in her place, I would."

He tries to get me to look at him, but I look ahead to Rebecca instead. I don't have the head space for Ian's blue eyes and dimples right now.

"There is one option," Rebecca says, a grin forming on her face. "It's the only thing I can think that bridges the gap between keeping the mall open and satisfying Matt so he thinks he's getting what he wants."

Ian and I look at each other. "Go on?" he says carefully.

"There is a way I can run the update as a test with only one dataset."

"Barbara's," Ian says with a nod.

"Yes, Barbara's. I can restrict the update to a test, but it means Matt will experience the destruction of the voice. He will be exposed to the toxins and it's beyond anything his vitamin IV detoxes can battle. I don't know how long it will take for him to show damage from the exposure, but maybe that's his problem and he alone? We need to do this."

"How will we get him to go first? He wants me to take the risk, to be the experiment."

"I'll talk to him and convince him to be the pioneer. The idea will appeal to him. To be the first."

"Are you sure he truly understands what he's about to do with this upgrade?"

"I've told him many times, but he is adamant. He's heartbroken and he wants to know for certain that Barbara forgives him. He will do anything in his power to ensure that."

"Well," I say, walking over to them at the table. "It's the only thing we can do. How can we help?"

"Matt is hands-on, even though he knows absolutely nothing about (para)normal or programming. I need someone to keep him busy so he doesn't notice I'm only running a short dataset. We have over five thousand test cases in Haunt Me, so he'll notice if something's up quickly."

"I can do that," Ian says. "I'll ask him for an interview for his memoir. He will just love it. I won't, but that's okay."

Just as we are starting to feel relieved there's a knock at the door, then the beep of a pass, and Matt enters the room.

"It's time," he says. "The investors are 'waiting' online and excited to be the first to hear about your work, Rebecca. I've told them amazing things about you. They are dying to see it. But first I need to speak with my love. Barbara always calmed me down. In a way, she was my advisor."

"Are you sure?" Rebecca says. "You know the risks."

Matt shakes his head. "It will be fine, my dear. Trust the process. Everyone, let's go. Carolyn, it's time for you to hear Jennifer. You go first."

I glance at Rebecca and she nods. Our plan is happening. We follow Matt back to Rebecca's desk. Matt is hovering over Rebecca's shoulder, watching every click she makes with her mouse.

"I assure you, an upgrade isn't that exciting. Can you give me some space?" She looks up at him. "You have nothing to be worried about. I've got everything under control. You can prepare yourself to see Barbara again."

"Carolyn is going first. She deserves it."

"I've been thinking about that," Rebecca says. "I have been running modeling of the upgrade to ensure everything goes well, and I think I found a way to mitigate the toxins I mentioned before."

Matt's eyes widened. "Are you sure?"

She smiles. "I'm sure."

"Don't you want to go first, Carolyn?" he asks suspiciously. "Unlike me, you don't truly know how your loved one passed. Hasn't that been picking at you your whole life?"

"I believe that you should experience it first. It only makes sense since Haunt Me is your vision. It's because of you that we have this app." I force a tense smile.

"It has been hard with Barbara offline these last few hours. I can't wait to see her and more importantly, I can't wait to hear her lovely voice." He sounds far away for a moment, then he snaps back. "Okay, I'll do it. Thank you for working through the little issue of the toxins. The investors will be thrilled. No one likes the bad press that comes with ecological disaster. Can you blame them?"

Once Haunt Me is destroyed, Jennifer will be gone, too. Our moment together in the bookstore. The words she shared come back to me. Before I can let myself replay what she showed me, I'm pulled back into the present. I need to stay sharp so I can support Rebecca.

"Okay," Rebecca says, swiveling her chair around to look at us. "I'm going to get the upgrade going."

Ian takes his cue to take Matt by the elbow to ask him something on the other side of the room. Matt launches in his polished Haunt Me elevator pitch.

I watch as Rebecca expertly opens her files and starts typing. The update has begun. As she waits, she looks around nervously.

"Is everything okay?" I whisper. "Can you do it?"

"I don't know how he he's going to react. Everything with (para)normal is new. Even though I hate him with everything I have, I'm nervous about what's about to happen with even just Barbara's Haunt Me functions updated. Any amount of toxins into the environment is not helping."

"We've got to get Matt in another room so we don't accidentally hear Barbara. We'd all be exposed." She rubs her belly.

I walk over to Matt and Ian. "Where will you connect with Barbara? She'll be back online shortly. She will be ready to talk to you."

Matt looks excited. "Um, how about in the garden? The new one, where no one has been stationed yet. I want to be surrounded by nature, but I don't want anyone around. This is a very special moment, but I'd like you to be there Ian, for memoir writing purposes. I want to record exactly how I reacted when I experienced the technology first. We must capture my genuine captivation. She is the love of my life."

"Wouldn't you want to exchange a few words alone?" I suggest. "Ian can always come in after."

"No, authenticity is key. I want my memoir to be as raw and real as I can make it. I will be hearing the love of my life's voice again after I lost her tragically. This is the biggest thing I can wish for. I might want Violet there, too. She misses her mom."

"No," Rebecca says from across the room. "Not Violet, and not Ian. Haunt Me is about *your* dreams coming true. After all, none of this would be possible without you. You should experience it without an audience to be as authentic as you can. Both Violet and Ian can meet Barbara first thing afterward. I'm sure you have things to tell her, in private. I'll set you two up in your meditation room. It's secure and private."

And far away from the residences and everyone else. It also has a large glass window looking into the Performance space so we can watch what's happening to Matt.

Matt looks at Rebecca and sighs. "Perhaps you're right, as usual. Barbara may have been my advisor, but you are my teacher. It may be too overwhelming to see her with someone else there. I know what I'm going to say and I'm eager to tell her. I want her forgiveness."

"Forgiveness for what?" I ask. I have wanted forgiveness from Jennifer for years. It has felt like an incomplete part of my life. What does Matt need forgiveness for?

Matt hesitates and then takes a deep breath. "I'm the reason she's dead. It didn't need to be this way."

Ian looks up from his notebook. "Why is that?"

"I was convinced she could fix her disease with juices and tinctures and sunshine and clean air. Feelings of gratitude. Cleansing yoga. She followed what I said because she trusted me. By the time she got to the chemotherapy she needed, the cancer had invaded every part of her body. It was too late. Nobody knows I gave her this advice. She always respected our bond. It's a secret that follows me. Violet doesn't know. I could have provided Barbara with the best cancer treatments in the world. If she got the treatment, there is a very good chance she'd still be alive. I need to make it up to Violet and Barbara. This is the only way."

Rebecca looks up from her screen. "Just a few more minutes and the upgrade will be complete. Are you sure about this, Matt? There's no turning back. It will be too impossible to roll back."

A soberness settles over Matt's face. "I'm sure," he says with a nod. "Let me hear her. I need to tell her I'm sorry. I need to know if she will forgive me. Then I need her to be with Violet. She needs her mom."

"Then it's time to get into your meditation space. She'll be coming there in the next couple of minutes. You need to be there waiting. There isn't much time. I don't know how this will all work out."

Matt turns and walks out of the room. But before he does, he thanks Rebecca. "With all of my heart, you are truly exceptional."

I know this. Everyone who meets Rebecca knows this almost instantly.

He shuts the door and is gone. I listen for Matt's footsteps to fade away and once I do, all three of us follow the hallway to his meditation room. "We need to lock this door so he can't leave." Rebecca walks up and flicks the latch shut. He sits on a mat with his legs crossed. He looks at ease. We sit outside the window on the Performance meditation pillows.

Within moments, Barbara appears out of nowhere. She's wearing a beautiful long white dress. He stands up and walks toward her. She winces when she sees him and closes her eyes. He takes her in his arms, and whispers something in her ear. And that's when we see her lips slowly move. I can't hear what she's saying. But Matt immediately lets her go. He falls to his knees and she continues talking, her mouth opening wider and wider. She's talking fast. She looks frustrated and angry. She stomps her feet. I'm not a lip reader, but I think she's swearing at him. He tries to get up to reach the door to leave. He starts coughing and then starts grabbing his throat.

"It's happening faster than I thought. I warned him, but you can't sway a self person. We all make our own choices." Rebecca gets up from her pillow and stands right outside the glass.

Barbara keeps talking. She doesn't know what's coming out of her body. She's stopped swearing and now looks like she's on the verge of tears. She puts her hand over her heart.

Matt lunges toward the window, and he covers his nose. He bangs the glass, throwing his body against it, but the glass holds. He screams, *help me*, then covers his face with his hands.

"No, we will not be helping you." Rebecca folds her arms and shakes her head. "Sorry."

I turn to Rebecca. "The glass might break soon. Rebecca. Should we get moving?"

"We need to destroy Haunt Me while we can. Every single line of it. It's the only way she will disappear and this will be over."

"This means I'll never see Jennifer again."

Rebecca looks at me, her face softening. "Yes, but maybe it's better not knowing. It's harder, yes, but seeing her the way you have been has been difficult, hasn't it? Something is missing. The time in between. The ghost cannot advance like we can. These manifestations aren't really them. You will never know what the spirit of your sister was truly and what was AI learning to be her."

"I saw her one last time when I went back to the old food court. She had a message for me."

"What was it?"

"She pointed to these words in an old book that had been lying on that bookstore floor for over a decade. The words were: *love you always*. That is the truth she wanted me to know." My eyes pool with tears.

Rebecca draws me into a hug. "That is the true power of (para)normal. A connection like that is how this technology should be used. Not the way that Matt wants it. I am happy you got to experience this."

The times I saw Jennifer earlier, before I knew what Haunt Me was, come back to me. Claw marks, cracked lips, pale skin, mud caked on her ripped jeans. All these images were my darkest fears of how Jennifer ended up and Haunt Me was learning from me to exploit them to make me more vulnerable. If Haunt Me thrived on fear, how was she able to connect with me on a true emotional level like this in the bookstore? Before I can ask Rebecca, she returns to her computer and nods at me and Ian, then she smiles.

"Haunt Me needs to end now. Matt doesn't deserve a moment's grace." With the help of Ian, we delete everything. All three of us stand there watching the computer screen while the script does the job or erasing the system. It feels good to watch all the code fly off the screen.

Once the code is gone, we find Matt exactly where we left him. He's laying on the ground in the fetal position. Barbara is gone, which is a good sign because it demonstrates our destruction of the code was successful. Ian unlocks the door.

"Matt?" Ian leans down beside him and checks for a pulse. "He's okay, I think."

Matt's face is pale and wet with sweat. He turns onto his back and looks up at the ceiling with a sigh. "It doesn't work," he whispers, rubbing a tear from his eye. "Haunt Me didn't work. It's not you, Rebecca, or what you created. I didn't expect Barbara to harbour so much anger and resentment toward me. She wouldn't accept my apology. She wouldn't even let me talk.

She said it was her time to tell me how she felt. It was worse than I thought. She said I never listened to her," Matt says. "I've failed this. I've failed Barbara again. I will be leaving this community. I can't be here like this. There is no space to reflect. There are too many shadows here for me to get lost in."

Matt slowly gets to his feet and dusts off his designer jeans.

Rebecca steps in front of him, her hands on her hips, to block the door. "We had a deal, Matt. If I did the upgrade, the mall would stay open for whoever wants to live here. You said you'd continue funding it. There are people here who have nowhere else to go. They quit their jobs to be here because they believed in what you were trying to build here. You need to keep up your end of the deal."

Matt looks at her blankly then shrugs. "The mall will remain open, but I am leaving. My work is done here and I've failed. I need to clear my mind and go on a radical detox. I don't feel right. I'll be leaving immediately. Please warn the others that my chopper will be landing shortly. It can be startling the first time they see something like this."

"Hold on. What about your daughter?" Ian asks.

He pushes past Rebecca toward the door. "Can you please stay and look after her? She always liked you. Sometimes I think she liked you more than me."

Ian's mouth opens in disbelief and Matt pushes past him and leaves down the hall. He's gone. We're left standing in his meditation room by ourselves. I can't believe it's finally over.

"I think the prescription of silence has concluded, and no refills," she says. "It was bad advice and not how people should live together. If people want to live quietly, they are more than welcome to."

That night, Rebecca gathers all community members into the workshop space to tell them what's going on.

"Matt," she says. "Matt is gone."

The room goes still. I thought people would be cheering, but I sensed an unsettling feeling of stress spreading through the crowd. It's as if everyone here took a single breath and are holding it until they find out one very important thing.

"The debt? What about our debt?" One person finally asks.

Rebecca nods. "The debts are paid. Don't worry. You can all stay. We will continue with aspects of the mall the way it is, but we will also work together to improve our lives here. The network is destroyed. If anyone feels like they need to have quiet, they are welcome to create their own silent retreat. But we can talk here openly now."

The crowd is quiet at first, but then a few people cheer. Then they all cheer. I hear a few "thank you's" over the clapping.

"I know a way we can make a difference with our work. I've been working on some prototypes."

She jumps into an explanation of the digital marketplace for good. She talks about using open source code to empower people to spend ethically. "There will be more on this to come," she says. "And unlike the project I was working on for Matt, this digital marketplace will be developed in the open. I'll be looking to assemble a team, and the more the merrier."

When the meeting is over, she looks at me and grins. This is the passionate person I know. This is the person I missed more than anything over the last six months.

"I want you to help me build this, Carolyn. I need you here."

"But, my personality was not right for the mall. That's why I wasn't invited the first time. I don't know if I can live in a community like this."

"That's not why," she says. "Diamond found your wounds and wanted to expose them for Haunt Me to exploit. She wanted to impress Matt so he would trust her. All she cared about was getting noticed. You are a perfect candidate for the mall and you always have been."

"I'll stay. I'm honoured you'd ask. Can I send for Sammy?"

"Please do," she says. "I've really missed him, too."

27

Six months pass and Matt hasn't come back to the mall, but he's still paying all the bills so at least he's been good for that.

Ian thinks Matt's on to something else by now since he knows there's no chance of being with Barbara ever again. There are rumours that Diamond is with him and they are expecting a baby. It may be his eleventh or twelfth, but it's none of my business. I've learned that!

Violet is here and she says they've been keeping in touch through messaging and she seems content with that for now. She's connected with Ian, and it's been nice seeing how they engage. He's writing a memoir, but not Matt's, his own. He's exploring a lot of personal history growing up in the shadows of the Maxis family. I've forgiven him for not telling me about his family ties. We're good colleagues now.

The mall has slowly taken shape as a real collective living space and looks much better than it did when Matt was here. There's a joy in this community that radiates somewhere within these old shopping store walls. It's wonderful to be a part of it.

Last month, Ian removed the blue security fencing and he and a team built a park for anyone in the larger community to come and enjoy. The locals have appreciated it. We call it "The Meeting Place." Kids from the neighbouring homes love to come play here, families have picnics, and older adults go for walks around the grounds. It's become a beautiful space.

My work also started in the garden. Rebecca recommended it since it would give me an important perspective on the foundation of the community. I weeded and harvested and watered. It was enjoyable, just like Rebecca said it was.

Rebecca and her team released the beta version of the app three weeks ago and it's already a hit. We've had over a million downloads. The idea of shopping and supporting local resonates with people. Everyone at the mall, including me, is an equal shareholder. We will start to receive dividends next quarter. I haven't looked back on my temping. Chris still calls me and I talk to him. My nieces have convinced him that a family road trip is in order to visit us now. With Matt gone, we allow visitors. In fact, we give tours quite frequently. People from all over the world are interested to see how we're transforming this old mall into a thriving community.

I might call my mom and dad, but I don't know. I haven't felt ready yet.

After four months in the garden, I'm now managing the marketing effort for the app. We've connected with intentional content creators searching for a slow life and I'm working on multi-national promotions. It's nice.

Over the last while, I've enjoyed getting to know someone new, James. He's handsome and smart and his hair always smells like he's just been outside. It's beautiful and we have the best conversations. My life at the mall has been better than I could have imagined for myself. I even help with cooking. It turns out I'm good at preparing meals in large quantities. I'm content and happy, but Jennifer never leaves my mind. That much has not changed, even with all the positive outcomes here at the mall. Her message to me in the bookstore, even if it was generated by artificial intelligence, keeps me going and that's enough.

Until, one day I see her. At least that's who I think I'm seeing, but it's impossible.

I look again. Jennifer is sitting on a bench in the courtyard with a book in her lap. It's her. I know everyone at the community, and even the kids from the neighbouring houses. This has to be Jennifer.

It's not the Jennifer of my fears. It's the Jennifer of my memories. The Jennifer from that last afternoon I saw her alive. A little nine-year-old girl. My twin sister, preserved in time. She's wearing her favourite pink jacket that looks as good as new. I'm instantly brought back with memories of my nine-year-old self. I look at my hands that have been with me for over three decades. I'm still this adult. She's still that girl.

But, it can't be. I can't be experiencing Haunt Me again. We destroyed it months ago. We double checked back-up servers. Everything was gone. We've had no reports of manifestations since. I haven't received any texts since then either. Haunt Me was successfully destroyed. I saw it all with my own eyes. It's gone.

Yet, I'm seeing someone. Is this the vision of the girl I saw in the beehive? Will her face glitch? So far, she hasn't glitched. So far, she looks perfect.

"Haunt Me is one hundred percent wiped out, right? There's no possible way for it to be working? Matt didn't have a secret backup you didn't know about?"

Rebecca is busy feeding her sweet baby, but she nods her head. I know this already. Of course it's gone. I was there. I can't be seeing Jennifer like this. It must be a coincidence, but it's so clear. Something is happening.

I look back at the bench and that's when my nine-year-old twin sister starts waving at me like she's been waiting for me to join her. She sees me, too. I need to get a closer look, so I know for sure my eyes aren't mistaken and this is just a friendly little girl from town, that's all. I get up and walk toward her. Rebecca doesn't notice me leaving. Jenny sweetly coos now that she's latched, and Rebecca starts scrolling through her emails on her phone. She always has lots of work to do with the app, but she's happy.

I walk slowly at first, worried I'll scare her away, then I walk faster. The closer I get, the more she looks like Jennifer. The more I think it just might be her. My heart fills with hope. But it's impossible.

"Lynnie," she says when I sit down beside her. Hearing this soft voice say my name brings me back to that summer and the last time I saw her. The tent that didn't set up right, the hidden books. Stumbling through the forest with my dad. The tears that wouldn't stop. Everything, including her last words to me before she marched into the forest alone: *I'll see you later. I need some time.* It's Jennifer's voice. She's sitting here with me, finally. I don't know how, but she is. "I've missed you. Stay with me this time.

Don't let me wander off alone again. It's taken me forever to find my way back to you."

My voice catches in my throat. I look over at Rebecca and she smiles.

"This simulation will last for another fifteen minutes," Rebecca calls over. "It's my prototype for a new and ethical (para)normal-based app called Remember Us. It draws on your memories to let you briefly and vividly re-experience a special moment you shared with someone who has passed. This is how this technology should be used. I started working on this when Matt was here, but he wasn't aware I was doing it. You gave me your consent when I started working on it ten years ago as a grad student. If you forgot and would like to be removed, please tell me."

"I saw something at the beehive in town once," I manage to say. "A girl, but the caretaker of the hive said it wasn't really happening."

Rebecca smirks. "It was happening. It might not have looked fully like her yet, but it was real. I've needed the focus time to figure out how to get the rendering perfect. And that caretaker was Michelle, my trusted field worker you met out there."

Rebecca figured out the technology on her own terms and she did it for me first, just like she said she would. Everything about this moment is worth waiting for.

Jennifer's in her pink jacket. She smiles at me. It's a smile I've wanted more than anything to see again. It's her, and even if it's temporary and even if it's only technology and I will never have Jennifer back, there's a strange comfort in this experience that I haven't felt in a long time and it's so satisfying.

And, so long as Matt doesn't come back to this mall, we'll live here collectively and we'll do it well.

But I do worry about Matt and his portfolio of dead malls across the country. He could easily redevelop this place into a strip mall or luxury condos for snowbirds. It's not out of the question. Certain aspects of our lives here will always be out of our control and part of my existence is to not let this fact eat at me anymore, even though it so easily could.

Until that day, I will enjoy my time here, with my community and my friends.

And my family.

"Jennifer?" I say, returning her smile, still familiar after all these years. "I've missed you so much. Love you always."

Acknowledgements

Thank you to Chris and Now Or Never Publishing for their fine work and incredible patience bringing this book to life. Thank you to my family, especially Esther and Nathan, for their unwavering encouragement and adorableness over the years as I wrote this book during small spurts over so many of their nap times. Thank you to the friends and colleagues who I've had the privilege of talking with about some of the themes I explored in this book, such as technology, affordability, and friendship. These conversations have meant everything to me.